T0110631

Ireland: This Land Is Ours

A Novelized Biography of Michael Davitt, Irish Patriot

by

Lewis M. Elia

Order this book online at www.trafford.com/06-0952
or email orders@trafford.com

Most Trafford titles are also available at major online book retailers.

© Copyright 2007 Lewis M. Elia.
All rights reserved. No part of this publication may be reproduced, stored in a retrieval
system, or transmitted, in any form or by any means, electronic, mechanical, photocopying,
recording, or otherwise, without the written prior permission of the author.

Note for Librarians: A cataloguing record for this book is available from Library
and Archives Canada at www.collectionscanada.ca/amicus/index-e.html

Printed in Victoria, BC, Canada.

ISBN: 978-1-4120-9198-5

*We at Trafford believe that it is the responsibility of us all, as both individuals
and corporations, to make choices that are environmentally and socially sound.
You, in turn, are supporting this responsible conduct each time you purchase a
Trafford book, or make use of our publishing services. To find out how you are
helping, please visit www.trafford.com/responsiblepublishing.html*

*Our mission is to efficiently provide the world's finest, most comprehensive
book publishing service, enabling every author to experience success.
To find out how to publish your book, your way, and have it available
worldwide, visit us online at www.trafford.com/10510*

Trafford
PUBLISHING™   www.trafford.com

North America & international
toll-free: 1 888 232 4444 (USA & Canada)
phone: 250 383 6864 ♦ fax: 250 383 6804 ♦ email: info@trafford.com

The United Kingdom & Europe
phone: +44 (0)1865 722 113 ♦ local rate: 0845 230 9601
facsimile: +44 (0)1865 722 868 ♦ email: info.uk@trafford.com

10 9 8 7

Dedicated to my wife's grandmother

Elizabeth Catherine Cleary
(Grandma Betty)

whom I never knew but whose spirit still lives in our hearts.

Acknowledgments

First and foremost, Patrick M. Davitt, grandson of Michael Davitt who kept me on the right track. His valuable input helped this poor American understand those tiny little cultural differences which make all the difference in this story.

The Michael Davitt Museum in Straide, County Mayo, Ireland for their help in pointing me to the right research materials.

Dr. Carla King, History Department, St. Patrick's College, Drumcondra, Dublin, Ireland who graciously supplied me with some of her valuable research materials.

To George E. Burns, cousin of Patrick M. Davitt, whose comments proved invaluable to the production of this book.

Rev. Fr. Anthony Curren, born in Ireland, who was kind enough to act as my cultural consultant in spite of his busy schedule.

My friend, Sally Magid, who acted as first reader and helped in the proofing.

Many thanks to my content editor and research assistant, Jeanne Finley.

A special thank you to my line editor, Jacklyn Wolf-Birch for her efforts and insights.

I would also like to acknowledge Bridget McGinty, a native of County Mayo whom I dated in college and who made me aware of the history of County Mayo.

Forward

Two elements were key to setting stage for the birth of Michael Davitt in Ireland.

In the year 1155, Pope Adrian IV issued a Papal Bull *Laudabiliter* giving sovereignty over Ireland to the English King Henry II. Gaelic Irish kings, as well as some of the Norman warlords who had settled there, were now forced to accept an English king as their overload. From the 13th century, English law was imposed upon the land and a feudal system was established.

In 1509, Henry VIII succeeded to the English throne. When the Vatican turned down his request to divorce Catherine of Aragon, Henry broke from the church. As a result, the Church of England was established. Later, Henry's daughter, Elizabeth I became Queen of England. She was at first tolerant of the Roman Catholic Church. However, on April 27, 1570, Pope Pius V, not recognizing her claim to the throne, excommunicated Elizabeth ending her tolerance for Roman Catholics. She began encouraging the settling of Protestants into Ireland. Protestants were given titles and eventually took ownership of much of the larger land tracts in the country. The Roman Catholic Irish population resisted this influx of Protestants. The problem would become worse over the next three centuries. Many laws would be passed against Roman Catholics and these would not be repealed until the 19th century. The result was a feudal system that would feed the Protestant-Catholic conflict.

This was the situation in the country when Christopher Columbus made his historic voyage of discovery in 1492. Among the treasures brought back by the Spanish from this New World, were two plants, the potato and tomato, native to South America. By the time Elizabeth I succeeded to the English throne, the Potato and the Tomato were destined to change the economy of Europe. The potato, in particular, would make profound changes in European and Irish history.

Potatoes, along with some milk, could supply most of the nutritional needs of a family. In turn, families could grow enough potatoes to feed all their members using a very small plot of ground. When introduced into Ireland, these factors would allow the Irish population to double. In addition to providing more food in a smaller space, potatoes also grew underground. They were able to survive warring factions in Europe who usually ended their battle campaigns by burning the enemy's crops. Families could now survive the ravishes of war.

Unfortunately for Ireland, only one type of potato was ever brought into the country. In 1845 a fungus would wipe out almost the entire crop. The resulting "great hunger" would have a profound effect on the country and the people. By 1846, at the height of the crop failure, Ireland had already been under the Protestant ascendency for about three hundred years and the English sovereign was now Queen Victoria.

It was under these circumstances and at the height of the crop failure that Michael Davitt was born in the village of Straide, County Mayo in western Ireland. This is where our story begins.

Lewis M. Elia, January 2007

Prologue

Mary tried to keep the funeral private. She arranged to have the body brought quietly to the Carmelite Friary on Clarendon Street in Dublin, but the word got out. The irrepressible news spread like a grass fire: Michael Davitt was dead. He was at the Carmelite Friary.

The next day, 31 May 1906, people began appearing at dawn. At first, Mary thought only a few would come. After all, she had made no public announcement. She gave in and allowed those who were waiting outside a chance to come in and pay their last respects.

But no one could have anticipated what was to happen next. The people kept coming, and then more and more. Great lines of mourners formed outside the friary as far as the eye could see. People stopped and wept in front of the coffin. They were old and young, healthy and infirm. There were old men walking painfully with canes, mothers with small children clinging to them, blind old women who had to be helped, young men in suits, middle-aged women in black veils, farmers, workers, clergy.

And they kept coming. There seemed to be no end to them. Some had to be stopped from touching the coffin. Others were weeping uncontrollably. And still there was no end. Hour after hour they came, well into the night. When it was finally over, a local newspaper put the count at over twenty thousand mourners.

Chapter One

March 25, 1846

The midwife looked at Martin Davitt. "You have a fine young fella," she said. "Catherine is doing fine as well."

"Thank the good Lord for that," said Martin, crossing himself.

Martin was a tall, slender man. Years of living the life of a tenant farmer during Ireland's worst farm years had made him thin. But when he saw his newborn son, a smile broke out on his face.

Catherine looked up at her husband. "Martin, 'tis a son the Lord has sent us. And he's as handsome as ever an Irish son was. The good Lord is watching over us."

"He could help us out a bit more with our crops, Catherine," replied Martin with a slight disdain in his voice.

"Don't you be saying a thing like that," Catherine retorted loudly, "or the Lord will send us worse. You should be counting your blessings, not blaming the Lord for your troubles."

"I suppose," said Martin. "I just hope I can feed us. Look at you, Catherine. Your face is thin and your body is tired."

"I'll manage," said Catherine. "Our son will grow up to be a strong, smart man, you can be sure of that. I'm not good at English as you are, so you will have to teach him."

Martin thought about Master Wolf, the hedge schoolmaster who had taught him how to read and write. Hedge schoolmasters had been given that name because classes were often held on the sunny side of a hedge. It was a dangerous profession and a lookout had to be posted to warn of any soldiers who might be approaching, since it had been against the law to educate Catholics in Martin's time. Basic education standards were high, and Martin had been taught the Latin and Greek classics as well as the Bible. Martin, a native Irish speaker, had proved to be an apt pupil who showed a gift for languages, and he could now read Latin, Greek and English.

"I'll teach him. I'll make sure he learns all the classic Latin and Greek stories, the King's English and be an Irish speaker as well. I want him to function in their world but not forget where he came from."

Martin took Catherine's hand in his. "Don't worry. Our son will make his mark in this world." He looked out the door of the mud cottage he had built with his own hands. "But if I don't make my mark on the land, none of us will be left. It's tough just to make the rent on this farm."

A slight anger began to swell up in Martin as he thought about the rent. If only he could own the land. It was seventeen years since the government passed the Catholic Emancipation Law, but it might as well not exist. How do any of them accumulate enough money to own land? "Perhaps I should appeal directly to Queen Victoria herself," Martin mused.

"And what would the Queen be doing with the likes of you?"

"I was at her coronation," said Martin, remembering.

"You were standing in the streets with thousands of others," said Catherine. "Better you spend your time in the fields and stop dreaming about the Queen."

Martin frowned. "It's not right, Catherine. This is 1846 and a man has a right to own his own land. The government is doing nothing to help us. We have a God-given right, I tell you, but we are forever under the yolk of these landlords."

Catherine put her finger to her lips. "Our people have been working the land under British rule for more than three hundred years, and you are not about to change that."

Martin turned his head and fixed his gaze out the door of the cottage, looking at the dawn that was just breaking over the Straide meadow. "Some day we'll drive the British landlords off our land," he said.

Catherine gasped. "Martin, please don't talk like that. Treason can get you hanged. I don't want to lose my husband and our children don't want to lose their father. Please!"

Martin's gaze turned sweet as he met her scared eyes. "You're right," he said. "I must be careful about what I say."

"What are we going to name our son?" asked Catherine, changing the subject.

"We shall call him Michael," answered Martin. "And some day, the Queen of England will know his name. Some day she will know the name Michael Davitt!"

* * *

It was time to baptize the new baby. The family walked from their farm to the church located next to the abbey and went into the chapel. Martin's two brothers, John and Henry, joined them. The church at Straide was small as befitted a rural church. The family brought Michael up to the baptismal font.

"Michael Davitt, I baptize you in the name of the Father, and of the Son, and of the Holy Ghost. Your son is now a member of the Body of Christ." Father McHugh ended the ceremony and everyone applauded.

* * *

It was more of a family gathering than a party. Martin's two brothers, had brought what food they could spare. Five-year-old Mary Agnes was sitting in a chair, holding her new baby brother. She looked up at her family with a glow in her eyes and a smile on her face.

Martin thought, *My poor Mary Agnes. Thin and pale she is. Having to work so hard at the age of five just for us to survive. It shouldn't be.*

"Da, Michael is beautiful," said Mary Agnes.

"Yes, he certainly is," said Martin. "And he's lucky to have a big sister like you to take care of him."

Mary Agnes acknowledged the recognition with an even bigger smile.

"How is your farm going, brother?" John asked.

"I suppose we have it better than most," said Martin. "Compared to some that I know, we are in easy circumstances. We have four milch cows, a male donkey, a pig and a few sheep. But I'm uncertain that I can pay the rent and still feed us. These landlords are driving us into the ground, John."

3

"Yes, I feel the pinch too," said John. "And with crops failing all over Ireland, the landlords are not willing to lower their rents. What will become of us Martin?"

"I'm sure the government will intervene," answered Martin. "They can't just let us all starve."

* * *

1847

The famine was becoming widespread. Most of the land in Ireland was owned by absentee landlords who had never been there, much less lived there. They hired agents, many of whom were ex-army officers, to act as managers and oversee the properties. They collected rents from the peasant farmers who actually worked the land. The feudal system was alive and well in Ireland.

Many landlords wanted to convert their land holdings to cattle grazing, a much more profitable enterprise . The only problem was that the farmers had leased the land, and they were in the way. Landlords resorted to the tactic of raising rents to the point where peasants, unable to keep up with these rent demands, were being evicted by the thousands all over Ireland. The practice became known as "rack renting," raising rents to the point where the landlord knew they couldn't be paid. This gave the owner the legal right to evict the tenant.

Martin and his family were eking out a living from their small holdings, however, his rent was now in arrears. Watching the bailiff come with an eviction notice was becoming a common occurrence in Mayo. Some people tried to resist but the bailiff would only come back with the Royal Irish Constabulary to enforce the "lawful eviction notice." Many of the RIC were rural farm boys themselves and did not like enforcing the evictions, but they had families to feed as well and could not afford to forgo the meager pay they were receiving. The landlords' agents were tearing down the meager mud homes from their properties and throwing the peasants and their belongings onto the road.

4

One day John visited Martin. "The landlords are clearing us from the land so they can graze cattle on the farms. They don't want us here. That's why they're refusing to lower the rents. There are people in the roads begging for food, Martin."

A look of desperation crossed Martin's face. "I don't understand why the government does not intervene," he said.

"Bah with the government," said John. "All they offer is the workhouse. I passed the Protestant soup kettle in Castlebar a few days ago and saw the Burke family down the road from my farm taking soup from the devils."

"Did they have to denounce the faith to get it?" asked Martin.

"They did," said John. "Burke plunged his soul and the soul of his family to eternal damnation doing it."

Martin pictured the Burke family taking the Protestant food. "A man will do any number of strange things when his belly is empty and his family is starving," he offered.

"True enough," said John. "But the priest says it would have been better to spill the Protestant soup on the ground than trade it for one's soul. Burke had to agree to send his children to the Protestant school, which he did."

"Burke could have gone to Westport and gotten soup from the Quakers," said Martin. "They are feeding anyone who asks with no such requirements."

"Yes, these Quakers are good people," said John. "They give without asking anything in return."

"They were also persecuted by the Anglican Church. Like us, they are required to pay the tithe to support the Church of Ireland," said Martin. "Even though they are Quakers and Protestants, they are Irish, just like us. They are not a violent people, but they do not like paying one tenth of their crop to a church to which they don't belong."

"Well, God help Burke and his family," said John. "I hope we never have to take the soup."

"And God bless the Quakers for what they are doing," said Martin.

John took an envelope from his pocket and showed it to

Martin. "A post from Brian McGinty," he said. "I cannot read the English as well as you, Martin, and I thought you could read it to us."

"McGinty, is it?" said Martin. "Didn't he go to Canada?"

"He did. This is the first letter we got from him since he left Mayo."

"I thought McGinty didn't know how to read and write."

"A priest wrote this letter for him." said John.

Martin opened the letter.

"Let's step outside in the light. It will be easier to read."

The men stepped outside and Martin began to read the letter out loud.

"It has a note from the priest who wrote the letter," said Martin. His name is Father Robert DuMortier, S.J., a French Canadian who speaks English. He was kind enough to write this letter for McGinty who was anxious to tell you his story.

Dear John,

It has been three years since I left Ireland. Even though I miss my country, I am doing very well in Canada and have no intention of ever coming back. However, it was a very difficult journey that I made and it is a miracle that allowed Mary and me to survive.

When I was back in Mayo, the Landlord's agent told me that I could have free passage to Canada for myself and Mary. If I took it, the landlord would forgive my rent arrears. If I did not take it, I faced eviction and all my belongings would be thrown into the road. He also offered to buy our belongings and get us a berth above deck. He told us the Canadian Government would give us ten shillings per head and one-hundred acres of land so we could start a new life. I did not know what else to do, so I took the offer and Mary and I went to Dublin to board the ship.

The conditions were miserable. We were among the lucky ones who had a berth above deck. There were five hundred and fifty people jammed onto that ship which was only

6

supposed to take four hundred. Most of them were already very sick with the fever and jammed below decks in steerage. Two children died before we set sail. We were given biscuits and water. I found out later that the law required all to be given a measure of oatmeal as well, but we never saw it.

It took fifteen days to cross the ocean. Many of the sick died in the steerage and were thrown overboard. I said a prayer for a two-year-old lad. The mate gave me an extra ration to go down in steerage to take the bodies out to be buried at sea. I was almost overcome by the stench. I tried to keep track of the number of bodies that I brought out, but lost count. The best I can remember is about one hundred, many of them small children.

When we reached the shores of Newfoundland, some of the sailors caught cod fish. The cook, taking pity on the plight of our people cooked some in a soup and passed it around. I believe it saved some people's lives. God bless that cook, he will receive his reward in heaven. As we sailed up the river we were able to get some fresh water, which was a Godsend since our supply was almost gone.

Soon I could see the homes and farms along the shoreline of Quebec. I felt relieved that our journey would soon end and we could feel solid land under our feet again, but our miseries were not over. Mary came down with the fever and an inspector who came aboard the ship said she would have to go to Grosse Isle, a quarantine station. He said I could go on to Quebec City but Mary would not be allowed to go any further. I would not leave her, and we were placed on a small boat, with about fifty others and sent to the Island. They were still taking bodies out of the steerage; the ship had become their coffin.

Grosse Isle was an island of death. There was not enough food to feed everyone and they only had a few doctors and nurses who could take care of the sickest among us. The Canadian government did nothing to help us and almost everyone who came to the Island died. Mary survived only because I was able to take care of her. The only ones who helped us were the French priests who did what they could,

7

risking their own lives to do it. I helped as much as I could, especially with the children. We had about two hundred orphans. About fifty died and I helped on the burial detail. More people were arriving on ships and so many died, their names were not even recorded. The French priests arranged for French-Canadian families to adopt the orphaned children who survived God bless every one of those French families. It was decided that even though they would be brought up as French Canadians they would be allowed to keep their Irish names. There is a place in heaven for all those French families.

Mary was lucky. She recovered and we were allowed to leave. We went to the city of Montreal where I found work on the docks and Mary worked as a maid. The promise of ten shillings per head and the one hundred acres of land was nothing but a landlord lie, the devil take them all. Eventually we were able to get a loan and buy a farm south of Montreal and we adopted two children, Kevin and Margaret, Mary not being able to have her own. I now have a small farm and there is enough to eat. I get some help on my farm from black men who were slaves in the United States and escaped. None of them stay very long. They are among the few around here who can speak English, although it is sometimes difficult to understand them. Mary and I are doing well with French and the children speak it as if they were born to it. I grow a variety of crops, and a plant called garlic is my money crop. The French use it all the time in their cooking.

God bless all of you. I do miss Ireland but I will never come back and work for a landlord again.
Your Friend,
Brian

"Well, John, what do you think about going to Canada or America now?" asked Martin.

"I don't ever want to leave Ireland," said John, "but I might take the chance if I were starving to death, and we are precious close to that. I've seen people go to the workhouse in Swinford and never come back. I once paid them a visit and saw a crew of men burying bodies in a mass grave across the road from the building. The bodies were wrapped and buried without coffins. If I decide to go to Canada or America, I think it would be a better choice than going to the workhouse."

Martin nodded his head in agreement. He knew that John was probably right for he too had known families who had gone to the workhouse and had never returned. In fact, he could not think of a single family who chose the workhouse that had ever come back.

* * *

1848

Despite all the poverty, things went well for the Davitt family in 1848. Another baby, Anne was born, and the crops were not as bad as they had been. The Davitts were certainly much better off than many around them. Some government relief programs were started and Martin, mostly because of his command of English, was appointed overseer of roads. He was responsible for the section between Castlebar and Straide. Along with his meager holdings, he was able to feed his family, which now numbered five. Mary Agnes, age seven, was a good worker and caretaker for Michael, now age two and the new baby Anne. Catherine was a strong woman, and with Mary Agnes able to help Martin work their small farm and pay the rent. Martin's overseer job made up for the farm's shortcomings.

The road between Castlebar and Straide was nothing more than a dirt path. Martin, read about the construction of roads from the documents provided him as overseer. He had the men working under him dig shallow ditches on each side of the road and slant it toward them, in order to provide proper drainage. He then had them clear the path of rocks, which he used to line the ditches so they would not collapse in the rain. The next step was to have the men cover the road with crushed sea shells, which another crew brought from the area near Clew Bay. The shells kept the road from turning muddy and helped it hold its shape when the weather was inclement. It also allowed for the water to expand when it froze, keeping the road useable all year round. Winters were short in Mayo, but sometimes very severe, and could be very hard on the roads. But Martin knew from his education that the ancient Romans had built roads throughout Europe that were still in use. One reason they had lasted so long was that drainage had been built into them.

Just as the road was beginning to look very good, things took a turn for the worse. A neighbor filed a complaint with the local authorities about Martin Davitt being given the position of overseer of the roads. The neighbor contended that Martin was better off than most of the farmers in the area: he had not been evicted from his farm and he had several holdings which kept his family from starving. This man contended that he himself was far worse off, and should be given the job. The case went to the authorities, who eventually sided with the man. Martin was relieved of his road duties.

The news hit Catherine very hard. Just as they were barely staying ahead, the family was thrown back on its meager resources. Martin began selling the livestock in order to pay the rent. They were forced to buy the yellow or Indian meal which was being sent to Ireland by America for famine relief. Unfortunately, the British government decided that the yellow meal could not be given to the starving Irish, whom they considered lazy, and decided it must be sold. The price was not very high, but many who had been evicted from their farms were sick and without income and had no means to pay for anything.

But it was not very long before the family was in arrears on their rent. The landlord began threatening the family with eviction. Martin decided that the only way he could hold onto the farm was to go to England and work as a harvester. Then they would be able to make ends meet.

"Please don't go, Da," cried Mary Agnes. She clung to her father's knee.

Catherine gently pulled her daughter away. "Da has to go, Mary Agnes. It is the only way we can save this farm."

Martin took Mary Agnes in his arms. "Da won't be gone

long," he said. "It will only be for a short time, just until the harvest season is over. Then I will be back." Martin took two-year-old Michael in his other arm and gave him a gentle squeeze. "You are the man of this house while I am gone, Michael," he said. "You take care of these women."

Michael babbled something, then reached up and grabbed his father's nose.

Catherine could feel the emotion swell up in her as she took Michael away from his da. But she would not let this emotion burst to the surface in view of her children. She simply hugged Martin and said, "We will be all right, dear. You go and do what you have to do and the children and I will take care of the farm."

Martin kissed baby Anne, and stepped outside the cottage.

Catherine left the smaller children inside with Mary Agnes and walked out with Martin. She needed a private moment with her husband.

Catherine, brought up in Turlough, had spent many an evening listening to the men tell stories by the fire. She had heard so many proverbs they became a permanent fixture in her speech.

"Even a small thorn causes festering," said Catherine, her arms around Martin while she gazed into his eyes. "I know you will only be gone for a short time and I suppose it is only a small thorn, but I feel it hurting."

"I feel its sting as well," said Martin. "Only necessity would ever cause me to leave you, even for a short time."

He kissed Catherine, confident that he could earn enough to save his home.

* * *

Not long after the harvest season was over, Martin returned home. With the money he had earned, he was able to negotiate a settlement with the landlord's agent which would allow his family to stay on the land for another twelve months. But it would prove to be of no avail. 1850 was a particularly bad

11

year for the crops, and the family had already sold most of the belongings that were not absolutely essential in order to keep the famine out. Still, Martin could not make the rent.

"Davitt!" called the landlord's agent. "Come out of that cottage and pay your rent."

Martin came out to talk to the agent. "Please," he pleaded. "Have some compassion, man. We have sold almost everything we own. The crops have not been good this year. Give us another season and we will make up the arrears."

"You've already had several seasons, Davitt," shouted the agent. "You'll only fall farther behind. The landlord will forgive your arrears and give you passage to America if you leave the land voluntarily."

"You want me to put my family on one of those coffin ships?" asked Martin. "We've already heard about them. I'll not have my family die at sea."

"Suit yourself, " said the agent. He motioned to a group of men who were standing about fifty yards away. One was a bailiff. He handed Martin a paper and said, "Martin Davitt, this is an eviction notice. It is being served by the owner of this land who has not been paid his reasonable and lawful rent, which is months in arrears."

"Reasonable!" said Martin. "These landlords are rack renters. The devils have deliberately kept these rents high knowing full well we could never pay them. Reasonable, you say!"

"Reasonable and lawful in any of the Queen's courts. Get your family out of the cottage or we will take them out by force," shouted the bailiff.

Martin got his family out of the house and some of the men went in and brought out what was left of the furniture: A table with some chairs, beds, a cradle and some kitchenware. They dropped them out in the road. Then the crowbar brigade went to work. They pulled the door off its hinges and began pounding on the walls of the mud cottage. The thatched roof fell in and landed on the fireplace, which immediately set the straw afire. The men threw the door on the fire and the rest of the cottage was knocked to the ground. The Davitt family clung to each other as they watched their home being obliterated.

"You devils! You'll burn in hell for this!" shouted Martin. "You've no right to be tearing down a man's home and throwing his family out in the road." He made a move toward the bailiff, who immediately stepped behind the men of the crowbar brigade. The men turned toward Martin clutching their crowbars and hammers in both hands, ready to use them as weapons if necessary.

Martin stepped back. He knew that if he decided to fight, they would kill him. He sat down on one of his chairs in the middle of the road and hung his head. Catherine sat down next to him holding baby Anne. Mary Agnes and Michael sat down on Martin's lap. "We have no choice, Catherine. We must go to the workhouse in Swinford or leave Ireland," he said.

He did not want to leave Ireland. It was his home and all his family had ever known, but going to the workhouse was hitting bottom for an Irish farmer. A man had to admit that he was poor if he chose the workhouse. It was the most degrading thing an Irishman could do. He remembered his conversation with his brother John where they'd agreed that people didn't come back from there. He recalled John, telling of the bodies being buried in the Swinford field, but at least in the workhouse, he would still be in Ireland. Perhaps things would get better and he would get back on a farm again. The crop could not fail every year. Sooner or later it would come back and he could rent another farm and have things the way they used to be. Yes, he would stay here--humiliating as it would be--and hope for the best.

It was a task to convince Catherine, but she finally gave in. Father McHugh made arrangements for them to store what little they had in the church's barn in Straide.

Walking along the road to Swinford presented sights that no human being should ever have to see. Adults with clothes rotting off their bodies, begging for food, the famine looking out from the faces of the people who were sick and dying. One family had dug a hole about three feet deep in the field next to the road and covered it with sticks, straw and pieces of turf to keep the weather out.

"They're living in a *scalp*," Catherine said, emotions clouding her features. "No one should be allowed to live like that."

Another woman, with two children hanging onto her, was digging in a field, gleaning for whatever potatoes or turnips were left.

"I see three of the four Horsemen of the Apocalypse riding through Ireland," said Martin. "Famine, Pestilence and Death are here. I don't see War, but he usually follows the other three."

Finally it came into view. There it was, standing like a huge, grey elephant in the field, that stalwart symbol of Victorian philanthropy, the workhouse.

* * *

The Swineford workhouse was one of the newer ones, having been finished in 1842. It occupied six acres of land just outside the town and could hold seven hundred inmates. It first admitted "paupers" in 1846. The largest part of the building was made up of two wings, for women's and men's quarters. Attached to the building was a separate infirmary. There was also a small fever hospital which had been added to accommodate patients who were too sick to work and had to be isolated. The entrance was on the south side of Barrack Street, while on the north side was the workhouse burial ground.

The workhouses were notorious for spreading disease. It was not uncommon for typhus and dysentery to become epidemic in the crowded conditions. In 1846,367 deaths were recorded in the Swineford workhouse alone and 600 bodies were eventually interred in a mass grave.

It didn't take long for the Davitts to be processed. The workhouse master and matron in charge of the building told the family that they would be assigned different quarters. Martin would bunk with the men and Catherine would be placed in the women's section. Catherine would be allowed to have Mary

14

Agnes with her and baby Anne, but since Michael was more than three years old, he would have to be quartered with the other boys.

Catherine stood up and snatched Michael to her chest. "I'll not be separated from my son!" she screamed.

"I'm sorry, but those are the rules," said the master. "It's the same for everyone. No boy over three is allowed to stay with his family."

"Then we won't stay," said Catherine. "I'd rather starve on the side of the road than be separated from my son."

"We went to a lot of trouble to get you processed, you ungrateful wench," said the workhouse master. "There will be another to take your place as soon as you go out the door, and if you go out the door, you will not be allowed back in."

"Then the devil take you and your workhouse," said Catherine. "If we starve, we will starve in dignity."

"Go then," said the master, "and see how much dignity there is in starving."

They had not been in the workhouse for even an hour. Once outside, the fear finally showed on Catherine's face. "Oh Martin, what did I do? Now what will become of us?"

Martin took Catherine's hand. She was still holding Michael, but had to put him down, for she was too weak to hold him with one arm.

"We'll go to England," he said. "I've been in England and there are factories there. In Lancashire there are cotton mills where we can find work. We will not starve."

The Davitts made the journey back to Straide. They went to the church and Father McHugh came out to meet them.

"What are you doing back here?" asked Father McHugh.

"We refused to stay in the workhouse," said Catherine. Father McHuch did not ask why.

"Martin," said Father McHugh. "Come over to the church barn. You can stay there until we can figure out what to do."

Martin complied. They went to the barn and settled in for

the night. Father McHugh brought some soup, and Martin was able to start a fire, since there was a fireplace in the barn. Father McHugh had built it. The Davitts were not the first family to stay there.

The next morning, Father McHugh talked to Martin. "The O'Lynn family is passing through and they are bound for England," said Father McHugh, "and they have a horse and wagon. I talked to them and they are willing to take you and your family as far as Dublin on the promise that you will pay them when you get work in England. I can get you some money for your furniture, and that should be enough to get you to Lancashire."

"Thank you, Father," said Martin. "Tell O'Lynn that I accept his offer, and he can be sure I will pay him back as soon I get work."

"Are you sure you can get work there?" asked Father McHugh.

"I have been there already, Father," said Martin. "The town of Haslingden in Lancashire has many cotton mills, and I know for a fact that many Irish have found work there. We will be all right."

The family said goodbye to the good Father when the O'Lynns arrived in their wagon. All the women and children sat in the back while Martin and Brian O'Lynn sat in front so they could share the driving duties. Michael was allowed to sit up front with the men. When it came time for Martin to drive, Brian took out a turnip and a paring knife and began whittling at the turnip. Michael watched in fascination as Brian fashioned the vegetable into the shape of a pocket watch.

After driving for several miles, it was time for Brian to take over again. Everyone got out of the cart to rest, and the horse suddenly bolted into the field. He was grazing when Martin and Brian caught up with him showing his unhappiness when he was interrupted.

"He's an Irish horse and doesn't want to leave Ireland," said Martin. "Just like us."

Brian's wife started a fire and tossed the turnip pocket

watch into the soup, and fed the peeling to the horse. The next day everyone said goodby and the Davitt's were off to England.

Chapter Two

It was a short trip across the Irish Sea from Dublin to Liverpool, where Martin had some friends who allowed the family to stay. After a few days, they walked to Lancashire and finally arrived in the town of Haslingden, about thirty miles from Liverpool, where they had a friend who agreed to take them in for a few weeks until they could be on their own.

This part of England was nothing like Straide. The beautiful hills surrounding Haslingden were a sharp contrast to the bogs and rocky fields of home. Haslingden had a population of about 9000, with more than 400 being Irish-born. Its main industries were cotton and woolen manufacturing and stone-quarrying. Both men and women worked in the cotton and woolen mills, and many were hawkers, selling everything on the street from fruit to hardware.

The Irish population was clustered in the poorer section of town. On the way into Haslingden, some English boys began taunting the family.

"Look, what are they?" one of them said pointing at Michael.

"They look like dirty Irish to me," answered the other.

"Why don't you filthy Irish go back home?" said the first boy.

Just then, a group of older Irish boys appeared and began yelling at the two boys, who immediately stopped taunting the Davitts and ran off.

"Thank you, boys," said Martin.

"They treat all of us like that," said one of the boys who was obviously the leader of this group. "Once in a while we have to beat them to make them stop, but they learn."

Martin noticed the boy's hand had several fingers missing. "What happened to your hand?" he asked.

"An accident," said the boy. "It happens all the time around here. I lost my fingers in one of the cotton machines. George there got his ear caught in it and it tore it off."

He pointed to George who turned his head so Martin could see where the ear used to be.

They finally reached the friend's house and settled in. The next day Martin found work as a day laborer. They hoped to be able to rent their own flat in a few weeks, but for now, this place was pleasant enough.

* * *

They were in the flat only two days when Catherine woke up in the middle of the night. Michael was crying. She put her hand on his forehead and found him burning up with the fever. There were large, flat brown blotches on his forehead. He was coughing and his nose was running. Catherine recognized the symptoms: measles. She went to the water closet in the hall and drew some water from the pump. She dipped a swath of cloth in it, wrung it out and placed it on Michael's head. She repeated her actions over and over and they seemed to be controlling the fever. But by morning, the blotches had spread down to Michael's face and neck and the woman who owned the house came in.

"What's the matter with him?" she asked.

"He has a fever," Catherine answered, deliberately avoiding the word "measles."

But the woman saw it anyway. "That boy has the measles," she shouted. "You'll have to take him out of here before he infects my children."

"Please," said Catherine, "we've nowhere to go. It's December and my son will die if we are left out in the cold."

The woman's husband echoed Catherine's plea, but to no avail. It was obvious that this man had never won a point with his wife, because he quickly gave in. The Davitts had no choice; they had to leave. They wrapped Michael in a sheet and took him outside. It was a cold December day, and snow began to fall as Martin rigged up a blanket tent next to a wall about fifty yards away from their former home. Catherine held Michael, still wrapped in the sheet, to her breast trying to shelter him from the cold. Martin tried his best to comfort the girls, but it seemed to him that God had abandoned them.

"Please help us God," he prayed to himself, since God didn't seem to be helping Michael.

Catherine began sobbing uncontrollably, still clutching Michael. "Jesus, don't let my boy die," she prayed through the sobbing. "Help us."

Just then, a man lifted up the blanket of the makeshift tent. "What in heaven's name is happening here?" he said. "Is that a child you have wrapped in that sheet?"

"Yes, it's my son," said Catherine.

"What is wrong with him?".

"He has the measles."

"But why are you out in the street with a sick boy?"

Martin answered the man. "When our landlady saw he had measles, she ordered us out of the flat. She was afraid we would infect her own children."

"Well, you can't stay out in the street like this. You'll all die," said the man. "Come with me. My family can make room in our home for you until you find your own place."

Jesus had answered Martin and Catherine's prayers by sending an angel of mercy.

"What is your name?" said Martin.

"James Bonner. I live just up the street from here. Now let's get that boy inside so he can start getting better," as Bonner took Michael into his arms.

Martin and Catherine were overwhelmed with this man's generosity. They must have looked incredulous, because Bonner said, "Don't worry, my children have already had the measles. We will take care of him and we can make the same

20

arrangement for rent as you had where you were living. We don't let people die in the street here. What are your names?"

"Martin and Catherine Davitt. This is Mary Agnes and Anne. My son is Michael."

"Well, come along now Mr. Davitt, and we will get you out of this December air."

Martin thought to himself how ironic it was to find a good Samaritan in, of all places, England. "God bless you, James Bonner," said Martin.

"The sky fell on us, and we caught a lark," said Catherine.

* * *

James Bonner was a tin-plate worker from County Armagh, and his wife contributed to their meager living by working as a hardware hawker. They had four children of their own, ranging from age three to five. It was a little crowded, especially when Catherine gave birth to another girl, Sabina, but they managed. By then, Michael had long gotten over the measles and was growing to be a strong boy. Eventually, Martin was able to save enough money and found a larger place. It was a tearful goodbye that they had to say to the Bonners.

"How does a man thank another man for saving his family?" said Martin.

"Looking at Michael running around healthy is my thanks" answered James. "He's such a fine-looking lad, and smart too. The Good Lord willing, Michael will grow up to become something better than we are, perhaps a teacher. That will add to my reward."

"We will never forget you, James Bonner," said Catherine. "As long as I live I shall remember the face of my healing angel, lifting the tent-blanket in the snow and taking my baby in his arms. Someday the Lord will take you in his arms and comfort you, James Bonner."

21

"We will always be friends," added Martin.

* * *

The Davitt family became lodgers in the house of Owen Eagan on Wilkenson Street. This section of town was a typical working-class neighborhood, populated mostly by Irish. Many, like Owen and his wife, were street hawkers, and Martin and Catherine joined in that trade, hawking mostly fruit.

Although larger than the Bonner place, it was very crowded in the Eagan house. They had taken in other lodgers as well, and there were as many as fifteen people living there at one time. The Davitts soon made enough money at hawking to rent a flat of their own. Martin heard about an "Irish Town" community made up of families from western Ireland, called Rock Hill. It was high up on the northeast end of Haslingden where the town ended, and contained several stone row houses. They were typical two-story stone dwellings and almost everyone was an Irish speaker. They could feel at home among the Gallaghers and Kellys, Morans and Timlins from western Ireland. All of them rented the houses and took in lodgers, and the Davitts decided they would take in lodgers as well.

It was a grand day when they moved in. After Wilkenson Street, this house seemed as if they were living in an open field. Eventually they were able to take in four lodgers. Mary Agnes was now old enough to take a job in a cotton mill and add to the family income.

"We are finally doing well by ourselves," said Catherine to Martin, who had just finished his meal and was enjoying a pipe. "And we will be adding to our family again."

Martin looked up and pulled his wife closer to him to give her a kiss. "That's wonderful, Catherine," he said. "There is no better blessing in a house than a child. Perhaps we will be blessed with another son."

1853

"I hope so," said Catherine. "I'm thirty-three years old.

One would think that I was coming to the end of my fruitful years. This will probably be the last child the Lord sends us."

"With five children, Catherine, I don't think anyone can accuse us of not doing our share on this Lord's earth of increasing and multiplying."

James Davitt was born on 30 June, 1853. He was a beautiful boy and resembled Michael.

"He looks a lot like Michael when he was a baby," said Mary Agnes, now age twelve.

"And just like Michael, he is lucky to have such a fine big sister to help take care of him," said Martin. "And of course, you now have help from Anne and Sabina."

"They don't help much," said Mary Agnes.

"I know," said Martin looking at his eldest child. "It has never been easy on you. You have always been there to share the burden of the family. You work in the cotton mill and share the burden of the younger children with your mother. You are an angel."

Mary Agnes put her arms around Martin's neck. He picked her up off the floor and held her tight. "I love you, my angel," he whispered in her ear. She clung tighter.

And so life got better for the Davitts. One of the lodgers was a stone mason and got Martin work as a day laborer. Michael attended the infant school. Mary Agnes took care of the children with her mother and brought home her wages from the mill. Eventually, Martin became a mason's laborer and they were more comfortable than they had ever been in their lives.

In the evening, Martin decided to help his neighbor's children to learn how to read and write. He remembered his old bush teacher, Mr. Wolfe who had given him a penknife as a reward for his good scholarship and so he always offered a reward for scholarship as well. His offer was a clay pipe. If anyone really did something spectacular, they could win the real prize: a copy of Archbishop MacHale's *Irish Catechism*. It was one of six books that Martin owned, and no intellectual feat by any student was ever judged good enough to win it.

Life in Irish Town was good. Everyone was earning a living, and the specter of starvation did not roam the streets. The houses were warm and reasonably clean and all the boys in the neighborhood attended the infant school with Michael, learning how to read and write. Younger girls were relegated to helping their mothers with household duties, and the older children, when they reached the age of thirteen, were able to get full time work in the woolen and cotton mills. Some children even found work at the age of nine and added to the family income, but children that young were limited to eight hours a day and many had to be part-timers, alternating their work schedules with their schooling.

Rock Hill offered a rich community life for the Irish. It was comfortable to be in a place where everyone spoke Irish, and the population, numbering about ninety, would meet at least twice a week to swap stories and sing Irish songs. The two best storytellers, Martin Davitt and Shemus Madden (who could not speak a word of English), were always vying for the title of the best storyteller of the *céili*, the Irish social evening of storytelling, music and dancing. Martin was usually awarded the title. One of their favorite entertainments was Dick Hallaran playing the fiddle while Molly Madden would sing the old love songs of Connacht, like "The Man Who Came Courting My Father's Grey Mare," and "The Red-Haired Man's Wife." Sometimes a patriotic song, like 'Roisin Dubh' (Black Rose) would strike a more somber note.

On rare somber occasions, someone would tell a story about the famine times in Ireland. In spite of the fact that all were now living in easy circumstances compared to the famine days in Ireland, there was always someone who just had to talk about it and get it off his chest: memories of starving people begging on the side of the road for food; families living in a scalp; bodies being buried in mass graves without a coffin or a prayer; the loss of dignity of the families opting to go to the workhouse; and the crowbar crews arriving to tear down the evicted peasants' houses. In these rare sessions, curses were heaped upon the landlords for their despicable and inhumane acts.

"It was easy for them," recounted Martin. "Most of them had never even been in Ireland and never saw the suffering they were causing. All they could worry about were their profits, curse them all!"

Young Michael sat listening to these tales, utterly fascinated. When the men and women talked about the landlords, the image of their old cottage in Straide rushed back into his mind. Even though it had happened when he was only four and a half, he could still see the straw from the thatched roof burning as the crowbar crews tore down the cottage that his father had built with his own hands. He could clearly remember the family's belongings being thrown into the road. He could see the men throwing the door into the fire. He remembered his father shouting at the bailiff over the eviction notice, and the crowbar crew stepping between the bailiff and his father when Martin's anger reached the boiling point. He could see Martin sitting on the chair in the road with his head down, powerless to resist. The eviction stood out in Michael's mind more than the incident at the workhouse, but, he had heard his mother tell the workhouse story so many times, that his mind filled in the details. He joined in when the men at the *ceili* cursed the landlords.

* * *

1855

Michael was nine years old. In the streets he had gained a reputation as a good fighter. English boys learned quickly not to taunt him, and everyone thought he was much older. The Davitts spoke Irish at home but Martin was very forceful about speaking English everywhere else, hoping his children would bridge both worlds. Even Catherine, who was uncomfortable with the language, used it more and more, finding it helpful when she was hawking.

Michael had developed an English accent, from his hours spent in Dan Burke's infant school the "spelling purgatory," as the children referred to it. Strangers did not even take Michael as Irish. Martin had mixed feeling about this development. He knew how important it was for his son to be able to function in the English world, but it tore at him that he might be losing his identity. Michael proved an apt pupil and was completely bilingual.

Suddenly, in February, baby James, now two years old, came down with a fever and severe cough. No matter what Catherine did, she could not get the fever down. James began to convulse violently, a condition which persisted for three days, and no amount of praying or anything else she or Martin could do made a difference. James died on the twelfth of March.

Martin and Catherine were devastated.

"How much trouble can God send us," said Martin, "before we break under the strain?"

It was an extremely difficult time. Funeral arrangements had to be made and neighbors kept streaming into the house. James was sent to the chapel and the funeral mass seemed to last forever. Catherine was a strong woman but kept losing control of herself as she wept.

The priest gave an eloquent eulogy, talking about the innocent that died at Bethlehem and how the baptized innocents were sitting on Jesus' lap. Once the mass was over, the body was brought to the church graveyard, hallowed ground.

After everyone left the graveyard, the family decided to stay for a few minutes. Catherine was looking down on the grave where James was now interred, Anne clinging to her.

"Is James in heaven, Mum?" asked Anne.

"Yes, James is in heaven," Catherine answered. "He died an innocent and is now an angel in heaven sitting on Jesus's lap.

And Jesus is smiling just as he always did when he was with children."

"Goodbye, Baby James," said Anne.

Martin and Catherine began weeping as they led their family back home.

Chapter Three

S pring began returning to the English countryside, and Michael thought he wanted to contribute to the family income. In spite of the orders he had received from his parents, he went looking for employment. He often passed for older than his actual age, and was able to convince everyone he was thirteen. English labor laws prohibited children under the age of thirteen from working longer than eight hours a day. After that they could work a full time schedule of twelve hours and Michael found a job at Parkinson's cotton mill about two miles from Haslingden.

"How old are you, boy?" asked the mill manager.

"Thirteen, of course," said Michael.

The mill manager looked at him; the boy certainly looked old enough. "Good. We can use a full-timer here. The job pays two shillings and four pence a week. You'll work sixty hours a week; you start at 6:00 a.m. and end at 6:00 p.m. Everyone gets an hour and a half off for breakfast and dinner, except Saturday when everyone gets half an hour off for breakfast and work ends at 2:00 p.m."

"That's fine," said Michael.

The manager took Michael to his new station and instructed him in his work.

"The first thing you need to do is read the mill rules which are posted on the wall there," said the manager, pointing to a faded poster.

MILL HOUSE RULES - PLEASE READ
(These Rules <u>Will</u> Be Enforced)

1. There will be a fine of 2d imposed for any of the following:

   > Arriving late.

   > Dropping a bobbin on the floor.

   > Wasting oil or spilling it on the floor. (Plus the replacement value of the oil)

   > Neglecting to oil at the proper time.

   > Leaving your work station and talking to other workers.

   > Using Oaths or insulant language.

2. You will be dismissed for any of the following reasons:

   > Smoking.

   > More than one person in the necessary together.

   > If any man or boy goes into the women's necessary.

3. You will also be required to wash yourself every Monday and Thursday or be fined 3d.

4. You are also being advised that anyone who wishes to leave the employ of this mill is required to give four weeks' notice.

Catherine was incensed when Michael came home and informed her that he had quit school and taken a job in the mill. But in spite of her anger and prodding, Michael refused to go back to school. It was not like Michael to disobey his parents, but he held steadfastly to his decision to work.

"I can contribute to this family," he insisted, "and I can do the work. We can always use the money."

Reluctantly, Catherine gave in. "He has a mind of his own," she said.

* * *

The mill foremen were charged with the task of making sure the employees were productive and filled their quota. Consequently, machines were constantly humming and always in need of oil and other maintenance. Accidents were common, especially among the child workers. The atmosphere was unhealthy, and little was done for the sake of safety. There were laws which were intended to protect the workers, but they were usually ignored. If any worker attempted to inform the authorities about a flagrant infraction of the rules, that person was summarily dismissed. Children were worked to the edge of exhaustion and if they dropped a bobbin or an oil can, they were likely to feel the boot of the foreman, as well as being fined.

Michael would come home at night utterly exhausted. He had to get up at 5:00 a.m. and walk the two miles to the mill. But in spite of being tired when he arrived, he proved to be a good worker. He learned quickly in spite of his age, but his stay at Parkinson's was to be cut short when the manager embezzled his wages. He got a job at Holden Mill, just outside of Haslingden. His friend and playmate John Ginty, who was thirteen years old, worked there and helped get him the job. The mill was owned by Mr. Lawrence Whitaker, who liked Michael right away and saw in him a lad upon whom some responsibility could be placed.

1855

It was a pleasant October morning, when Michael and John walked to work, as usual. There was an autumn chill in the air, and brown leaves were swirling and crackling around their feet as they walked.

"We're lucky," said John, "to be working for Mr. Whitaker. He is much better to us than most of the other mill owners around here. I can't believe those rules you had to live by in Holden."

"Or the man taking my wages," added Michael.

"That won't happen here," John said. "Mr. Whittaker will pay us."

"I hope so," said Michael. "I like working in Holden much better anyway. We don't get kicked when we drop a bobbin."

The boys arrived at the mill, went in, and manned their work stations. The machines began to hum and the noise drowned out everything else.

In the afternoon, John was working near Michael's location and was about to oil a belt. Michael turned his back to get another worker a tool and he heard John scream. When he turned around, he saw that John was caught in the revolving belt and his head had entered the cogwheel. Michael ran to him but John's limp body fell out of the machine, his head crushed and his blood spattered everywhere. The machines were stopped. Everyone was told to go home for the day.

That night he sat trembling in his mother's arms recounting the awful experience of seeing his friend die. Catherine did what she could to comfort her son.

"John has gone to heaven," she said. "It's his mother who has to live in this world without him."

Michael, feeling a little more comforted, decided to go outside. When he looked down the street, he saw John's mother sitting by her son's dead body, rocking in her grief and singing an old Connaught *caoine*, to him in Irish.

Deaw near to the tables, ye that wear the cloaks;

Here ye have flesh, but it is not roast flesh,

Nor boiled in pots, nor cooked for feasting,

But my dear John—och, och after been slain.

Michael finally could not hold back his tears. The sight of John's body, and his mother singing over it, was more than he could bear.

That night the whole Davitt family sat down together and

decided that Michael would not go back to work at Holden. Then Mary Agnes said that Stellfoxes's Victoria Mill at Baxeden, where she was employed, needed a spinning-room handylad. It was also only about two miles away. The next day, Michael went to Stellfoxes and got hired. The pay was better then Holdens, five shillings a week, and he would be working in the same mill as Mary Agnes who could watch out for him..

* * *

The year went very well for the Davitt family. Mary Agnes was now sixteen, Michael was eleven, and both were bringing home their share of family income. Catherine still had her hawking license and made a fair contribution selling fruit, and Martin was working as a stone mason's helper. Haslingden was encircled by several other towns like Blackburn, Burnley and Bolton and was a good spot for hawking and getting masonry work.

Yet Martin and Catherine still yearned for home. They would often talk about their farm in Straide and of Mayo in general. Michael could not understand why they got so depressed when they talked of it. After all, weren't they much better off here? Could they really miss a windowless cottage and the windswept landscape of Mayo which consisted of bogs and boulder strewn hills? Could they really miss lining up to buy the yellow Indian meal when they were all eating so well now?

"It was home," Martin told him. "I know that cottage wasn't much, but I built it with my own hands. You and your sister were born there. They had no right to tear it down."

It was difficult for Michael to understand, but all the Rock Hill families felt that way. Ireland was their country; in spite of the famine, rocks, boulders, rain, and bogs, it was home. It was the land of their ancestors and it was as if the land were a part of them. They were made out of Irish soil, an no one had the right to take it from them. Even Michael could feel the fierceness of their emotions. He had left Ireland at four and a-half years old,. No matter how long he would be in England, and no matter how much he assimilated, he would always be

Irish.

1857

May turned the hills around Haslingden deep green. Michael had been working in Victoria Mill for eighteen months along with Mary Agnes, and they were long used to working the twelve hour days.

Martin sat down that evening and talked to his neighbor, Kelly over a pipe.

"Things have been going well for our families," he said, "thank the good Lord."

"Aye," said Kelly. "We are prospering around here compared with what we would have been facing in Mayo."

"But as much as I miss Mayo, we would have probably died in the Swinford workhouse if we had stayed. I can't say I like the English much, the way they treat us, but we're not starving."

Kelly nodded his head in agreement.

"And yet, I can't help thinking that somehow my good fortune is always followed by disaster."

"What do you mean?" asked Kelly.

"The last time my family was doing this well, my baby James died," answered Martin. "Sometimes I feel like Job. I can't help feeling that God keeps testing me with one disaster after another. When things begin to get better, look for them to get worse."

* * *

It was just another ordinary day at Victoria Mill, and Michael was being his usual reliable self, oiling the machines and performing other duties when the overseer, a man named Proctor, called him. Proctor was an unusually tough boss and was prone to beat the children who did not follow his orders strictly and immediately. Today, Proctor had a problem. A boy named Mitchell had not shown up for work. Mitchell was seventeen and had the job of minding a doffing machine which spun cotton fibers into yarn. Proctor decided that Michael would take Mitchell's place for a day. Michael knew how the doffing machine worked, but was too small to be assigned to this job.

"I'm not supposed to run that machine," he said. "I've seen what Mitchell does, and I can't reach up as far as he can."

Proctor looked at Michael scornfully. Someone had to mind that machine, and Proctor was certainly not going to do it. "Get yourself over there, Davitt, or you'll find yourself out of work."

When Michael repeated his objections, Proctor sank his boot into Michael's bottom. "You heard me! You're wasting time and costing us money. You can run that machine. Now get yourself to it."

Michael did not want to lose his job. He reluctantly went to the station. He had been on the job for only about half an hour when something obstructed the cotton that was being fed into the doffing comb. It was the minder's job to pick out the obstruction without having to stop the machine. Stopping the machine would cause a stoppage throughout the entire plant and would plunge the profits down for the day, so the machine had to be keep turning.

Michael was not tall enough to reach the obstruction, so he stood on his toes. He still could not reach it, so he stretched out as far as he could. Then he lost his balance. The whirling comb caught the sleeve of his shirt, which he had rolled up over his elbow, and pulled his arm into the machine.

Michael screamed as he tried to get his arm free, but the cogwheel of the machine picked him right off his feet. When he finally got the arm free, it was a bloody, mangled thing. Then an adult co-worker got a piece of cotton cloth and wrapped the arm in an attempt to stop the bleeding. Mary Agnes was immediately summoned. She went nearly hysterical when she saw Michael until a worker calmed her down and told her she had to get him home. The worker picked up Michael and took them outside the mill where he had a horse and wagon.

"Take the wagon and get the boy home as fast as you can," he said.

Mary Agnes and the worker helped Michael into the cart. She took the reins and began the two-mile journey to Rockhill, a trail of blood on the ground marking their way. Michael began to lapse in an out of consciousness, the memory of John Ginty's death flashing across his mind. I'm going to die, he thought, just like John. My Mother will be singing a *caoine* over my body tonight.

Suddenly, a stranger, seeing the blood dripping on the road, ran up to the cart. "Hold up there," he said. "What on earth happened to that boy?"

"He caught his arm in a machine," said Mary Agnes, weeping as she yanked on the reins.

The stranger climbed up into the cart and looked at Michael's arm. Then he removed the bandage and re-tied it so it would do a more effective job of stopping the bleeding. "You get him home and have your parents get him to a doctor right away," he said. Then he looked Michael in the eye. "Keep your spirit up, lad. You won't die."

By the time they got home, Michael's arm had almost stopped bleeding. All he could think of was the story his mother had told him of another good Samaritan, Mr. Bonner who had saved Michael from the measles. Now he knew that it would take more than a good Samaritan to save him from this.

Catherine was in agony when she saw her son, sure that he was going to die of the loss of blood. She pushed Mary Agnes aside, scrambled into the cart and drove to the local doctor, who was able to stop the remainder of the bleeding and then sent the boy to the hospital. Two days later, he examined the arm again and could not decide if he should amputate or try to save it.

"We should bring in Dr. Taylor of Rawtenstall to look at this," he advised. "He is well known for his limb setting and surgical skills. He should make the decision."

Dr. Taylor was called. It took a week for him to get there. He examined Michael and declared that the arm would have to come off immediately if they wanted to save Michael's life. "Gangrene has already set in. If we don't amputate right away, the boy will die."

It was an agonizing decision, but Catherine knew the doctor was right. She would never choose death over amputation. She told the doctor to go ahead.

A friend of the family, Molly Madden, heard of the news and came to visit Michael. She tried to convince Michael not to let the doctors butcher his arm. "Don't choose to become a cripple for life, Michael," she said. She made a long speech about joining Jesus in heaven, which would be better than living a life without a right arm.

Michael decided that he, not the doctor or his parents, should make the decision. He decided that Molly was right. He would rather be with Jesus in heaven than live without his arm, unable to work or even defend himself. He decided that he would not let the doctor cut off his arm.

Catherine was incensed when she heard of the incident. "The old hag! What business does she have telling my son to end his life? If I weren't a Christian woman, I would send her to be with Jesus."

Michael protested vehemently. He was not going to let anyone cut off his arm. It was his arm; what right did anyone have to tell him how he could live in the world. He was very strong and the adrenaline in his body made him much stronger. It took several people to hold him down and force the chloroform on him. When he woke up, his arm had been amputated just below the shoulder.

Chapter Four

The world was hazy when Michael woke up. He could see his mother's face and feel the tender touch of her hands as she began stroking his forehead and cheeks.

"My right elbow hurts," he said.

Catherine went to get the doctor. "He said his right elbow hurts. How could this be if he has no right arm?" she asked.

"This is not uncommon in amputation cases," answered the doctor. "The brain has not adjusted to the loss of the limb yet. The pain he feels is real to him. It will take time for him to adjust."

Michael was wide awake and sitting up when Catherine came back to his bedside. When Michael saw her coming, he tried to reach out with his right hand. His brain jolted when he remembered he had no right arm. He laid back down, depressed.

"The doctor said it is normal for you to feel your arm. The pain will go away in time," she told him. Catherine probably felt the pain more than he did. But at least he is alive, she thought to herself. Somehow we will see that he gets along with one arm.

"I wish you had let me die," said Michael. "I will be good for nothing now, a hopeless cripple. I won't be able to earn wages or do any kind of job."

"You are still alive. And you will now have to work with your brain. People with one arm have done many things. You will stand up and account for yourself. You will go to school and it is with learning that you will make your living. A scholar's ink lasts longer than a martyr's blood."

But Catherine's words were of little comfort to Michael. He could not think of going to school or making something of himself. All he could think of was the pain he was in. Sometimes it got so unbearable, the doctor had to prescribe morphine.

Long hours in the hospital followed as Michael began his

rehabilitation. In a few weeks, his arm had healed and he was finally allowed to go home. It was a long, painful process, but Catherine took care to complete his rehabilitation. Michael proved he had inherited Catherine's strong will by responding quickly.

One advantage of being a British subject was that handicapped people were eligible for government assistance. However, not many good schools would have been available to the Davitts. Mr. John Dean, a local cotton manufacturer and prominent Wesleyan offered to send Michael to the Wesleyan school conducted by Mr. George Poskett, a well-known and respected teacher. Martin and Catherine told Mr. Dean how much they appreciated his offer and said they would let him know.

The Davitts decided to consult their parish priest, the Reverend Thomas Martin.

"Mr. Dean has offered to send Michael to the Wesleyan school," said Martin. "I must admit I am tempted to take his offer, even though the man is a Protestant."

Fr. Martin was of an extremely liberal mind set when it came to the mingling of the different denominations. He believed in '...social harmony and brotherly love–no distinction between Protestants and Catholics, English and Irish, but all blending together in one social brotherhood,' as he once said in a speech he gave at a Catholic school.

"Schoolmaster Poskett is the best teacher to be had in Haslingden," said Fr. Martin. "We have other Irish who went to school there and he never made them feel ashamed of themselves as either Irishmen or Roman Catholics. Michael will learn a great deal and Mr. Poskett will not try to influence Michael as to religion."

That was enough for Martin and Catherine. It was a Protestant school, but the priest was sanctioning it. If it was good enough for him, it was good enough for them. They took Michael to the school and enrolled him.

* * *

It took a few months for Michael to recover from his accident. In that time, he was able to begin the term at his new school. His first task was to learn how to write with his left hand. It was like starting over in infant school, but Michael painfully worked on his letters and penmanship until he mastered it. Inside of a year's time his handwriting was almost as good as it had been with his right hand. As a factory worker, he had not done much reading and writing, but now as a student he did more in three months than he had ever done in his life.

Mr. Poskett lived up to his reputation. He was a creative teacher and everyone in the school loved him. Michael proved to be one of his best students. Mr. Poskett, although a Protestant Methodist, taught Michael to accept religious diversity and not see it as a factor that divided people.

"We should all learn to respect and accept each other for what we are and not let our religious differences fuel hatred toward one another," he said.

Michael was greatly influenced by Mr. Poskett. He remained in the school four years and at the age of fifteen, he left to seek employment.

* * *

1861

Not able to return to mill work because of his handicap, Michael found work as an errand boy for Mr. Henry Cockcroft, the postmaster of Haslingden and an owner of a print shop and stationary store. Mr. Cockcroft, a little wary at first about just how useful Michael would be to him, quickly changed his mind after Michael started work. It was not long before he found him to be an intelligent, reliable and resourceful employee willing to learn anything. And Michael learned quickly. In a very short time, he was able to set type just by watching the other workers do it, and he was often asked to assist them when he was needed. Mr. Cockcroft promoted Michael to assistant letter carrier. His first job was to carry the mail bags to the railway station every day. Later he delivered the mail when the regular postman was off for the day.

During these mail deliveries, Michael got to meet some of the English working class residents of Haslingden. The handsome young man with one arm, speaking with the Haslingden accent, was an instant favorite on the mail route. Many of the customers loved talking to him. He noticed how much like his own people they were–poor working families struggling to make a living. A few mentioned how some of their relatives had to go to the workhouse when they couldn't find employment, which conjured up the half-memory of his mother telling the workhouse master to go to the devil.

* * *

Autumn, 1863

Michael had been employed by Mr. Cockcroft for two years. He attended night school (one of only two Haslingden Irish to do so) at the Mechanic's Institute trying to better himself while he continued to work as a letter carrier and print shop helper. In night school he had access to the library and newsroom where he could read the leading newspapers and periodicals of Great Britain. This helped him greatly in his relationship with the people on his mail route, many of whom went out of their way to comment to Mr. Cockcroft about what a smart and well-informed lad he was.

He also surprised Cockcroft one day when he took over for one of the regular printers. A posting bill had been ordered, and Michael, in spite of working with one hand, completed the task in three and a half hours, a shorter time than the regular printer had taken with his two hands. Cockcroft remarked later that he had been in the business since 1820 and had never witnessed anything like it. Michael performed this feat once again by printing five hundred pulls of an advertisement in an hour and a quarter, exactly the time it took the regular, two-handed printer to do a similar job.

His night school education started to become useful in another way. Being one of the few educated Irishmen from the over two hundred Irish families living in Haslingden, he was sought out for his knowledge of current affairs, and it was this quality of leadership that led him to think he might get involved in politics.

A big push in this direction came from an unlikely source. A man named Ernest Jones, who had spent two years in a British prison for making seditious speeches, came to the Mechanic's Institute to talk with the students. He immediately took a liking to Michael.

"There is only one way out of the land problem for Ireland," said Jones. "Ireland must become independent and nationalize the land."

Michael was stunned to hear this non-Irish man speaking of Irish nationalism. "What good would nationalizing the land do for Ireland?" he asked.

"It's the only way it can be taken from the landlords and given to the people," Jones answered. "If Ireland is independent of British rule, the landlords will not be able to own those estates and exploit the small farmer. Most landlords don't live in Ireland anyway, so they won't miss anything but their profits. Don't forget, we have the same problem in England. This is a fight of the working class against the privileged royalty, not just an Irish question."

This was the first time that Michael had heard an Englishman denounce landlordism, and not only in Ireland but in England as well.

Chapter Five

Mr. Cockcroft was like a second father to Michael. He promoted him to chief letter carrier mainly because of how popular he was. People marveled at how well he could function delivering mail with only one arm. But also he could discuss with them, some of the issues facing the English working class and sometimes offered solutions for their predicaments. These short meetings convinced Michael that the English and Irish working classes had much in common. He was beginning to feel that these workers were as much victims of the system that built a privileged class in Great Britain as was the Irish minority.

It was at this time that a co-worker's father, Martin Haran, became very friendly with Michael. Some years earlier, Michael had asked Mr. Cockcroft to hire Martin Haran, Jr., and Mr. Cockcroft had obliged. The younger Martin had turned out to be a good worker and became an apprentice in the printing office.

The elder Martin, a cloth hawker, lived on George Street with his family. They had been former next door neighbors of the Davitts when they had lived at Wilkenson, and they had remained friends. Martin Haran's wife had died and left Martin with four children to support. One of them was Frank, who had lost his right hand in an industrial accident and had met Michael at the Wesleyan school. The elder Haran appreciated the fact that Michael had used his influence to get his oldest son a job, and Martin Haran and Michael, despite the difference in their ages, became good friends.

Haran was a member of the Fenians, a secret revolutionary society formed in 1858 in Ireland and the United States in order to achieve Irish independence from England by force. The name was taken from ancient Irish history. In Irish Gaelic, the *Fianna* was a professional military group that served the Irish kings in the third century. The Fenians were also known as the Irish Republican Brotherhood and were being heavily financed by Irish and Irish-Americans in the United

States.

"Let's take a walk," said the elder Haran to Michael. "First, I want to thank you for getting my boy a job at Cockcroft's shop."

"He's doing a good job," said Michael. "Mr. Cockcroft likes him."

"Cockcroft is a good man," said Martin. "Not at all like those English aristocrats who make life miserable for our people."

"True enough," said Michael. "But there's nothing we can do about the aristocrats. It's the system in Great Britain. We're caught in it."

"It doesn't have to be true forever. I'm a member of an organization called the Fenians and we aim to change that system."

"I've heard my father and the men at Rock Hill talk of your organization."

Martin saw his opportunity. "We need young Irish like yourself if we are ever going to have an Ireland that is free and independent of British rule."

Free and independent of British rule. Michael pondered the words. He thought of Ernest Jones, whom he had heard lecturing at the library.

"What can I do?" asked Michael.

"We have a Fenian cell here in Haslingden, said Martin. "Join us. A young man with your kind of talent would be very useful to us."

"I will have to discuss it with my parents," said Michael.

"Of course," said Martin. "Talk with them about it and let me know what you decide."

Michael did indeed discuss it with Martin and Catherine, and got his Martin's instant approval.

"I never told you this Michael," he said, "but when I was young, before I met your mother, I was a member of a secret society and had to flee Ireland to avoid prosecution. I went to England and worked as a harvester until they stopped looking for me. That's how I got so familiar with England"

Michael looked at his father with surprise. Catherine was a little more cautious, but thought that any young Irish man should be in the fight to make Ireland free.

Michael joined the Fenians.

The Lancashire district, which included Haslingden, was a stronghold for the I.R.B. Haran belonged to what was known as the Rossendale centre. About fifty men belonged to the centre, organized into cells spread across four or five small towns in the valley. Michael proved to be a prize recruit. It did not take long for the members to recognize his leadership abilities. His command of English, the fact that he could easily pass for a Haslingden native, and his in-depth knowledge of civic affairs were impressive. Not long after he took the Fenian oath of obligation, he was elected "centre" (leader) of the Rossendale circle. This added to his income, and he was able to keep his job at Cockcroft's as well.

* * *

1867

Michael had been a Fenian for about a year. With the financial backing of the membership in the United States, the movement was growing. A year earlier, a Fenian armed force had tried to invade Canada and take Campobello Island. The plan was to hold the Captive island hostage while demanding freedom for Ireland and independence for French Quebec. A group of about 700 armed Fenians launched an attack from Maine, but were stopped when the U. S. President Johnson, working in cooperation with the government of Great Britain, dispatched an American military force and disbursed the Fenian soldiers.

So it was time for a new plan. This time they would hit England itself. The centre brought in an Irish-American military officer named Captain John McCafferty. He had been an officer in the Confederate army during the American Civil War and was a specialist in guerilla tactics. He had formed a group of men from the Fenian cells of northern England, most coming from Michael's area. They would be organized and led by

44

experienced American officers. The plan was to have one party raid Chester castle, in Cheshire England and seize the store of arms there, while another group would commandeer a mail train so the arms could be transported to Holyhead. Another party would tear up the rail lines behind the train and cut the telegraph wires. Once in Holyhead, they would capture a boat and transport the arms to Dublin, where they would be used to fuel an uprising.

So as not to arouse suspicion, the raiding party would enter Chester in small groups and muster after all had arrived. Captain McCafferty reasoned that one thousand men could easily take over the lightly guarded Chester Castle. This number would be more than enough to do the job.

But this plan would go astray thanks to a mouse who was sitting in on the meetings, an informer, Corydon, who gave the British the details of the Fenian plan. British troops were immediately rushed to Cheshire by special trains. When the Fenian troops arrived, they found British soldiers waiting for them. Michael was leading a detachment of Fenians from Haslingden. Seeing their position was hopeless, they began retreating and many were captured. Michael, however, remained cool and was able to avoid capture. He led his troops away from the battleground and out of harm's way.

"We were betrayed," he told them. "I didn't bring you here to walk into martyrdom. I am ordering you all to go home. We will live to fight another day."

Not all the commanders were as calm and calculating as Michael, however. The commander of the Manchester detachment, Arthur Forrester, ordered his men to regroup and led them on to Dublin in the hope of joining the planned insurrection. All were arrested as soon as they set foot in the city.

* * *

Safely back home in Haslingden, Michael sat back in his chair and contemplated his position with the I.R.B.

"I don't think it's possible for us to overthrow the might of the British Empire by force," he told his father. "They're too strong. We need to think about leading the movement in another direction."

Martin looked at his son with admiration. Leading a group of armed men in spite of his disability. But he could see that Michael was dispirited from the experience and needed to be consoled.

"Jesus of Nazareth was able to change the mighty empire of Rome with twelve unarmed men," Martin said. "It took more than three hundred years and cost many lives, but it was done. He did not bring down the Roman Empire with a sword. He brought it down with an idea."

Michael thought long and hard about this. *But what kind of idea?* He was still a Fenian and had sworn an oath to the organization. He would do what he was ordered to do. If that meant more military action, so be it. But it bothered him that such military operations could cause the death of innocent civilians. He did not want that. Some of the victims would surely be from the English working class and he was not out to hurt them.

But British public opinion would turn against the Fenian movement after more events were planned. The first of these was late in 1867, when the brotherhood decided to free two Fenian prisoners, Thomas J. Kelly and Timothy Deasy from a police van on its way to Salford jail via Manchester. As a result of this attempt, a police office named Charles Brett was killed. The other event was an explosion outside the walls of Clerkwell prison, London. The Fenians were trying to free their member, Ricard O'Sullivan Burke. The overzealous band of rescuers planted an explosive charge outside the prison walls. Since they had not calculated the charge correctly, the resulting explosion was too large and resulted in the deaths of twelve innocent people.

Michael was appalled at the clumsy attempt of these men in doing a job which should have been carried out without the bloodshed.

"We are losing discipline in the ranks," he told Martin Haran. "If we go on like this, killing innocent people, we will lose the sympathy of the British working class and probably some of our backers in America. We must find other ways to work."

Everyone in Britain felt threatened by such random acts of violence. The London police arrested three men, William Phillip Allen, Michael Larkin, and Michael O'Brien. They were held responsible for the bombing and were executed.

"This execution has satisfied the anti-Irish clamor that is growing in England," Michael told Haran.

"Would you have gone on that mission if ordered?" Haran put the question to Michael, almost as if it were a test.

"Yes, I would have," Michael answered, "But I would have not resorted to killing to achieve it. Certainly I would not have killed a police officer and would not have hurt innocent bystanders."

The execution of the three Fenians, who were being called "The Manchester Martyrs" by the Fenians (and being billed as such by the pro-Irish and English liberal press) stemmed some of the resentment against the Irish, but not all. Anti-Irish demonstrations still took place, and one such incident hit Haslingden.

It was at their Roman Catholic Church, St. Mary's. on the day of the church's first confirmation service. A band of Protestants converged on the church, probably with the intent of burning it down, incited by a demagogue named William Murphy. Michael organized a body of young Irish men to protect the church. They confronted the mob and many times disbursed it by firing over their heads. And so the "Murphy Riots" and other similar incidents were thwarted, and many Catholic churches in the area were saved from desecration.

* * *

With Ricard O'Sullivan Burke still in prison, the Fenians needed someone to take his place. Burke had been the chief arms agent for the I.R.B. in England and Scotland, so it would have to be a person who had intellectual ability as well as nerve. Everyone was pointing to Michael Davitt. He was now twenty-two years old and mature beyond his years. He was tough and reliable and had an excellent command of English. His English accent would allow him to pass unnoticed throughout the British Isles without arousing suspicion. He was just what the brotherhood needed.

This was a big step up for Michael. He would receive more money but would have to resign from Cockcroft's employment, since serving as an arms agent was a full-time commitment. He regretfully told Mr. Cockcroft of his decision to resign.

"What are you going to do, Michael?" asked Cockcroft.

"I'm going to hawk cloth," he said.

Cockcroft looked at Michael in astonishment. He could not believe what he was hearing. Give up his good job in printing and carrying mail to hawk cloth! Was he mad? Nevertheless, he tearfully bid Michael goodbye and wished him luck.

"If it doesn't work out for you, Michael," said Mr. Cockcroft, "you can always come back to the shop. I will always have a job for you."

Michael wished he could tell Cockcroft what he was doing. But he knew that was impossible, not only because he would compromise the mission but because he did not want Cockcroft to be involved in any way.

"Thank you Mr. Cockcroft," said Michael, "I will never forget you."

Chapter Six

The new job carried with it some heavy responsibilities. Michael was a key link between all the Fenian cells in Great Britain, which numbered over 100. He reported directly to James Fox of Leeds who headed the division and who in turn reported directly to the supreme council of the I.R.B. The members of the supreme council were not known to Michael, since information that sensitive was only given on a need-to-know basis.

The post was making Michael financially secure. Since Michael's job was to procure arms for the Fenian cells and included considerable personal risk, the position was well compensated. Under the guise of being a cloth hawker, Michael was able to move around the North of England and handle the financial transactions required in procuring arms.

Belgian revolvers were the preferred arms of the Fenians. They were well engineered and reliable. They could be broken down and easily shipped inside other goods, and their parts were interchangeable. They could also be easily hidden on one's person. Rifles were also needed for larger military type operations, but were more difficult to buy and transport.

"Buy them without stocks," instructed the cell leader. "That way they won't take up as much room and we can make our own stocks when they arrive."

It was a splendid idea, and one which James Fox would pass on to the supreme council. Eventually it would become standard procedure for buying and shipping rifles.

Michael got word that Forrester had been released from jail in Dublin. He was only seventeen years old and stood only five feet one inch tall. He was as dangerous as any Fenian, but because of this he was not taken seriously by the authorities in Dublin.

Michael admired Forrester's courage but thought he was foolhardy. He needed discipline, or he would get himself into trouble. After his release, Forrester began attracting the attention of the police. His name was constantly showing up in the press. Michael himself made a deliberate effort to stay out of the headlines, not wanting to attract the attention of the police.

* * *

March 1869

Michael sat down with James Fox to give his routine report of arms activity in his district.

"What do you think of the new prime minister, Gladstone, announcing his new 'justice for Ireland' program?" asked Fox.

"I'm not impressed," Michael answered.

"He's released forty-nine Fenian prisoners," said Fox.

"True," said Michael, "but only because he's yielded to the pressure being put on him and his party by the Irish Amnesty Association. He's also made it clear that if they're caught in Fenian activities again, they can expect no mercy. Releasing prisoners does not address the problem in Ireland, namely the landlords. I would be more impressed if he did something about the rights of peasants."

Fox nodded in agreement. No matter how many prisoners they released and how much "reconciliation" Gladstone and his party were spouting, the fact remained that the government was not addressing the fundamental cause of the problem, landlordism. Gladstone was attempting to treat the symptom of the disease rather than eradicate the cause. The Fenian movement had to go on.

* * *

Chief Superintendent Ryan of the Dublin Metropolitan Police was looking at the file in front of him.

"So this Michael Davitt of Haslingden is a centre for the Fenians?" he asked to the inspector who was sitting in front of him. "Yes," said the inspector. "Our informants tell us that he has been supplying arms to all the cells in the north of England."

"Have we been able to trace the source of their funds?"

asked Ryan.

"The bulk of it comes from Irish and Irish-Americans in the United States. We can't get at the accounts because they're using a bank in Paris to deposit the money, turn it into pounds, and smuggle it into England and Ireland. Some funds have been used in Scotland, but Davitt has been concentrating mostly in his area in England."

"How reliable are these informants?"

"We pay them well," said the inspector. "We have our own men follow up on their leads, and so far they have been giving us extremely valuable information."

"What has your informant turned up on Davitt?" Ryan asked.

The inspector picked up the file and shuffled through some of the papers. "He was working as a letter carrier and printing apprentice for an Englishman named Cockcroft in Haslingden. After working there for several years, he quit to become a cloth hawker. We have reason to believe it was at that time he became a centre."

"Unless hawking cloth has become a much better business than I thought it was,"

"I'm sure the Fenians are paying better. We have reason to believe that Davitt is planning another arms shipment soon," said the inspector. "We have assigned two detectives, Joseph Murphy and Thomas Welby in Liverpool and Manchester to track Davitt's movements. If there really is a shipment coming in, we will intercept it and catch Davitt red-handed. The Crown also has secret agents in America who will inform us of any movement of funds which could be used to obtain arms."

* * *

Arthur Forrester sat in the pub with all of his Irish friends, a pint of bitter in his hand. The alcohol loosened his tongue, and he began bragging about his exploits as a Fenian commander.

"They put me in jail in Dublin," he boasted, "but let me

out after a short time. They were probably afraid my friends would come and rescue me and blow up the prison like they did in Manchester. That must be why they didn't hold me. Now I'm an assistant arms dealer for the Birmingham region and we are shipping arms to our members all over England and Ireland."

In truth, the magistrate in Dublin could not take seriously a seventeen-year-old who claimed to be a Fenian commander, even though it was true.

"Have another pint," the man sitting next to him said. "When are we going to get these guns?"

Forrester was getting too drunk to stop talking now.

He assured the man that the guns would arrive shortly. They were being bought in large quantities in Birmingham and were to be assembled at a secret depot in Manchester. They would be smuggled to Dublin via Liverpool.

"That's fine for Dublin, but when do WE get them?" the man persisted. "Do our commanders want us to just call the English names, or do they want us to fight?"

"Some of those guns will get to you. Be patient. I'll see to it personally," Forrester said.

He did not know that his drinking companion was actually one of Constable Murphy's spies who had infiltrated the Fenians several years ago.

The additional alcohol kept Forrester talking. He told the man about his plan to raid all the gun shops in Liverpool.

"It would speed things up considerably," he said. "We wouldn't have to wait for guns to be manufactured and assembled. We could just seize them and start the revolution now."

"Have you made this proposal to your superiors?" asked the man.

"Yes, and they turned it down. Said it wasn't the right time. Well, what is the right time?" said Forrester.

"Davitt turned down the plan?" asked the man.

"Yes," said Forrester, "and he is the arms agent for my section and my boss."

The spy already knew about Davitt turning down

Forrester's plan. When Forrester brought up the plan, Michael told Forrester that a raid on Liverpool gun shops was premature, rash and lacking in judgment and that it should only be done in conjunction with an uprising in Ireland, or it was doomed to failure.

"I don't like working for a person who is so careful about everything," said Forrester. "I want action, not words."

The next day, Forrester met with Michael, telling him that he had an urgent topic to discuss. Knowing he would not get Michael's support for the Liverpool raids, he turned the conversation to the traitors within the ranks.

"We need to kill the informers who are selling us out," he said.

"That privilege is solely in the hands of the Fenian ruling council," said Michael with a bit of scorn in his voice. "They have forbidden us to take that kind of action at this level. Don't forget that!"

Another rebuke. Michael was beginning to make Forrester angry, but he held his tongue.

* * *

Forrester seemed to be under control for the time being, but Michael was worried Forrester was a loose cannon and was capable of taking matters into his own hands. But Michael let it go and left England for a trip to Scotland, where he was going on an organizing tour. The next day, in Glasgow, Michael received a letter from Forrester stating that he had "overwhelming proof" that a young Fenian named Burke was a traitor, and if the north of England executive of the I.R.B. did not take action, Forrester would shoot Burke himself.

Michael knew that Forrester meant what he said. In an attempt to at least delay his actions until he returned, Michael decided to write him a letter in response. His approach was not to actually bar Forrester from such action, but make him wait until he could get approval from his superiors. He added that if such an approval was obtained, then the deed would be done. In an attempt to appeal to Forrester's vanity, Michael told him he was far too valuable to the family and was needed, even at the risk of letting a rotten sheep exist in their midst. He closed with the following line: *"Whoever is employed, don't let them use the pen we are and have been selling"* thus avoiding any direct reference to the revolvers

Michael also informed Fox.

When Michael returned to England, he learned that Forrester had been arrested the day after he had received the letter and was in jail for three weeks. It was almost a relief to get him out of the way for awhile. When he was released on bail, Forrester still insisted that Burke was guilty of treason, but Michael calmed him down considerably.

"We can watch Burke, and even use him to give misinformation to the police," said Michael. "Let's use our heads and not draw attention to us at this time. We have many more important things to do here, and Burke is only a small thorn."

The strategy seemed to work; Forrester seemed to accept this, but Michael was still concerned about him. He wanted to inquire at the jail about the charges against Forrester, but knew he must be careful about how much interest he showed so as not to expose himself. He was able to use a friend to find out why Forrester had been arrested, and learned that he was charged with having revolvers in his possession for which he could not satisfactorily account. There was no doubt that he had four revolvers in his possession, including one that was loaded and found on his person. His explanation was that he had purchased them in Birmingham for cash from a gunmaker named Robert Minningham. His intent was to sell them to Englishmen; and he could produce English witnesses who had purchased revolvers from him. As for carrying a loaded weapon, he had on one occasion been robbed, he said, and he had to carry it to protect himself.

The Chief Magistrate listened carefully to Forrester's defense. When it became time for the prosecution to make its arguments, the police simply said that they had information that

Forrester was a Fenian, and they would make available only what information they had which would prove only that. They did not intend to go any further, so as not to compromise any of their sources. They would, however, produce enough information to justify that Forrester be held.

The main piece of police evidence was a letter they had confiscated from Forrester when he was arrested. It was in four pieces, and had been carefully pasted together. The police claimed that Forrester attempted to tear up the letter when he was apprehended. They were fast enough to snatch it from him before he was able to tear it more than twice. The police entered the letter into evidence, claiming that it showed Forrester in correspondence with another person and that the two were discussing and planning an assassination of a third person whom they suspected of being an informer.

After a short deliberation, the Chief Magistrate ordered Forrester held over for further investigation, citing a 1360 English law that allowed a magistrate to bind over any prisoner, even one of good behavior, if the court had good cause to believe the person could be dangerous. The magistrate, of course, did rule that Forrester, being a suspected Fenian, belonged in that category.

In spite of a vigorous self-defense, the court was persuaded by the prosecution which made the argument that the accused's claim to have been a gun hawker was unlikely, and, that his attempt to destroy the letter implied that he was aware that it could incriminate him. As it turned out, Forrester had to spend Christmas in jail but was technically acquitted of the charge. The prosecution did not need to pursue the Fenian connection, which would have necessitated exposing their informants. They were saving them for catching a much bigger fish: they were after Michael Davitt.

Chapter Seven

Once again, the police inspector briefed the commissioner on the Davitt file.

"We have him under surveillance," he reported. "He spends a great deal of time away from home. He leaves for long periods of time, sometimes a month or six weeks. When he does come back, he meets frequently with a Martin Haran, also a cloth hawker. However, my men observed that this Haran, who also has a hawker's license, carries a pack of cloth, while Davitt never does."

"Is this man Haran a known Fenian?" asked the commissioner.

"Our informants tell us he is, although he is not very high up in the organization."

The commissioner stood up and looked out the window of his office. "If this Davitt never carries a pack, he must not be selling much cloth. You would think the man would at least make it look good."

"We don't think he is aware of the fact that we have him under surveillance," said the inspector, "but he's a slick one. Our surveillance team has to be very careful when they follow him. If he thinks he's being followed, he can slip in and out of a house so quickly that he seems to evaporate before their eyes."

The commissioner sat back down at his desk. "Yes, he is a cunning lad. Keep up the good work, inspector. Slippery as he is, we will still catch him."

* * *

Michael's arms trafficking was intensifying. He was purchasing revolvers and rifles, depositing them in a secret depot in Leeds, and then smuggling them to destinations in England, Scotland and Ireland. These were always paid for in cash, and many were purchased from gun makers in Birmingham who sold arms to anyone with the right amount of cash, no questions asked. Invoices and bills of lading were being changed at Leeds, where the arms were repackaged and marked as industrial goods and merchandise. So many goods were being shipped in and out of this area, it was difficult for the police to catch anyone. Only a small number of shipments were ever confiscated in port areas and many of these were shipped under the names of eminent English industrialists and then intercepted at their destination by Fenians. Sometimes the Fenians acted under fictitious names. It became difficult for the police to identify which arms were legitimate and which were meant for illegal purposes. It was not against the law for citizens to bear arms, and many Irish landlords insisted on carrying them for their own protection.

Michael met with his main suppliers, a group of partners named Minningham, Wilson and Gill. They were gun finishers and repairers, working mainly from unfinished specialty parts made by other manufactures.

Minningham, a gun finisher, held up an unfinished rifle to Michael. "We get some of these parts from Belgian and some from England," he said. "Then we put them together here and make a working revolver or rifle." He put down the rifle and picked up two pistol parts, one that had been purchased in Belgian and one made in England. "Belgian pistols are the best," he said. "They are manufactured to more exacting tolerances than the English models. However, the English models are getting better as the craftsmen get more experienced and the manufacturing equipment gets better. The English are still cheaper."

Michael took one of the finished Belgian pistols in his hand. Minningham watched in amazement as Michael opened and spun the revolving barrel and then clicked it shut while it was still spinning. Minningham had never seen that done with one hand.

"I'll keep this one for myself," he said. "We'll buy the Belgian revolvers for the officers and the English models for the regular soldiers, unless the soldiers want to pay for the Belgian variety themselves."

"We can produce the English types faster," said Minningham, "and they're not bad. If a soldier keeps them cleaned and oiled they will prove to be reliable. They are not of the same quality as the Belgian, but they will kill a man."

"I would like to make a purchase today," said Michael.

"See Wilson," said Minningham. "He's English and has no idea that Gill and I are Fenians. He never asks any questions. He's simply in the business for the money and we keep him innocent. His shop is next door." He pointed to a closed door in the middle of the room. "You can go through that connecting door."

Michael did not know whether his being Irish would have made any difference to Wilson, but he was not about to find out. Wilson seemed to be interested in the money, and never asked where the guns were going. He even at times helped deliver the pieces to various addresses, and never questioned whose addresses they were. To make sure that Wilson was kept apart from the purpose, Michael used the name W. R. Jackson when he purchased the guns.

* * *

The smuggling system was working much better under Michael's direction then it ever had under Forresters. Michael was much more clever and articulate than the young Forrester, and was much more detail-oriented. The police in Dublin had picked up on a mistake made by Forrester before Michael took over and streamlined the operation.

The inspector handed some papers to the commissioner. "We confiscated a shipment of arms being sent to a Mrs. Kennedy, a grocer on Sheriff Street in Dublin. We have had this address under surveillance for months, suspecting it to be a meeting place for Fenians. The place is used by a number of sawyers and carpenters who we suspect are making the rifle stocks for illegal arms. They were supposedly a tontine society, but our investigations disproved that. The labels on the shipment said the contents were sauce and pickles coming from a Mr. J. Reeves in Birmingham."

"Did your men check out this Reeves?" asked the commissioner.

"Yes," he said, "He was an Englishman, and we found out that he did have a sauce and pickle business at one time, but had emigrated to America nine months earlier. We opened the crates and found the arms."

The commissioner looked puzzled. "It doesn't sound like Davitt to make such a blatant error."

The inspector smiled. "You're right, commissioner. It was Forrester who made the shipment, before Davitt took over the operation."

"Well, it seems that the little Mr. Forrester has been the bait that is going to catch the big fish," said the commissioner. "Now we know how and from where they operate. We have them."

"But we cannot inspect every case of merchandise that leaves England for Ireland," replied the inspector. "We were lucky to have intercepted that one, but we need to be more intelligent in our approach. Since we now know that the Birmingham area is their source, we need to station a detective there."

The recommendation went to the inspector general, and he, in turn, appointed Head-Constable, John Bodley to the Birmingham position. Bodley had a sterling reputation as a police officer in Belfast.

Detective Murphy of Liverpool briefed Bodley on his assignment.

"There are three men who seem to be running the Fenian organization in Birmingham: Forrester, Davitt, and one William

Hogan. Forrester is a young hothead and will probably get himself killed sooner or later. Hogan runs the St. Patrick's Burial Society in Birmingham and seems to be the one who handles the funds for the area. But Davitt is by far the mastermind of the operation, the head of the snake, so to speak. Get him, and you will set back the whole operation for years. He's your priority."

"From what I read in his file," said Bodley, "it won't be easy to catch him. He's crafty and intelligent and has a gift for paying attention to details. Forrester seems like the most likely to make a mistake. I might use him to get Davitt."

"He's a foolhardy kid," said Murphy. "It should be easy to get him. Using him to get to Davitt might work. But I would let Forrester go if I could get Davitt."

Bodley shuffled some of the file papers in front of him. "First, I would like to see one of the revolvers and one of the rifles you confiscated in that last shipment. I might be able to trace them back to their source."

* * *

Bodley took the pieces to Birmingham and showed them to a well known gun maker, Mr. Webley.

"There is no doubt that this is the work of Robert Minningham, the gun finisher," Webley said, turning the revolver over in his hand. When Bodley showed him the rifle, he said, "I'm pretty sure about this, too. But you should ask Williamson the gun-maker about it. He employs craftsmen who specialize in rifling for this type of weapon. He could tell you more."

"You can tell that much even without the pieces bearing their identifying marks?" asked Bodley.

"Every craftsman has a slightly different way of doing things," Webley instructed. "Robert Minningham is the only

60

gun finisher who can produce work of this quality. Anyone in the business can tell you that."

Bodley went off to find Williamson.

Williamson's plant was not far from Webley's. It was a much bigger operation, employing over sixty men. When Williamson examined the rifle, he recognized the work at once.

"The rifling was done by Thomas Bembridge, who works for several gunsmiths," he said. "He is generally considered the best in his field outside of Belgium. His place of business is within walking distance from here."

Bodley thanked Williamson for the information and walked to Bembridge's in a few minutes. He found Bembridge working on a gun barrel. Bodley showed Bembridge his credentials, and then the confiscated gun barrel.

"It's my work," he admitted, "and I know exactly where that piece came from."

"Remember, Mr. Bembridge, this is part of a police investigation. This rifle is evidence," Bodley said.

"I did that work for Minningham, Gill and Wilson. It was Minningham who brought them in. It didn't seem like there was anything wrong. Minningham makes his living as gun finisher and he's a good one. Why do you say it is evidence? Evidence of what?"

"We believe they were sold to Fenians who were shipping them to Ireland."

Bembridge nodded. "We have so many customers come in and out of here purchasing arms," he said, "it's quite impossible to tell who is doing what with them."

"I quite understand, old man," said Bodley. "I thank you for lending your expertise to the police. It is much appreciated."

"I would be happy to help in any way I can, sir," said Bembridge. "You might need more information at a later time. Most of these gun dealers don't like talking to the police. Let me know if I can make further inquires for you."

Bodley understood what Bembridge was saying. He was right about gun dealers: Most were just taking money and looking the other way. They didn't want the police snooping into every deal they made. They were more likely to talk to Bembridge than to himself.

"I thank you for the offer, Mr. Bembridge. I will certainly let you know if I ever need your services again."

Bodley left, the first part of his investigation over. Now he knew the source of the weapons. It was time to set a trap.

* * *

First, Bodley had to find out who was purchasing the weapons from Minningham, Gill and Wilson, how they were transporting them out of Birmingham, and for whom they were intended. He enlisted the aid of Detective-Sargeant John Seal of the Birmingham police.

"They are almost certainly using the railway express," said Seal. "There's no other way to ship an order that large in so short a time. I suggest we enlist the aid of the railway officials. With their help, we should be able to stop this."

"You are most certainly right," said Bodley, "and using the railway express leaves a paper trail. But tracing the movements they were looking for was not easy. Buyers from everywhere were constantly coming and going in the Weaman Street area, where most of the dealers were located. Dealers were constantly in and out of each other's shops. Huge amounts of money would change hands, and guns were constantly being packed and shipped to many destinations. Gun-making was a big business.

Even Bembridge was giving false leads. Several times he alerted Bodley about suspicious transactions involving guns being shipped, all of which turned out to be legitimate. It was becoming very frustrating.

Bodley sat down with Seal and tried to find a better solution. "Perhaps we can approach Minningham, Gill and Wilson and offer them amnesty in return for testifying against the others?"

"I doubt they would do that," offered Seal. "If they did, they would wind up dead. The brotherhood would kill them in an instant."

"Well there, I don't know how we are going to do this, Seal. We need a break."

Just then, a note arrived from Bembridge. He wanted to see Bodley. "I hope it's not another dead end," said Bodley.

"I saw Minningham's younger brother take rifles away from his shop in a handcart," Bembridge reported. "I figured this might be a secret shipment. If it were legal, why use his brother and a handcart? I followed him, making sure he did not notice me."

"And just where did he go?" asked Bodley.

"He delivered them to a cottage at the end of an alley off Caroline Street about a mile away," he said. "Here's the address."

"Good job, old man," said Bodley. "Now get back to work like nothing happened. We'll take it from here." Bodley did not want anyone to get suspicious of Bembridge. The man was too valuable And perhaps this was the break he was waiting for..

Detective Seal handed the address back to Bodley "It belongs to a man named J. Rafferty, a dipper and silverer in the jewelry trade. He is on our list of suspected Fenians. We should set up a surveillance immediately to watch what happens to that shipment. "

"I'll bring Bembridge with us just in case they're picked up by someone we don't recognize," Bodley said.

The three men set up the surveillance at 5 p.m. the

following day. They watched all through the night, taking turns sleeping. The morning sun lit up the street but still no one had visited the cottage. " J. Rafferty" did not even venture outside. The team watched all day and still saw no one. Finally, at about 7 p.m. the vigilance paid off. The younger Minningham, accompanied by Wilson, arrived with a handcart. They took a packing case out of the cottage, loaded it on the cart, and began pushing it down the street, Bembridge and the detectives following at a distance. The men took the packing case to the goods receiving office of the Midland Railway in George Street Sandpits, located about a half-mile from Rafferty's cottage.

Alerting the railroad officials of their investigation, the detectives examined the package. It was addressed to 'John Wilson, Midland Good Station, Leeds- from John Wilson- to be called for.' Upon opening it, the detectives found it contained twenty rifles and bayonets. They were unfinished, and the gunmaker's markings had been removed. They were clearly illegal, there being no invoices or other documents which were required by law to accompany such a shipment. Bodley had the crate resealed and instructed the railway officials to send the package on to its destination. The next day, he boarded the train to follow it.

In Leeds, the package was collected by John Wilson, and a man who identified himself as Henderson. They loaded it onto a handcart and began pushing it away, followed at a short distance by Bodley, who saw Wilson walk away while Henderson went on to a small and well concealed warehouse. This location was not on Bodley's list. He was sure he had uncovered a clandestine Fenian gun depot.

There was no activity until the next day. Then Bodley observed a one-armed man walk up to the warehouse. He had hit the jackpot! It was Michael Davitt himself! Bodley watched as Henderson left, and returned with some empty wooden barrels. Later, he saw Davitt and Henderson emerge from the building and load two heavy wooden barrels onto the handcart. Henderson then took the barrels to the railway station and returned to get two more, and repeated the operation until six barrels were delivered. Once the six barrels were in the rail station, Bodley intercepted them and had them examined. They were addressed to John Flannery, Ballaghadereen, Co. Mayo, and Martin McDonnell, Tuam, Co. Galway. The other four were also addressed to various locations in Ireland.

Bodley had his evidence. He telegraphed the Inspector General in Dublin about his findings, and the next day all six barrels were confiscated by Superintendent Ryan's men in Dublin. All contained rifles, bayonets and revolvers as well as over six hundred rounds of ammunition.

Bodley's further investigation showed that the warehouse had been rented by Davitt under the name of W. R. Jackson. The home office had matched Davitt's handwriting to documents signed by W. R. Jackson, and determined them to be one and the same. They also had been able to determine that the "pen" letter, which Forrested had tried and failed to tear up, had been written by Davitt.

The police allowed Michael to conduct business as usual in order to build up a case against him. The news of the barrels being confiscated in Dublin got into the press, and Michael attempted to be more careful. He did not know he was being watched closely for every hour of the day. The police finally arrested him as he was attempting to take delivery on a gun shipment at a railway express office in Paddington.

Chapter Eight

The news of Michael's arrest hit the Fenians hard. They met at the beerhouse, and opinions varied on what course of action to take. One centre resigned his position, certain that since Michael had been caught, the police must have informers in the Fenian ranks, which would make it impossible to carry out their duties. If Michael got caught they were probably next. Others were blaming Forrester for their troubles, stating that he was too irresponsible to occupy the position he held. Others claimed that Michael, having one arm, was too easy for the police to spot and should never have been given the position of centre. They were also concerned about the £153 that Michael had on his person when he was caught. After all, that was Fenian money, and would probably be confiscated by the police. But after all the discussion, it was agreed that they still should support Michael.

Michael was very concerned about his family staying in England. He did not know what repercussions his arrest would have on them. Mary Agnes had married and her husband, Cornelius Padden, had gone to America, to Scranton, Pennsylvania, where he had found work in a coal mine. Mary Agnes was about to make the trip to join him.

"The whole family should go to America," Michael told his parents. "I don't know how safe it will be for you if you stay here."

Martin and Catherine looked at each other, as if they had a secret which they were reluctant to tell. "We had always planned to go back to Ireland some day," said Catherine.

"Mary Agnes, please tell them that the only sane thing for them to do is go to America with you!" Michael implored.

"You know Neil has already agreed to take you, Anne, and Sabina in until you get established in America," Mary Agnes said to her parents.

"We knew what a good man that Neil was when you married him," Catherine said. "He is like a son to us. But if we go to America, I'm afraid we will die there and never see Mayo again."

It was not easy for Michael to convince his parents, but with Mary Agnes' help he finally got them to agree that America was the only choice they had. Things were still pretty bad in Mayo and there was nothing to return to. Reluctantly, they agreed and sailed to New York in April of 1870.

* * *

With his family now safely in Scranton, Michael prepared himself for his trial. Standing before the magistrate, he was surprised to see that Wilson, the gun dealer, had also been charged with felony-treason, even though Michael had taken great pains not to get Wilson directly involved in the movement.

The first to testify for the prosecution was the informer, J. J. Corydon, who swore that he knew Davitt and had seen him at Liverpool in the company of well know Fenians right after the attempt to storm Chester Castle.

"Do You know most of these Fenians?" asked the prosecutor.

"Yes," replied Corydon. "I lived in Ireland for a number of years working for the Dublin police as an informer. I came in contact with many Fenians during that time."

The usually reserved Michael could not hold back his anger. "YOU could not live in Ireland---reptiles cannot live there!" he shouted.

"Mr. Davitt, I must warn you against further outbreaks in this courtroom," said the magistrate. "You will get your turn when the time comes. In the meantime, if you do not control your behavior, I will order you gagged."

Michael slumped back into his seat. It was a childish show of emotion, and he knew he had to control himself if he were going to get through this.

Several police officers were then called to testify. They detailed evidence, mostly from surveillance teams that had been set up by Bodley, about arms trafficking. Michael was astounded at the amount of information they had. It seemed that, despite all his precautions, they knew just about everything. They must have been watching him twenty four hours a day.

But the most damaging of all was the testimony given by handwriting experts, who testified that the names and addresses listing the recipients of several arms shipments were in Davitt's handwriting, although bearing the signature of W. R. Jackson.

The defense argued that in spite of the assumed name, the arms shipments were legal and intended for legal owners in England, Scotland and Ireland. After all, it was not illegal to bear arms in Great Britain. Michael also maintained that he was working at Mr. Cockcroft's printing shop at the time of the Chester Castle incident, and therefore Corydon could not have seen him there.

Mr. Cockroft himself testified on Michael's behalf. He gave an impassioned plea, claiming how well-liked Michael was and what a good and reliable employee he had been.

The print shop work log was subpoenaed but unfortunately it did not back up Cockcroft's insistence that Michael had worked there continuously.

After several days of testimony, the verdict was still in doubt. It was at this point that the prosecution introduced their best evidence. They showed a torn letter which they had pasted together, and which had been confiscated from Arthur Forrester, whom the police had arrested for arms smuggling. Forrester, they testified, had tried to tear up the letter but was only able to get two tears before the police snatched it from his hands.

And so the "pen letter," along with the testimony of the informer and the police, convinced the court of Michael Davitt's guilt. The same verdict was also returned on Wilson. When

Michael heard the verdict on Wilson, he asked for permission to speak. He pleaded with the court not to punish Wilson.

"He is innocent of any wrongdoing," he testified. "It would be a miscarriage of justice to punish him. Place his sentence upon me, but please let him go."

His plea was to no avail. Wilson received seven years of penal servitude. Michael was not so lucky. His sentence was also to penal servitude--but for fifteen years.

Chapter Nine

During his trial, Michael had already spent two months in prison: first at Paddington police station, then in the Clerkenwell House of Detention, and finally at Newgate prison. He had been detained in these places in spite of the fact that he was still at trial and not yet proved guilty by a court of law. The judge had determined that being a Fenian made him too high a risk to set bail. After he was convicted, he was removed to Millbank Penitentiary which handled sentences of penal servitude.

1870

Michael arrived at Millbank at the age of twenty-four, on the 29th of July. He was a good-looking, strapping young man, fully six feet tall and sported the popular look of the day, a black mustache and long, trimmed sideburns. He looked up at the wooden prison gate and glanced at the grey granite walls in which it was set. It was a huge place, the long, grey line of stones extending down almost as far as he could see on both sides. It was also high, several stories high. A look at the iron bars set strongly into the windows made him shudder. There would be no getting out of here. He told himself he would have to make the best of it. He was going in as a political prisoner, but he would walk into it proudly, for his cause was just. *Let them make a martyr out of me,* he thought to himself. *I will wear it like a badge of honor.*

The prison gate door opened and Michael was ushered into the waiting room. There were benches on which other prisoners sat, about a yard apart from each other, waiting to be processed. Michael was instructed to sit in a designated spot. Talking was prohibited. He was told to ask no questions and not to look at the other prisoners. Everything else he would need to know would be told to him in time.

Sitting at a big desk in front of the room was the turnkey,

who enforced the no communications rule. He chastised one prisoner, who obviously had been there for some time, for looking around the room. Michael thought it was best to just put his head down and stare at the floor.

"Make no mistake about it," said the turnkey in a loud voice which echoed off the grey stone walls, "You are now part of the Queen's livery."

Part of the Queen's livery, thought Michael to himself. *What were we Irish before? We have never been other than a part of the Queen's livery.*

The turnkey called up the first prisoner. He was a sickly-looking lad, probably about eighteen years old.

"Empty your pockets on the desk," said the turnkey in his sternest voice.

The boy did not have much, a few buttons and a chain. All were confiscated and recorded in the property book. The boy was taken away.

Other prisoners had a variety of objects in their pockets: chains, pipes, watch fobs, a hair brush, a toothbrush.. All were confiscated by the turnkey.

"You won't be needing any of these items where you're going," he said with a smirk on his face. He seemed to be enjoying himself, passing out the indignities. He purposely dropped a hair brush on the floor and broke it into pieces by stomping on it with his heel.

The prisoner who owned the hairbrush looked at the turnkey with an angry scowl.

"In two months you won't be scowling at anyone," said the turnkey, scowling back.

Michael had only a small purse with a few shillings. The turnkey confiscated it and wrote it in the property book.

"Where do you think you're going, W82215? Shopping in the Queen's bakery?"

This brought a small laugh from the other guard.

Michael stood firm and continued to stare at the floor. He was then moved out to the next section, and here he was instructed to remove his clothes and stand in a stall. The stall was a cramped space, hardly able to fit a person six feet tall; he had to bend over to get himself into it. He was given a bucket of water and told to dump it on himself.

"Make sure you include your head," said the guard.

The water was a sickly, yellow color and looked like chicken broth. The slime that he felt under his feet on the cement floor made his skin creep. He splashed the water over himself. He was then handed a dirty towel and told to dry himself. Although the towel was dry, it was a sickly, brown color. He moved on to the next room, carrying his clothes which he handed to the guard.

"Do you identify these as your clothes?" said the guard.

"Yes," said Michael, bewildered.

The guard took them and tossed them into a great pile of clothing in the corner of the room. "They now belong to the Queen," he said, and proceeded to give Michael the prison clothing, which were nearly rags. The shirt was a bright scarlet and the pants were grey, both severely worn. There were no undergarments.

Michael felt as if his old life had been torn from him. It was worse than hearing the prison door closing and locking him in. Now he truly felt like a prisoner.

"What will happen to my suit?" he asked.

"Her Majesty's prison will sell it to help defray the cost of your incarceration," said the guard.

The next step was the examination by the prison doctor. This was mostly to determine which prisoners were fit for hard or light labor. Due to his status as an amputee, Michael was to work in his cell picking oakum, a loose, stringy hemp fiber obtained by taking apart old ropes. The stuff was used mainly for calking boat seams. Michael saw that he would spend his prison time helping the Royal Navy dominate the high seas.

It seemed to him that the day would never end. Finally, after being fed a measure of oatmeal, he was taken to his cell. It was ten feet long and eight feet wide. The bed was nothing more than a supported plank. Stacked neatly in the corner was a lidded bucket (for holding water), a pint tin, and a chamber pot. He was to spend ten hours a day here in solitary confinement with nothing to do but pick the oakum that was brought to him.

* * *

Millbank prison was situated on the north banks of the Thames, near the Houses of Parliament and not far from Westminster Abbey. Above the susurrus of voices from the Londoners passing by under the windows of his cell, were the sounds of the London streets: horses, crates being unloaded, ships passing on the river. Even though he could not see any of these things, they were actually pleasant sounds to him, but for one thing: Every fifteen minutes, the chimes of Big Ben would shake the very prison walls. It was both impossible to ignore it and not to think about it; the anticipation of it was worse than the sound itself. Michael did not know if he could take it. He felt his mind bend under the strain.

During the next few weeks, he prayed. "Please don't let me lose my mind," he implored the Almighty. "I can feel the strain, Lord. I don't want to go mad."

Each night, after his work was done, his mind began wandering. Deprived of any human interaction, he retreated into the past. He began to see things that had happened to him in his childhood with remarkable clarity. They were just short of being hallucinations. He was four and a-half, in Straide. The bailiff was yelling at his father, telling him that he was being evicted. He could see his Martin stepping toward the bailiff and the men with the crowbars barring Martin's way. He could feel the heat

75

of the fire as the thatched roof fell into the hot embers of the fireplace. He saw his father sitting helplessly in what was left of their furniture in the middle of the road with his head in his hands. He felt his mother's hand holding him close to her leg as he was clinging to her while she held Mary Agnes in her other arm. Once again, he made the journey to the workhouse and heard his mother say, "I'll not be separated from my son!"

He could see, with perfect clarity, the man in the wagon who carved the turnip into the shape of a pocket watch, and the horse who did not want to leave Ireland. He remembered the trip to Haslingden, and the boys who tormented them. He saw the face of James Bonner, lifting the blanket that was providing the shelter for his family when they were thrown out of the flat because he had the measles. John Ginty's mangled body fell out of the cotton machine in front of him. He heard John's mother singing over her son's dead body. He felt the boot of the foreman who made him work on the cotton machine, and relived the pain of the accident which took his right arm.

After a while, even these images began to fade. He began looking around his cell when his work of picking the Oakum was done. He had only a few daylight hours which he could spend on himself, and the guards would not let the prisoners pace. He began to stare at the wall in front of him. It was made of grey, unfinished stone and therefore contained many natural cracks and crevices. These became canyons and valleys in his mind, and he imagined himself leading Fenian troops through them, surprising the British. A small crack running about six or seven inches became a river, and a bump in the stone became a British fortress. With his imagination running wild, Michael was sure he was losing his mind.

Next he began examining the door to his cell. It was made of heavy English oak, and several prisoners had scratched their names into it for posterity. Michael recognized the name "John Devoy." He had never met Devoy, but had certainly heard of him. A well-known Fenian, high up in their inner circles, he remembered when the man was arrested. He also recalled the newspaper article that reported on Devoy's release from prison on the condition that he be exiled to America. So this was the cell that Devoy had occupied!

It would have been more tolerable if he had been given books to read. But the only books allowed to prisoners was the Protestant bible and the serials *Good Words, Leisure Hours* and *Sunday at Home.* These were solid, Protestant, Victorian works which the Catholic Chaplin would not allow the Catholic prisoners to have. The only other books given to him were two elementary school books, *Naughty Fanny* and *Grandmother Betty.*

Just when Michael thought he would lose his mind forever, an unexpected thing happened. He received a letter from his family in America. It was from his mother, written in his father's hand since she could not read or write. Prisoners in solitary could receive only one letter during this period, and this was it.

Michael ripped open the envelope and began to read hungrily. He could see his mother's face as she told of their new life in America. They were living with Mary Agnes in Pennsylvania and Mary Agnes's husband, Cornelius was making a good living as a coal miner. Martin had found steady work as a mason. The United States was beautiful and no one had to go hungry. Everyone got the chance to go to school. The rest of the letter described ordinary events like attending church and taking care of the grandchildren. Mundane as it was, Michael kept reading it over and over every chance he got. He could see his mother's face whenever he read it, and he drew strength from her memory. He thanked God for the letter, and then for his family. It kept his sanity. He had been allowed to write one letter during the first six months of his solitary confinement phase, and he had done so, to his family, on his arrival. He

77

would not be able to do so again for five more months.

He was also denied visitors, even though he was entitled to at least two visitors during this first phase of his sentence. Two had come and been turned away. One was James Haran, a close friend. The other was Ellen Forrester, Arthur Forrester's mother.

* * *

Michael had spent ten months in Millbank when the prison governor came to his door. "Davitt!" he shouted. "Get your things together. You're being released."

Michael felt his heart jump from sheer joy. He was getting out! Amnestied! He would go to America and join his family! He would see his mother's face again and talk again with his father. He would see how his nieces and nephews had grown. Perhaps he would get a job in Pennsylvania like the rest of his family, and he would be happy.

When he arrived at the prison gate, the wagon waiting for him. "Where are we going?" asked Michael of the wagon guard.

"You're being transferred to Dartmoor," he said, "to serve out the rest of your sentence."

Michael's heart grew sick. It was a cruel joke. He was just going to another prison. He thought back on the actions of the governor. How could a man like that live with himself? How could anyone be so cruel? Did it make him feel good to do this to another man? Michael made a vow to himself while he was riding, locked up in the cell of the black maria carriage: If he ever got out of this, he would work for better treatment of prisoners here, and everywhere in England.

* * *

On 25 May in 1871, Michael entered Dartmoor Prison for the second phase of his sentence. In this phase, the prisoners were required to work at hard labor. The prison physician deemed Michael well enough to perform heavy manual labor, in spite of his disability. He was immediately assigned to breaking rocks with a sledge hammer, which he was barely able to swing with one arm. The increase in physical labor was not accompanied by much of an increase in food, only about three ounces of bread more than he had received at Millbank. He began to lose weight.

Still, as difficult as life was in Dartmoor, it was a welcome change from solitary. Even though he could not converse at length with other prisoners, he could at least have contact with them. The work was hard on all of them, but even a short, "I'll get that," from another prisoner sounded like an encyclopedia to Michael. Even though his physical condition seemed to be deteriorating, his mind was again growing sharp.

One day the guard decided to have Michael pull a wagon filled with rocks. They hooked him up like a beast of burden with a harness around his shoulders. He was barely able to move the cart but he strained to it, not wanting the guard to see him break under the weight. Anther prisoner offered to help him or even take his place, and was loudly told not to interfere. Michael pulled and strained as hard as he could. He moved the cart.

That night, the stub of his arm began to ache. The pain became so intense that he asked to see the prison doctor. When the doctor saw the redness of the arm stub, he placed Michael on lighter duties. This meant pounding in the bone shed. Bones were gathered from various dead animals both from the prison itself and the surrounding farms. Michael's job was to pound the bones into as fine a powder as possible. The powder was then used for fertilizer in the fields surrounding the prison.

It was loathsome work. The bone shed was located just outside the prison cesspool, which gave off the most awful smell imaginable. The smell of the bones would have been bad enough, but the stench of the cesspool which collected the human waste of the entire prison was nearly unbearable.

Chapter Ten

Prime Minister Gladstone looked at the food being placed on the table in front of him. The choice was among beef, pork, or lamb served with mint. Potatoes, peas, carrots, and gravy also adorned the table, all served on the finest silver plates and dishes.

"Sometime I would like some French cooking as well," said Gladstone, directing his remarks to the butler.

"Sir, we have hired a French chef from Paris who will be cooking at the end of this week," said the butler. "You must remember, sir, that it will take him about three days just to make the sauce for his first meal. He will be serving...."

"Don't tell me," interrupted Gladstone, "I want to be surprised. It will take some of the drudgery out of these meals."

"As you wish sir," answered the butler, bowing himself out of the room.

After the meal, Gladstone turned to his secretary and began drafting the new act, soon to be introduced, about which he had already had many conversations with supportive members of Parliament. The new law would provide for the protection of tenants who had no recourse to the government if they were abused. It would provide compensation to tenants for improvements made to a farm if the tenant surrendered his lease, as well as compensation to tenants for damage for "disturbance", which meant for tenants evicted for causes other than non-payment of rent.

"Read it back to me," said Gladstone, and the secretary obliged.

Gladstone then thought about the next clause, which the members of his party had drafted but which he was very reluctant to accept. It was known as the "bright clause" and allowed tenants to borrow from the government two-thirds of the cost of buying their holding, at 5% interest mortgaged over thirty-five years. This, of course, assumed that the landlord was willing to sell but the act would not compel a landlord to do so. Gladstone thought that few landlords would be willing to sell and therefore the clause would be useless.

The secretary read the clause back and noted an important point.

"In my earlier notes," he said, "you stated that you were contemplating a solution to rack-renting and asked me to do some research on the subject. Sir, I found out it is a very widespread practice. The landlords raise the rents so high, that they insure the tenant cannot pay them. They then evict the tenants for non-payment of rent."

"Yes, thank you for reminding me of that," said Gladstone. "These provisions will be of little use unless we can curb that practice. Making landlords pay compensation and exempting them from it in the case of non-payment of rents will only induce them to raise the rents and avoid the intent of law. Let us put in the phrase that rents must not be 'excessive,' and leave the description of excessive for the courts to decide."

"Well done, sir," said the secretary. "I will draft this bill under the title 'The Irish Land Act,' and have it ready for your signature in less then an hour."

"Good! I'll be by the fireplace." Gladstone summoned the butler. "Bring me a snifter of our finest cognac," ordered Gladstone. "I believe I have changed history tonight and I wish to celebrate."

What Gladstone did not know was that the House of Lords would later substitute the word "exorbitant" in place of the word "excessive," and thereby take the teeth out of the act that would have stopped rack-renting.

* * *

Michael Davitt sat down to his meal at Dartmoor Prison.

This was the evening that the best meal of the week was being served: three ounces of meat, bread, water, and oatmeal. Michael looked down at the oatmeal and saw a cockroach struggling in it. He picked the insect up and tossed it aside. The bug made a mad dash for the end of the table when another prisoner, sitting right across from Michael, picked it up, put it in his mouth, and swallowed it.

Michael stared at the man.

"It's a source of nourishment," the man said. He offered that he had been a chemist, and had been convicted of trying to poison a rival. It was only through the skills of a good lawyer that he had narrowly escaped the death penalty. He was in Dartmoor for life.

"What does it feel like to eat a cockroach?" asked Michael.

"The best thing is to swallow them whole. You can feel them squirm in your stomach for a moment until the stomach acid kills them, so it's not so bad. When I was in India, I saw many people eating insects. I got over my revulsion long ago."

Michael thought about the people in India and how the British Empire had exploited them.

"I read much about India and how the British defend their interest there," said Michael.

"British interests, indeed," said the chemist. "I can assure you that the British do not run India for the sake of the Indians. You are eating better in this prison than most Indians ever do."

"I can imagine, if they are eating insects to survive," said Michael.

"Not all of them do, of course. India has a strict caste system. If you belong to the upper caste, you eat well. If you are in the lowest caste, the Untouchables, you would be better off in this prison."

"So their system is not much different than the one we

live under here," Michael offered. "As you know, they do not treat our Irish very well. It appears we are the British equivalent of the Untouchables, at least if one is an Irish Catholic."

"You're Irish?" said the Chemist. "You don't speak like an Irish."

"I was brought up in Haslingden," said Michael. "I lost my arm in an industrial accident there."

"I see," said the man. "I would gladly give up my right arm if I could serve only fifteen years."

"That's enough conversation," shouted the guard. "What do you think this is, a tea party at the Queen's court? Finish up your meal and let's get ourselves moved."

Michael thought he would like to converse more with this man, but was grateful for even this small interlude. Normally prisoners could not talk to each other. It was a rare moment when a guard was occupied elsewhere. Otherwise, a conversation of such a length would never have been allowed.

Michael went back to his cell for the night. It was a cold evening and he wrapped a blanket around himself. He sat in a corner with a tin cup of water and contemplated the conversation he had just had with the chemist. It was so cold, and he was so tired, that he fell asleep. He did not even hear the cup clank on the stone floor when it fell out of his hand.

* * *

December 1871

Michael had been in Dartmoor for ten months. Working outdoors in the bone yard, he felt the winter chill bite at his face and hand. He could even feel it in his shoulders. All the pounding was causing his hand to ache regularly. He stopped for a moment and tried to warm his hand under his shirt, and noticed that he could feel his ribs. He pulled his shirt up and looked down at his side, and could see that his ribs were beginning to show prominently. He was losing weight. It was all he could do to finish his work that day; fatigue was overwhelming him.

When he got back to his cell, there was a letter waiting for him. He felt the blood rush to his head, anticipating another letter from home. Michael tore open the envelope and read the sad news. His father was not well, but the letter did not say what was wrong. His mother quickly got off that subject and began speaking about the new grandchildren. He remembered that Mother could not write and it was Martin who was actually writing the letter.

I guess the illness is not serious, Michael thought to himself. *If it were, Mother would certainly have found a way to say it.*

Martin had been sick before. Michael remembered him being out of work several times in Haslingden, but he always recovered. The longest he was ever out of work was a week. Michael put the thought of his father's illness out of his mind and enjoyed reading the rest of the letter and hearing about his nieces and nephews. He read it over and over again, trying to picture their faces and hear their voices.

The letter kept up his strength. About three weeks later, another letter arrived. Immediately Michael noticed that this one was not in his father's hand. He would not allow himself to think the worst, but when he read the letter he learned that his father had died.

Michael's initial reaction was denial. The last letter said that Martin was ill, but did not mention that the illness was serious. It could not be! He read the letter again, hoping that he had misread it, but it was true. Martin Davitt was dead.

Michael was overcome with grief. It had been a long time since he had cried, but with this event he was unable to control his emotions. He began blaming himself. Perhaps if he had not sent his family to America, Martin would still be alive. He had not been with him at the end. Catherine did not say if he had received the Last Rites of the Church, but Michael had to assume that he did.

He began to curse being a convict. He had always borne the suffering that came with being in such a place because he thought himself a patriot. He was there serving his country: a political prisoner. Now, for the first time, he cursed being a prisoner because it kept him from being there when his father needed him most.

Under the circumstances, he was allowed to write back to his mother. When he received her response, she said that she wanted to come to England to visit him. Michael immediately answered her. "It would be folly to travel 6,000 miles just to visit with me for a few minutes," he wrote. He went on to say that just thinking about her making such a trip would be more than he could bear, given the fact he would feel responsible for her having to undertake such a journey. He made it clear that he would be very unhappy if she attempted such a trip.

But Catherine was persistent. She wrote back, insisting that she had to make the trip to comfort her son who had just lost his father. Once again, Michael wrote to dissuade her from doing such a foolish thing. He assured her that making such a journey would do neither of them any good.

Much to Michael's relief, Catherine finally relented and gave up her plans to visit her son. She began writing about the rest of the family and keeping Michael abreast of the latest family news. Michael's uncle Henry and his son, Michael's cousin and also named Michael had moved to Albany, New York where there was a large Irish community and where they could get work. Catherine and Michael's sisters, Anne and Sabina moved out of Mary Agnes' house and went to Manayunk, Pennsylvania, outside Philadelphia. Mary Agnes now had seven children, and the house could not accommodate everyone. Catherine and the girls had found work in Manayunk and were getting along fine. Mary Agnes and her husband Neil kept in close contact with them, and there was also a large Irish community in Manayunk, so they had plenty of support.

At least they are all right, Michael thought. Catherine had Anne and Bina with her and was not far from her grandchildren. She was fifty-one years old now, but Michael knew she was a strong woman and she would get along well. She was even able to send him $20 from time to time so he could bribe the guards into giving him pen and tablet. As long as he kept the guards satisfied, he was able to keep a journal and smuggle out an occasional letter to her.

To him, America sounded like a wonderful place. Every child was being educated and even his illiterate mother was able to find work and take care of herself. It seemed that almost anyone could own a home. People were not starving, begging and dying in the streets of America, and the crops never seemed to fail. Michael thought he would like to go there after he got out of Dartmoor.

Yet, Catherine kept writing about going back to Ireland. She was torn now that Martin was gone. On the one hand, she wanted to be buried with him, on the other she wanted to go back home to Mayo. Yet she knew that she would never leave Martin alone in the soil of America, and therefore she would never see Ireland again. Bitter as it was, she had made up her mind to stay and die in America. She would be with her husband when her time came. Besides, her grandchildren had now become Americans. They would never know the ache of hunger, the humility of the workhouse, the sting of the eviction, the poverty, the illiteracy, the death. Many times, she wrote, they would ask her what life was like in Ireland, but she would never talk about it with them.

"Those days are gone," she would tell them. "This is a new country, a new land. You all know how to read and write. The old ways are gone."

In her letters, she went on to say, "those who are full do

not understand the wants of the hungry, and these children are full. Why should I disturb them with tales of our poverty?. And did we not have it better than most? True, we lost baby James, but that was from sickness, not starvation. We did not live in a hole in the ground or beg alms to bury our dead child. These children will never know that and I will never tell them of it."

As he was reading these words, Michael began to cry. With all that his family had gone through, his mother still considered herself fortunate. Once again, his mother had became his pillar of strength. He felt ashamed that he had ever felt sorry for himself, that he had thought he would never make it through prison life. He could feel his mother's strength surging into his body as he resolved that no English prison would ever break him.

Chapter Eleven

Isaac Butt was a Protestant and a Tory Member of Parliament. He was also a brilliant barrister who had made a name for himself defending Fenians after the 1867 upising. The poverty of Ireland had twinged his conscience, his conservatism slowly giving way to a more liberal view. He thought that only way to solve the problems his country was facing was for Ireland to have home rule and legislative independence. He had formed the Amnesty Association for the release of Fenian prisoners. This organization had some success freeing several Fenians like John Devoy, but it was too late to help Michael Davitt. In 1870, Butt founded the Home Rule Association and was elected to Parliament on the Home Rule ticket as a representative for Limerick.

Isaac sat in Prime Minister Gladstone's private quarters. "Your Land Act is only the beginning of what needs to be done," he said, "but it leaves too much power to the landlord. They are still causing hardship to the peasantry, still exploiting them legally."

Gladstone knew that Isaac was right. "It is difficult to get anything passed in the House of Lords," he answered. "We were very lucky to even get them to consider the Land Act, and still they managed to change the phrase 'excessive rents' to 'exorbitant rents' against my will."

"Yes, and they made your Land Act quite useless in doing so," said Isaac. "These lords are legislating in their own interests. Most are major landlords, and they will continue to support legislation designed to protect their profits. The only answer for Ireland is home rule and a right to legislate independently of the British Parliament. We must see to it that the House of Lords is stripped of the power they have over the Irish peasants."

"But the lords are not just going to hand over their power to an Irish Parliament," said Gladstone. "They know what that would mean. Such a body would pass local laws that would eventually drive the absentee landlords out of Ireland and give the land to the Irish peasants. It would upset the entire structure of the British Empire. Even worse, the idea could spread to other lands, like India."

"And India is a good example," said Isaac. "The Indians need salt to preserve their food, and salt is a royal monopoly in India. It is against the law for an Indian to produce or sell salt. The Royals hire Indians to enforce this law against other Indians."

"But It has been like that since Roman times," said Gladstone. "I don't think we can break the entire system upon which the British Empire operates."

"If we don't, the Fenians will. If we're going to have a peaceful Ireland, we must make the citizens of Ireland full-fledged citizens and not feudal serfs."

"You're right, of course," said Gladstone. "However, this so-called 'feudal' system is working for the British upper classes, and won't be easy to break."

"Slavery was working for the American plantation holders and the system was broken," said Isaac.

"True, but not without a fight."

* * *

Michael received another smuggled letter which nearly drove him to insanity. He learned that his friend and former employer, Cockcroft, had died. He felt a grief similar to what he had felt upon learning Martin was dead. Cockcroft was sixty-five years old and had continued to run his shop in Haslingden for forty years. Michael remembered the first time he had met Cockcroft He remembered the look on Cockcroft's face when

Michael, an amputee, had set the type for the advertising bill with one hand as fast as the shop's other worker had with two. He remembered the day Cockcroft promoted him, and saw again his face when Michael told him he was quitting to become a drapery and cloth hawker.

It took awhile for Michael to get over Cockcroft's death. Mercifully, It would be several years before he would find out that Cockcroft's death was ruled a suicide due to an unsound mind, and that it was the doctor's opinion that Michael's arrest and conviction had contributed to the deterioration of Cockcroft's mental condition.

* * *

August 1876

Four years had passed slowly for Michael. He had survived several long, icy Dartmoor winters in the bone yard when his requests to be moved to indoor work had fallen on deaf ears. Suddenly, in August, he was moved to the prison washhouse. He did not know that the police had informed the governor that Clan na Gael was planning to rescue him and possibly other Fenians. The governor took this news seriously and had Michael transferred to the washhouse, where it would be easier to keep him under surveillance.

The washhouse turned out to be a mixed blessing. It meant that he could finally be out of the yard where the cold winters and summer sun were taking a toll on him, but the washhouse was very hot and caused excessive sweating. Therefore he would be given the privilege of bathing once a week instead of once a fortnight. He was set to work on the wringing machine, which was much harder labor than the bone yard. Working the wringer machine with one hand was almost at the limit of his physical abilities, but he was able to perform as well as anyone else. When the end of the week came and the washhouse prisoners were led to the bath, they were forced to bathe in water already used by other prisoners.

Nights in the new section proved to be a hardship as well. His new cell was located next to the punishment cells, and he was constantly kept awake by the cries of the prisoners, which often lasted into the night. To add to his misery, the warder in charge of the section would open a trap door located right above Michael's bed and shine a lantern on his face. This often interrupted his sleep, and so he had to face the long, hard days at the wringer with little sleep.

All of these prisoners in the punishment section were on bread and water rations only, and many were insane. Michael was never allowed to spend more than twelve days in one cell, and every time he was moved into a new cell he had to deal with the mess left by the last prisoner. In some cases the stench from vomit was so bad it almost overcame him. His weight had dropped badly, and the mental anguish was also taking its toll.

Once again, his mother's strength sustained him. He kept thinking about her not letting go of him in the workhouse and clinging to him in the blanket tent in Haslingden when he had the measles. He survived then, and he could survive now.

His only break came when he bribed the guards. He was able to obtain pencil and tablet and write to his family. He managed to smuggled out some of his writings, some of which were published in the Irish newspapers. He even received two pounds for one of the pieces.

* * *

October 1877

It had been more than seven years since Michael first went to prison. In October he received a letter from home stating that his sister Anne had gotten married. Her new husband, Edward Crowley, was a laborer and a son of Irish immigrants from Cork. They were making their home with

Michael's mother, and this was a great help to Catherine and Sabina. The extra money helped put food on the table, and life was a little better for everyone.

This news lifted Michael's spirits. Knowing that his sisters and his mother were being taken care of lifted a heavy burden from him since he could not help but feel responsible for their predicament. He was in prison and unable to help them. He hated taking money from them to bribe the guards so he could continue the letter smuggling. But his penal servitude was about to end.

Thanks to the increased activities of the Amnesty Association and people like Isaac Butt, Michael was informed that he would be given a ticket of leave. The conditions required him not to get into any trouble, or he would have to forfeit his ticket and serve out the remainder of his time. Michael did not fully understand why he was being released. When he was told, he didn't believe it. He remembered the prison governor at Millbank, who told him he was being released when he was merely being transferred to another prison. But when it became apparent that he was actually being released, he could not contain his joy.

Michael was now thirty-one years old. Outside the prison walls where he had spent seven years, wearing a new suit and looking up at the sky he was finally free. But still Ireland wasn't free. So much had changed around here, with his family, and he had changed too. He had gone to prison for smuggling some rifles to Ireland without even knowing if any had actually been used. Seven years and nothing was accomplished. There had to be another way. He thought of what his father had told him years earlier.

"Jesus of Nazareth was able to change the mighty empire of Rome with twelve unarmed men," Martin had said. "It took more than three hundred years and cost many lives, but it was done. He did not bring down the Roman Empire with a sword.

He brought it down with an idea."

Michael thought, *I must change people's minds about how to bring down the British Empire. The Fenian way did not work. If we shoot at the landlord, we must hit him in the purse!*

Chapter Twelve

1877

Isaac Butt was sixty-four years old and still a Member of Parliament when he and the other members of the political prisoner's welcoming committee greeted Michael Davitt on his arrival in London. The others were Richard O'Shaughnessy, also an MP, F. H. O'Donnell, and John Ryan. Ryan was the only person that Michael knew. They had both been Fenians and had done business in gun running some years before.

Isaac was a short, stocky man, clean shaven with long flowing, white hair. Most of the others had the characteristic mustaches and long sideburns common to the fashion of the times.

"Welcome, Michael," said Butt as he extended his right hand out to Davitt, forgetting that Michael had no right hand. Michael reached out with his left hand and grasped Isaac who looked embarrassed for having made such a mistake.

"Oh, I'm sorry," said Butt.

"It's all right," said Michael. "People need to get used to me. It's a simple reflex action."

Butt's face flushed a little red as he took his hand away. Michael was deceiving. He had lost a great deal of weight in prison and looked more like a starving poet than a revolutionary, But Isaac noticed how strong his hand was. He proceeded to introduce Michael to O'Shaughnessy and O'Donnell. After the amenities, O'Donnell wanted to talk to Michael privately.

"I would like to take some of the recently released prisoners to Ireland to talk about their prison experiences." said O'Donnell. "We would certainly like to have you along. We will pay your expenses, of course. I handle the funds for the prisoners' visiting committee, and the others have authorized me to make this offer."

It was a nice offer Michael thought. *Since I have little money and no prospects.* "I have a lot to say about how the prison system is run," Michael said aloud. "I welcome the chance."

"Wonderful," said O'Donnell. "I'll make the arrangements right away."

"You mentioned there were others. Might I ask who they are?"

"Certainly. Thomas Chambers, Charles 'Happy' McCarthy, and John Patrick O'Brien."

Michael thought he recognized these names, but it had been a long time. He wasn't sure just who they were. Then the thought hit him: He was going to Ireland! He had not set foot in his native land for twenty-seven years! He was four years old when his family had crossed from Dublin to Liverpool. He felt the excitement gather in his chest. He thought he would never see the Old Sod again. Yet the memories he had were so sad.

Once again he saw his family's house being torn down and the roof burning. He remembered the horse who ran off and his father's comment about "He's an Irish horse and doesn't want to leave Ireland." *Strange, he thought, all these years my parents wanted to return and they never could.* Now his father was gone and his mother was dedicated to staying in America with her grandchildren to comfort her. Only he would get the chance to return.

Michael looked at O'Donnell. "How soon before we leave?" he asked.

"Right after Christmas," said O'Donnell. "In the meantime, John Ryan will put you up. You needn't worry. Your earnings on this lecture circuit will pay for your keep."

It was a comforting thought. Michael did not want to be a burden to anyone, but knew he did not have much choice. Earning his way by lecturing would renew his own sense of worth and make him feel as though the seven years of prison could contribute something.

* * *

Michael found out that two men, an MP by the name of Charles Stuart Parnell and another by the name of O'Connor Power, with some help from a few others, were responsible for the release of several political prisoners, including himself. He decided to seek these men out and thank them in person.

He and Parnell hit it off right away. Parnell was an aging Anglo-Irish MP who had been educated in England and had an American mother. Although he seemed to be a typical Englishman in manner and speech, he was certainly pro-Irish. In fact, he seemed to hate all things English. Michael had already been told that Parnell had joined the Home Rule movement, and found out later that he had a reputation as an obstructionist in parliament, where he had made many long and boring speeches simply to annoy the members.

Parnell was also a landlord, but not the type that Michael had come to despise. He was a champion for tenants' rights. He and Michael had a long and intense talk about the situation in Ireland and what should be done to correct it. Michael also found out that Parnell was an admirer of his, who told him that if he ever had to serve in penal servitude and face solitary the way Michael had, he would murder a warder and get hanged rather than endure such a thing.

"Will you continue to work in the Home Rule movement?"

"I think home rule is the only solution to the land problem," said Michael. "At least it's a first step. I'm beginning to believe that the Fenians cannot solve the problem."

"Well, we have a future for you," said Parnell. "We will talk when you return from Ireland. Perhaps together we can plan a strategy that will save our Irish people."

* * *

Christmas came quickly. The Ryan house was full of cheer and Michael was enjoying the good food. Ryan thought it strange that Michael did not drink, but respected Michael's strong temperate views. Michael was having a wonderful time. It was his first Christmas outside of prison in seven years. If only he had been with his own family, it would have been perfect, but right now he would enjoy the holiday. Yet as much as he was enjoying freedom, he could not help think of the convicts still in prison and how they were celebrating. If they were lucky, they were getting three ounces of meat and perhaps a once-a-year serving of pudding if the warder was in a holiday spirit.

It was not long before a man named Patrick Egan showed up with the tickets and itinerary of the four ex-prisoners: Michael, Thomas Chambers, Charles 'Happy' McCarthy, and John Patrick O'Brien. They were scheduled to take the mail steamer from Holyhead to Dublin.

When the four ex prisoners arrived in Dublin, they were surprised to be welcomed as national heroes. It was 6 p.m. when they arrived. The harbor had been lit up for the occasion, and the four stepped ashore to the rousing cheers of crowds, to brass bands, rockets and bonfires on Howth and on Dalkey Hill.

Michael stood in awe as the crowd greeted him and his associates. Such a spectacle was the last thing he had anticipated. Although he had been gaining weight and felt much stronger over the last month, this huge greeting was beginning to overwhelm him physically.

It had been a long day and an even longer seven years. Yet he was not as affected as Charles McCarthy. After some patriotic speeches, which had been written for him, McCarthy took sick and had to retire. On the 15th of January, he died of heart failure. His funeral was long, and many speeches were made, extolling him as a hero-patriot who had given his life for his country.

After the remaining three got some needed rest, it was decided that they should visit their native countics. Michael would return to Mayo.

* * *

Just before he left for Mayo, Michael was informed that his election to the Irish Republican Brotherhood, the Fenian supreme council, had been approved. As he sat waiting in Dublin for the train to take him to western Ireland, he began to form a plan in his mind. Perhaps he could use his influence to make the IRB a constitutional movement. Could the Home Rulers and the IRB movements be persuaded to work together? That was a tall order, but what could be more difficult than what he had already been through in his life? He would have to work on it.

He boarded the train and made himself comfortable. As the train pulled out of the Dublin station, he felt tired. The constant clicking of the wheels on the rails was putting him to sleep. His eyes finally closed.

"Ballyhaunis, next stop Ballyhaunis," cried the conductor, waking Michael from his state of semi-consciousness. He looked out of the window of the train and saw a huge crowd waving at him and screaming his name. He was forced to step to the back platform of the train to wave. The same happened on every stop.

At Clairemorris he was met by two well-known nationalists, John W. Walshe and John W. Nally, who boarded the train to greet him. "Welcome, cousin Michael," said Nally. "Welcome to Clairemorris!"

Nally was indeed Michael's cousin. He was from Balla, about ten miles from Straide, where he kept a public house. Michael had heard of him, though his parents had considered

Nally a person who would never be taken seriously by anyone. "His problem is the drink," his mother had told him. "It's the curse of the nation, and he's got it."

Between his mother and the Methodist school he attended in England, Michael had come to hate the drunkenness that seemed to hang over the nation like a vulture. But he was very civil to Nally, and he found him a likeable fellow. Walshe was Nally's brother-in-law, and he seemed a perfect fit for the role of Nally's companion.

"Come with us, Michael," said Nally, "as our guest." Michael was about to turn down the offer, but Nally and Walshe had already picked up his luggage and were holding him under the arms, practically dragging him off the train. Before he knew it, he was standing on the station's passenger platform as the train was pulling out. Walshe already had his bags on the carriage, and in a second they were off for Balla.

When they arrived, a group of people was there to greet them. They all went inside Nally's public house. Walsh and Nally got a pint for him but Michael refused it despite all their badgering. Then they ordered him a pot of tea. They introduced him to several of the local nationalists, who assured him he had attained the stature of Irish national hero. Many had read his articles in various Irish newspapers and journals, and were well aware of his incarceration. This was somewhat of a surprise to Michael, who never realized that the articles that he had smuggled out of prison, and for which had been paid two pounds, had enjoyed such a wide circulation.

Next came a group of "patriotic" young ladies, friends of Nally, who wanted to meet him. One in particular, whose name was Margaret, seemed particularly and suddenly beautiful to Michael.

"These girls consider you a great hero, Michael and they are very patriotic, if you know what I mean," said Nally.

Margaret was a beautiful, dark-haired Connaught Irish

girl with beautiful blue eyes. She could have been a young version of his mother. It was obvious that Margaret was attracted to him as well.

Michael's obvious attention to Margaret seemed to upset the others. She grabbed him by the arm and led him upstairs.

* * *

After about an hour, Margaret came back down into the pub. Michael was still upstairs, she said, freshening up and getting dressed. The other girls could not wait to question Margaret.

"What was he like, a man with one arm?" asked one.

Margaret looked at her and smiled. "Well, it's only his arm that's missing, dear," she said. "I can tell you, he's sure a man who spent the last seven-and-a-half years in prison."

Michael finally came down stairs, walked over, and kissed Margaret's hand.

"And such a gentleman, he is," she said, drawing jealous stares from the other "patriotic" girls.

After their goodbyes, Michael, Walshe, Nally and other nationalists boarded a horse and carriage, which took them on to Castlebar. Cheering crowds waved to them at every village along the way.

Chapter Thirteen

At Castlebar, Michael was met by a man named James Daly, who invited him to be a guest in his house. Daly was the editor of the *Connaught Telegraph*, a weekly, pro-Irish regional newspaper.

After settling in at Daly's home, Michael found out that Daly was a founder of the Farmer's Defense Association, which advocated that tenants not pay more than a fair rent to the landlords or they would refuse to work. In his newspaper they had urged farmers not to take tenancy of any farm from which the tenant had been evicted, and had tried to set up a fund to help evicted tenants. Unfortunately the plan had had only limited success. The farmers were just too poor to refuse work of any kind, and there was never enough money in the fund to take care of evicted families for very long.

But Michael thought the plan had merit. All it needed was organization and funding. Here was one way to defeat the landlords. If enough money could be raised to take care of the farmers who were out of work, the plan might work. Perhaps a league could be formed along those lines. Without the peasants to work the land, the landlords would not be able to make a profit on their holdings, and would have to give in eventually.

After a brief speech on the commons of Castlebar, Michael decided to make a trip to his home town of Straide. Meeting him at Straide was his cousin, Mary Davitt, the daughter of his Uncle John. He also met his Mother's brother, Uncle Pat Kielty, and Pat's son, Tony. Various other children gathered around him, delighted to be related to a great Irish hero.

Michael led them to the spot where he was born, a place he had not seen for twenty-seven years. The stones that once were part of his house had been gathered together to make a wall, marking the boundaries of the land which the landlord had consolidated. There was nothing else there but an old poplar tree.

Michael could not stop the flood of memories. Hc heard the steel tearing into his parent's home and saw the roof burning when the straw hit the fireplace. He saw the anger on his father's face as he made a move toward the bailiff and the crowbar crew. He felt his mother's arm press him to her leg as he watched his home disappear.

"Cousin Michael, is this where you lived?" asked Mary Davitt.

Michael snapped out of his dream state. "What's left of it," he said. He turned and looked at the horizon. "Let's leave this place."

* * *

The rest of the week was filled with travel and speeches. Michael spoke all over Mayo, always to warm and enthusiastic crowds. When his tour ended, he wrote to his mother, "I was received like a prince."

He said goodbye to Daly and headed back to Dublin. It was time to plan for his future. He would have to get work. He had an opportunity to become an agent for a wine and whiskey merchant. This was in conflict with his strong temperance views, but he might have to do it out of necessity. Just then, some good news arrived. He had sent a manuscript of his prison writings to a publisher who accepted it for publication. He had called it, *Leaves from a Prison Diary*. Being a published author, he would now be in demand on the lecture circuit. Royalties from his book and payment for his lectures would be more than enough to support him over the next year. He began speaking all over Great Britain on prison reform. He thought of making a trip to America to see his family but he would have to save a bit more money.

June, 1878

Just as his finances were at the point where he could think about the trip, he was summoned to testify before the Kimberly Commission on prison reform, assembled by the British government. It had been established at the insistence of O'Connor Power in the House of Commons, to investigate the conditions in prisons which, for one thing, had contributed to the death of Charles McCarthy. After a long and drawn out investigation, which had been harshly criticized by O'Connor Power, the commission finally questioned Michael in June.

One of the commissioners began by asking, "Mr. Davitt, in your book you state that you had seen ravenous men eat old moldy bread found buried in heaps of rubbish. Is that true?"

"Although I did say that in my book," Michael replied, "I actually saw only one man do it. Other prisoners told me that many men did it and I assumed it was a more widespread practice. But I saw many men eating candles, one of which had been retrieved from a prison cesspool."

The commissioner winced visibly, and then called Prison Governor Harris to the stand.

"Governor Harris, is it true that many men in your prison ate candles out of hunger?"

"It was not out of hunger," answered Harris. "It was rooted in a belief among prisoners that candles melted into coca and made the gruel more palatable."

"And was the gruel so unpalatable that men had to take these extreme measures?" asked the commissioner.

"I admit that prison food is not fancy," replied the governor, "but it was always sufficient according to the workload assigned to specific prisoners."

The commissioners shot unbelieving looks at each other and dismissed Harris from the witness stand. Then they recalled Michael.

"Mr. Davitt, you state in your book that the cells were too

104

small, the ventilation and lighting were bad, and the waterclosets could become offensive. Do you wish to add more to that statement?"

Michael thought for a moment and then answered. "The waterclosets were especially offensive on Sunday after they had been used all week and not properly cleaned. Coupled with the bad ventilation, the cell blocks became almost intolerable."

On his rebuttal testimony, Governor Harris stated that the atmosphere was bad, but that most of the criminals had come from a class of society that was used to close quarters, and actually preferred closeness to fresh air.

The commissioners could hardly believe that a man trusted with such authority could even think like this. They immediately recalled Michael who testified that prisoners were supposed to bathe once a week but were allowed to bathe only once a fortnight, and then in the dirty water used by other prisoners. Harris countered that what happened was neglect by a warder and not prison policy. If caught in this type of negligence, he said, the warder would have been punished.

Michael then told the story of the guards checking on the prisoners with the lantern every hour, even through the night, thereby interrupting the prisoner's sleep patterns. Many of these men were expected to perform hard labor the next day, and their health deteriorated as a result of this excessive surveillance.

Harris admitted that hourly inspections with a lantern were done as a matter of policy, but insisted that constant inspection was necessary as a precaution against escape attempts. He also stated that the men had become used to it, and therefore it did not disturb their sleep.

The last person to testify was the Rev. James Francis, a former prison chaplain who had resigned his post. The commissioner asked if he had resigned in protest over the way prisoners were being treated. Rev. Francis testified that his resignation was a result of a strained relationship with the then-governor, R. F. Hickey, who was solidly backed by the visiting director, Captain W. J. Stopford. Hickey had introduced harsh punishment as a normal means of running a prison, which included long periods of detention on bread and water. He stated that he knew of one man who was kept on bread and water for over a year. He also stated that punishments of various types were summarily administered by the guards and were tolerated by the governor.

Michael did not know at the time just how far-reaching his book and subsequent testimony at the Kimberly Commission would influence the prison system. Davitt's testimony would shake the prison establishment and would be the forerunner of change for a system badly in need of reform. In the years to come, he would become known as the one person in the British Empire who had most influenced prison reform.

With the commission ended, Michael gave a few more speeches. With some additional money from the "testimonial fund" for released prisoners, he finally had enough money for a trip to America.

Chapter Fourteen

July 1878

Clan na Gael in America wanted Michael. It's head, Dr. William Carroll, wanted him for a lecture tour, and the IRB was sending him with their recommendation. It was a shaky financial footing to go on, but it was either that or stay in Dublin and work as a wine and liquor merchant.

So, Michael started on his first journey to America. However, he wanted to take at least a day to see some of Ireland beforehand. He took a train to Cork and visited Blarney Castle where he kissed the Blarney Stone. After spending most of his life in England, and not having seen much of his own country, Michael felt he had to do at least this. Now he felt like more of an Irishman.

He was having trouble tearing himself away from the beauty of the country. He lingered for three hours just taking it in. It was like looking at a painting. He began to understand why so many of his countrymen were so infected with Ireland. July was a good time of the year, and he could remember how his parents always wanted to return. He remembered his father's remark about the Irish horse who did not want to leave. He reached down and scooped up a handful of soil.

It's made out of two hundred generations of Irish who lived and died here, he thought. No matter how many invaders come, they can never change that. It makes no difference what they do, they can't take the Irish out of us.

* * *

The White Star liner *Britannic* was an impressive sight as she sat docked in Liverpool. She was the newest ship in the company's fleet. A four-masted, single-screw, iron ship displacing 5,000 gross tonnage, she combined her sails with steam propulsion and held the Atlantic crossing record of seven days, ten hours and fifty three minutes, which she accomplished in 1877.

Michael climbed aboard the forward gangplank and showed his cabin-class ticket. As he entered the opening to the forward deck, he glanced back at the steerage passengers who were using the gangplank in the rear. He settled into his cabin, and could hear the crew releasing the gangplank as the boatswain shouted, "Single up all lines." He could feel the movement as the tugs towed the ship out into the deeper water, and the vibration as the steam engines began turning the screw and propelling the great iron hulk out to sea. At last they were under way. He was headed for America.

He was determined to enjoy the trip. He was a bit seasick at first, but this passed quickly as he walked about the deck. He walked forward and saw the huge rope wrapped around the stem post, and the image of picking oakum from rope, which he had done so much of in prison, flashed unwanted into his mind. He turned and walked away, heading back to his cabin.

While lying in his bed trying to rest, the incessant blowing of the ship's foghorn kept him awake. He could not help but think of Big Ben and how it had kept him awake in prison. He walked out on the deck to clear his mind. Would he be forever gripped by these images of his past? The next day, he got to meet and talk with some of the other passengers. There was an American woman, strong-minded, rich and fairly unsophisticated, who had spent eight months traveling in Europe with her daughter. The woman was determined that her daughter would grow up more cultured than herself and she thought a trip to the cultural centers of Europe would insure this.

There was also a Yankee lawyer who was returning home from the Paris exhibition. "It was far inferior to the one we held in Philadelphia in 1876," he stated.

A Scot, who mistook Michael for an Englishman, was intent on talking religion. Michael did not let on that he was a Roman. The Scot stated that there were Catholic and Christian religions.

"What do you think a Christian is?" asked Michael.

"Why, a Presbyterian, of course," he answered.

Michael then struck up a conversation with an Irish priest, Rev. Patrick Murry, who had spent thirty-four years among the Chippewa Indians and spoke their language. "I never found better Christians anywhere," said Father Murry.

There were also four young priests of Irish heritage who were going home to America after studying for three years at the University of Lauvain, Switzerland.

But Michael found interesting a Canadian who had been a captain of volunteers who had fought the Fenian invasion of Campobello Island. Michael let the man ramble on about the evils of the Fenians and their separation movement, and never let on that he was a member of the IRB supreme council.

Michael was happy with the food, accommodations and the interesting passengers. He also took pleasure in watching dolphins, which were following the ships, and even a spouting whale about 150 yards away. He also paid a visit to steerage, where he met a man he had known in Haslingden and who remembered Michael working in Cockcroft's print shop. When Michael saw the meager and crowded accommodations of the steerage passengers, he thought it unjust, because they had paid half the price of cabin class.

He held, many more discussions with the Irish priest, the Yankee lawyer (who was of Irish extraction), and the young priests. Father Murry did not hold with the Fenian movement, and thought the country could not survive on its own. The Yank took the opposite side, although Michael determined that he knew very little about Ireland. The young priests would not commit themselves to the question and were more concerned about the liberal movement in Belgian, which they concluded was making rapid progress at the expense of Catholicism.

It all helped pass the time. Before anyone knew it, the journey ended and the ship anchored in the narrows of Staten Island. It was 9 p.m., and Michael came out on deck to observe the spectacular sunset. What a welcome to America! The next morning, they sailed up the Hudson River and docked at the White Star wharf in Manhattan. Michael said goodby to the passengers, got a blessing from Father Murry, and set out to see New York.

* * *

When Michael stepped out of the horse driven buggy, he walked along lower Manhattan taking in the sights along Broadway, Fifth Avenue, and the Bowery. He noticed the streets were in need of repair. Then he boarded a ferry and headed for Brooklyn. He stared up at the imposing sight of the Brooklyn Bridge, which was under construction..

"It's going to be the longest suspension bridge in the world when it's finished," said a man standing next to him.

"It's truly amazing," said Michael. "I hope the people who are capable of building such a thing can also manage to fix the streets."

"You must be new to New York," said the man.

There was not much to see on the Brooklyn side of the bridge, mostly farms that seemed to feature sheep and chickens. Michael walked around for a short time, thinking how the bridge would help all these farmers get their sheep, eggs and produce to the Manhattan markets more quickly and at less cost then by using the ferryboats. He marveled at a city that would do such a thing.

Having taken in the sights, Michael went back to

Manhattan and called on the one man in New York that he knew personally, James J. O'Kelly, whose office was at *The New York Herald*. O'Kelly was delighted to see him.

"Come in, come in," said O'Kelly ." Have you eaten yet?"

"Not yet," said Michael.

"Good. We'll go down the street to an Irish pub I frequent and get something to eat."

The "pub down the street" was a stronghold of Irish and Irish American-nationalists and the back room was the main meeting place for the top men in Clan na Gael.

"Michael, this is John Devoy," said O'Kelly, standing behind Devoy, who was still seated.

Michael stuck out his left hand and Devoy got to his feet and grasped it.

"I've heard a lot about you in a lot of places, Davitt. Sit down and have lunch with Cunningham and myself."

O'Kelly sat down with them, although Cunningham seeing that Devoy wanted to talk to Michael privately, excused himself and left.

Michael looked at Devoy. He was only thirty-six years old, but looked at least ten years older. He had a hard face and a stern look.

"When I was in Millbank prison," Michael began, "I saw your name scratched on the door of the cell I was occupying."

A little of the hardness left Devoy's face. "So it seems we occupied the same hotel room in London."

That brought a smile to Michael's face.

"Have some lunch," said Devoy pointing to the food on the table. "How about a pint?"

"Sorry, but I don't drink," said Michael. "You can bring me a pot of tea."

"A pot of tea?" said Devoy, with a disbelieving look on his face.

"Yes, if you would."

Devoy got up to leave the room and signaled for O'Kelly to follow him. At the bar, Devoy ordered a pot of tea, much to the surprise of the bartender.

"First pot of tea I've ever served in that room," he said.

"This Michael Davitt," said Devoy looking at O'Kelly, "he looks like a Spaniard, talks like an Englishman, and he doesn't drink! Can we trust him?"

"He looks like a Connaught Irishman. In the part of Ireland where he comes from, they mostly have dark hair and dark eyes. And they tell of the old days, when the Spanish Armada crashed on the shores of western Ireland, many Spanish took refuge among our people and blended in with the Irish Catholic population."

"How about his English accent?" asked Devoy.

"He was brought up in Haslingden, England where his family moved when he was four years old, escaping the famine."

"I see," said Devoy. "How about him refusing to take a pint?"

"Why don't you ask him about that yourself?" said O'Kelly. "I know he attended a Methodist school in England. Perhaps that had an influence on him. Remember, he's a member of the IRB supreme council and is here on their recommendation."

They returned to the room and sat down with Michael again. Devoy looked straight at Michael. "What do you have against drinking a pint?" he asked.

Michael stopped eating. "My mother always told me, 'Drink is the curse of the land. It makes you shoot at your landlord–and miss him.'"

Devoy and O'Kelly burst out laughing. "He's an Irishman alright!" shouted Devoy.

"That's an Irish mother if I ever heard one," O'Kelly agreed.

"She lives in Pennsylvania," said Michael. "I'm anxious to see her. It's been eight years. My two sisters are there too, and I have nieces and nephews I have never met."

"We'll go tomorrow," said Devoy. "We have clan business in that area, and Dr. Carroll wants to meet you. He lives in Philadelphia."

Chapter Fifteen

The train ride to Pennsylvania was beautiful and gave Michael a chance to get to know Devoy. They talked about Irish nationalism and life in English prisons. Slowly, Devoy was beginning to ascribe to Michael's view, which blamed Ireland's trouble on the landlord system. However, Devoy could not adopt the constitutionalist view that some Irish had proclaimed was the only way to save the country. He held fast to the belief that only a free Ireland could ever be the solution to the problem the Irish were facing.

"Don't you feel the freedom of America," asked Devoy "and how liberating it is to be free of English rule here?"

Michael did indeed feel it. He had felt it as soon as he walked off the ship and set foot in America. In fact, he had begun to feel it even on the voyage, when he talked to the Yankee lawyer.

"Certainly, I do," he answered. "But remember, Ireland is a poor country. If we make a total break from Great Britain, we may not be able to survive. Perhaps we will be ready sometime in the future, but I don't think we have the resources to survive independently right now. We need to solve the landlord problem first."

Devoy conceded that might make sense. He would see what Dr. Carroll and the other members of Clan na Gael thought, but he would not give up his dream of a free Ireland. Privately he thought Michael Davitt was a very convincing fellow. He was beginning to like this Connaught Irishman who looked like a Spaniard, talked like an Englishman, and only drank tea. Davitt's intelligence and smooth manner evoked an admiration and a trust even among strangers–and Devoy was not immune.

* * *

Catherine threw her arms around her son as soon as she

saw him, and would not let him go.

"A merciful God has answered my prayers and brought you back to me," she sobbed.

"Yes, Mother," said Michael as he embraced her. He could not hold back the tears, either. She had gained weight and was stronger. America had been good to her.

"Mother, you seem in very good health. In fact, I don't ever remember you looking so well," he said.

Mary Agnes wept openly when she saw her brother.

"So long," she cried, "so long."

Then she paraded the "new" nieces and nephews before Michael. They were like little princesses and princes introducing themselves to the king.

"I am certainly glad to meet all of you," he said, bowing formally with an exalted flourish. "I have been reading all about you, but I never thought you were all this beautiful."

This brought smiles to the children's faces, who were then excused so the adults could be alone.

"Mother," he said, "tell me the truth about America. Is it really to your liking?"

"America is a very bountiful land," she replied. They sat down at the kitchen table but refused to let go of Michael's hand. "We never have to worry about crop failures or diseases wiping out our livestock. In fact, we simply use our wages to buy what we need at the farm markets. But you wrote that you were in Mayo. How are things there?"

"I found it a little sad when I stood on the place where our cottage used to be," he said, remembering. "There is nothing there now. But everything is better off than it was when we lived there. The famine is over. But the people of Mayo are still poor. The landlords are still a problem, but the new Land Act has at least made them a little more reasonable."

He could see the hint of sadness on his mother's face when he talked about Mayo. And the sadness led to the memory of Martin, who was palpably missing from their reunion.

"I wanted so much to be here when Father died," said Michael. "I wanted to comfort him in his final hour." He feared he would cry again.

"He understood," said Catherine. "He was proud of the fact that his son was an Irish patriot. More proud then he could ever tell you."

Michael looked down. "Someday I will make him even more proud, when I drive the landlords out of Ireland."

* * *

Devoy had a meeting planned with the high ranking members of Clan na Gael. Michael made his apologies to his family and assured them he would be back to spend more of them with them. Michael was not sure how the Clan would accept him and his ideas, but the meeting went even better than he had expected. He had not really known just how much of a celebrity he had become. Dr. Carroll was anxious to talk with him. They shared views on what the next step should be on solving the problems in Ireland, and Michael made a convincing argument about what to do with the landlords.

"I saw a movement in Mayo which I believe could take Ireland out of this feudal system which the British lords have created," he said. "A man named James Daly, the editor of the *Connaught Telegraph,* had some limited success in action against the landlords. I believe it only needs better financing and organization to be a significant approach."

"And you think this non-violent approach will break their will?" asked Carroll. "If you look at history, Michael, you will see that nothing ever changes tyranny but violence."

"Times change, Dr. Carroll," said Michael. "I can tell you that having been brought up in England, the members of the English working class are also the victims of the British

116

aristocracy. Not as much as we Irish, of course, but victims nevertheless. The non-Irish English working class is saved somewhat by the fact that they are Protestants, but they get mangled in industrial accidents and go to the workhouse as well. We need them on our side. Public opinion will be very important in this fight."

"And you think they will be on our side?" asked Carroll.

"As long as we keep the movement non-violent," said Michael. "I have known many English who see the domination of the aristocracy as unjust. We must keep them with us."

"And you want Clan na Gael to finance your scheme?"

"I want to combine the resources of the home rulers, the nationalists and the constitutionalists into one organization to concentrate on the fight with the landlords. A national land league. It would withhold services to any landlord who does not charge a fair rent. It would provide funds for people who are evicted for withholding services and ostracize those who would move into a farm from which a family was evicted. Eventually the landlords will find out that they cannot survive without the peasant labor, and will have to come to terms with us."

"These landlords won't go down without a fight," said Devoy.

"Of that I am sure," said Michael. "If we hit them in the purse, they will fight back at first, but they'll have to realize that sooner or later they cannot get along with us."

"We won't be able to control all the violence," said Carroll.

"I suspect that is right," said Michael. "But we must do what we can. We need to get public opinion on our side or we won't win this fight. Violence will only make people fearful, and could turn the tide against us."

"We'll not give up our dream of a free Irish State," said Devoy.

"That will be another day," said Michael. "First we need

to make our people strong and eventually get the land out of the ownership of the aristocracy."

"And will you head this land league?" asked Carroll.

"No, I don't think that would be a good idea. I suggest we ask Charles Stewart Parnell to head the league."

"Parnell?" asked Carroll in surprise, "The obstructionist in Parliament? Why him?"

"Several reasons," said Michael. "One, as you stated, he is a Member of Parliament. He has political connections, and as an MP, he has a voice. He will be listened to by the press. He is also a landlord, albeit not as bad as most of the ones we will go after. He has always treated his tenants well. And he is a Protestant, who is nevertheless, still very Irish. This will be a war against the landlords, and having a Protestant head the league will keep it from becoming a religious war."

"It seems you have thought this out well," said Carroll. "The Clan will have to think about your proposal."

But Carroll already knew he would endorse the plan. He was succumbing to the Michael Davitt charm, just like everyone else.

Chapter Sixteen

December, 1878

The lecture tour that Clan na Gael had prepared for Michael lasted until December. His talks concentrated on the evils of the British government with regard to their treatment of the Catholic population of Ireland. He talked about nationalism and the various political movements in the country. He was well received wherever he went and was often quoted in the newspapers, especially those that were pro-Irish.

Carroll and Devoy were delighted with the tour. It raised a great deal of money for the cause, and netted Michael a tidy sum. Finally he had enough money to be comfortable. He had also seen a good deal of America. He marveled at the political structure, the non-sectarian public schools, and the abundance of goods.

Just before his return to Ireland, he spent a few more days with his family. He was delighted to meet a new born nephew who was named Michael, after him. He said goodby to Mary Agnes, his other sister Bina, and hugged his mother.

"Some day I will take you back to Ireland," he promised.

When she heard this, the twinkle in Catherine's eye made her seem twenty years younger. Michael knew she would probably never move back to Ireland permanently and leave her grandchildren, but he could see that even the thought of a visit made her heart leap. He left her $130 to pay for the trip. She would never use it.

* * *

When Michael arrived back in Ireland, he found much unrest in the rural areas. Editor James Daly in Mayo had been publishing editorials endorsing political candidates who were sympathetic to home rule and land reform.

"We must stop sending landlords to Parliament," he wrote.

He was also instrumental in forming the Mayo Tenant's Defense Association. Rack renting had become epidemic, and evictions were common. The association was the means by which some of Mayo's leading citizens were banding together to meet the crisis. Daly had enlisted John James Loudon, a barrister in Castlebar, to act as its chairman and had himself appointed as secretary. O'Connor Power, the well known MP, attended and endorsed the organization and coined a phrase that would soon become its battle cry: "The land of Ireland for the people of Ireland." He advocated that all the clubs in the area unite and support the association.

At Ballinisloe, several others showed up to voice their support. One significant speaker was Chalres Stewart Parnell, He openly criticized Isaac Butt's moderation in Parliament and called for more action on the part of the tenants. Supporting letters were read from Archbishop MacHale of Tuam, Bishop Duggan of Clonfert, and Mitchel Henry, MP for Galway County, a moderate home-ruler and land reformer.

It was Parnell's first visit to Mayo. He was astounded by the conditions he found. Riding in his horse drawn carriage through the rural areas of the county, he remarked to his secretary, "We have been driving through this county for miles. We have seen rich, fattened grazing land and not a single person or horse. How could this be?"

"This land is owned by a few landlords who mostly live in Scotland or England," his secretary answered.

"I have not even seen a house," said Parnell, "only the ruins of what once must have been houses here. Just ruined walls and roofless cottages."

"They used to belong to the tenant farmers who once worked this land," said the secretary. "They were evicted by the landlords and their houses torn down to make room for grazing cattle."

They came upon a settlement, hilly and barren of vegetation and very congested, its population huddled into a few houses, which were totally inadequate to accommodate them. Parnell could not believe what he was witnessing. He had had no idea of the wretched conditions of the people and the squalor of their homes.

"Where is the conscience of these landlords, their sense of right and wrong?" he exclaimed. "Do they have any idea of the conditions they have created with their rack-renting?"

"Sir, most have never set foot in Ireland, no less in Mayo," the secretary replied. "They simply don't care. All they care about is protecting their profits."

Parnell was beginning to see things differently. The three F's of the tenant farmer—fair rents, fixity of tenure, and freedom to sell his interest in his holdings—was meaningless to most of these people. Most of the good land was not being utilized, and a great many of the people had no interests to sell. He saw that more aggressive action needed to be taken.

* * *

Michael was to attend a meeting of the supreme council of the Fenians in Paris. When he arrived, he met John Devoy, who was already there. It was a happy reunion, Devoy having become one of Michael's most influential supporters. A few days later. John O'Connor, the secretary of the council, arrived. Michael tried to convert O'Connor to his new ideas, a new departure for the Fenian movement, but found him to be insensitive. O'Connor considered all constitutional agitators to be unpatriotic, and was totally committed to the more traditional role of the Fenian movement.

"It appears to me that you were influenced by O'Connor

Power," said John O'Connor. " Is this some plot of his?"

"Absolutely not," said Michael, with a mixture of anger and offense.

The new plan to consolidate all the groups into a Land League did not sit well with many of the other Fenians. After the conclusion of the essential business of the organization–which included the election of Michael as the representative for the district of Northern England–the organization took up the question of his new plan. Everyone except Davitt, Devoy and a man named Harris saw it as a departure from the traditional goals of the Fenian organization. Some saw it as a betrayal, and others as a retreat from their traditional views.

The meeting was presided over by Charles Kickham, who was both deaf and blind. Everything had to be interpreted to him through an aide, who communicated through the fingers of his left hand by a "deaf-and-dumb" alphabet. Kickham was very intelligent and alert, but the situation became explosive, with Devoy, Davitt and Harris in the minority. The usual Davitt charm could not be brought to bear on the unseeing and unhearing Kickham, who was a member of the Fenian "old guard" and who wanted nothing but a revolution. Michael became so frustrated with his inability to convey his thoughts to Kickham that he broke down and wept.

"I must leave the room," he stated to the group.

"Please don't go," someone said with the others concurring.

But Michael got up to leave, and Devoy joined him. They went out to the lobby of the hotel where Devoy tried to console him.

"I don't know what came over me," said Michael. "I never shed a tear for myself in prison, but just now I could not contain myself."

Devoy said, "Perhaps in prison they were abusing your

body, and that you could take. Here they were abusing your ideas, and that's much harder to accept."

"You're right, John," said Michael, looking up at his friend. "But I won't get anywhere breaking down and running away from meetings. I must control myself or I will accomplish nothing."

The two men spent the remainder of the evening talking about the incident. Perhaps they had pushed too hard. They decided to get some rest and see if they could start anew the next day.

* * *

In the morning, Michael and John Devoy were having breakfast when John O'Leary joined them. O'Leary was not a supporter of the new departure, but convinced the men to rejoin the meeting.

"We cannot lose the support of Clan na Gael or a celebrity like Michael and expect to survive," said O'Leary. "I've talked to the others and we want you to come back. I can't promise you'll receive their support for your plans, but they will at least listen. Perhaps there is a compromise here somewhere."

Michael and Devoy looked at each other.

"There are bound to be disagreements within any organization," said Devoy.

The atmosphere in the meeting had totally changed. There was an aura of calm that prevailed, and everyone was allowed to speak without being shouted down. However, Michael, Devoy and Harris were unable to convince the council to join forces with the constitutionalists. The council considered the constitutionalist stooges of the British Empire, and could see only revolution and independence as solutions for Ireland's troubles. Joining forces with the constitutionalists would be the same as endorsing the British Empire, which they hated. They would not become part of it and the meeting ended with their saying so.

Chapter Seventeen

Devoy said goodby to Michael. "I'm going to stay in Paris for awhile," he said, "What will you do now?"

"I'm off to London," Michael answered. "Hopefully, I'll meet with Parnell and set up a meeting between the two of you."

"I'd like to meet him and plan out our strategy," Devoy said. "Regardless of what happened here, Clan na Gael is supporting the formation of the land league."

Michael had a thought. "Suppose we set up a Mayo league first? We would have plenty of support there, and if it's successful we could turn the tide and expand to other counties. Besides, Mayo is the most needy of all the places in Ireland."

Devoy had to agree. "Excellent idea. Set up a meeting with Parnell and we can discuss it. I want to relax in Paris for awhile. I'll join you later."

* * *

After a few days in London, Michael arranged to see Parnell in Dublin, at which he arranged the meeting between Parnell and Devoy, who was now in Dublin at Morrison's hotel. That meeting went better than Michael expected. Parnell was impressed by Michael's argument that the agrarian crises in Mayo needed attention. Devoy kept arguing for a national movement. Eventually, all three decided on the Mayo plan and asked Parnell to take over the leadership of the new Mayo league, which Devoy hoped would become a national movement. Parnell not only saw the opportunity to help the people of Mayo, but also thought it would be a good political move for him as well. It would certainly keep him in the headlines. He did not agree to the role right away, however.

Michael returned to Mayo and stayed with relatives at

Balla. He began studying the state of affairs in the county, anticipating the formation of the new league. The situation he found was becoming grave. The 1877 crops had failed badly, and the 1878 crops were even worse. The Mayo spring had been bleak and cold followed by incessant rains. Farmers were falling deeper into debt to the landlords and shopkeepers. The Landlords, unable to get their rents, were evicting peasants in larger numbers, causing much resentment and unrest. The specter of famine was looming over the county again, and action had to be taken immediately.

Michael decided to meet with some of the leaders in Mayo. He and Devoy called upon two well-known local figures, Eagan and Brennan and discussed having a meeting to bring the problem out in the open. They decided to hold the forum at Irishtown, a small village located at about the dead-center of Connaught that they considered a perfect location. Speakers would be drawn from Mayo, Dublin, Scotland, England, and would include several sympathetic members of Parliament..

Such an array of civic leaders was sure to attract much attention and receive wide press coverage. It was decided that Michael would not attend the meeting, since he was still on a ticket of leave and his attendance might be used to send him back to prison. However, he would write several of the resolutions to be considered.

After drafting these resolutions, Michael returned to Dublin, and the local leaders were left to plan the meeting. They began by printing a flyer which would be distributed throughout Connaught.

THE WEST AWAKE!
GREAT TENANT RIGHTS MEETING IN IRISHTOWN
TO COME OFF ON SUNDAY, 20ᵀᴴ APRIL
Charles S Parnell, Esq., M.P., John O'Connor Power, Esq.,
M.P.
Edwin Dryer Grey, Esq., M.P., Joseph Giles Bigger, Esq., MP
John J. Loudon, Esq. Westport, John Barry, Esq., Manchester
John Ferguson, Esq., Glasgow, Thomas Brennan, Esq.,
Dublin
Matthew Harris, Esq., Castlebar, are expected to attend.

From the China towers of Pekin to the round towers of Ireland, from the cabins of Connemara to the kraals of Kaffirland, from the watted homes of the isles of polynesia to the wigwams of North America the cry is: 'Down with invaders! Down with tyrants!' Every man to have his own land–every man to have his own home.

It was not bad for a local production. Farmers in the Irishtown area, hard-hit by the evictions, wanted editor James Daly to write more about rack-renting and expose the landlords. Daly was reluctant to do this, fearing a libel suit might result. He decided that he would cover the meeting in Irishtown as a reporter and in this way not editorialize. Reporting on what others were saying would serve the same purpose.

In Dublin, Michael met once again with Devoy and Parnell. Devoy was getting to like and respect Parnell even more in spite of the fact that they held somewhat different views.

"I'm opposed to fighting England unless we have a reasonable chance of success," said Parnell, "and I don't think we do. We must find other ways to fight."

"Clan na Gael has changed its views on that as well," said Devoy. "Our present stance is for peace at home but a vigorous attack on England abroad whenever possible."

127

"You're not thinking of another fiasco like Campobello Island, are you?"

"Nothing that stupid," answered Devoy. "We might send aid to any people who are fighting against England, but we don't yet know what that aid would be or to whom it will be offered."

"That's not something I would be a part of," said Parnell. "But I think it is important that these various factions with differing philosophies not impede each other."

"Such as Nationalists and home rulers?" Devoy asked.

"Yes, precisely. I don't think we necessarily have to work together, but I believe it is absolutely essential that we do not work against each other."

Devoy nodded in agreement.

* * *

It could not have gone any better. Upwards of seven thousand people attended the meeting at Irishtown. James Daly presided over the opening with the quote from O'Connor Power, "The land of Ireland for the people of Ireland." He also singled out the "land grabbers" as they were called; "Those who take the land of the evicted are enemies of the country, and are as culpable as the landlords." This was followed by speeches from all the prominent politicians and the passing of three resolutions, the first two written by Michael.

Be it resolved that "Ireland–our misgoverned and impoverish country–a dictum of The Times that rulers who failed to govern in the interest of their subjects forfeited all claim to allegiance, declared the 'unceasing determination' of those present 'to resort to social, can be regained from our enemies.'"

Be it resolved that "As the land of Ireland, like that of every other country, was intended by a just and all-providing

128

God for the use and sustenance of those of his people to whom he gave inclination and energies to cultivate and improve it, any system which sanctions its monopoly by a privileged class, or assigns its ownership and control to a landlord caste, to be used as an instrument of usurious or political self-seeking, demand from every aggrieved Irishman an undying hostility, being flagrantly opposed to the first principle of their humanity—self-preservation."

The third resolution simply called for an immediate reduction of rents, deemed to be unjust, pending a settlement of the land question.

Thomas Brennan of Dublin made a particularly eloquent speech. He talked about the misgoverning of Ireland and stated the need for self-government was to be taken for granted. Then he focused upon the question of the land system. "You may get a federal parliament, perhaps repeal of the union, nay more you may establish an Irish republic on Irish soil, but as long as the tillers of the soil are forced to support a useless and indolent aristocracy your federal parliament would be but a bauble and your Irish republic but a fraud." He went on to state that the only solution was to abolish the landlord system and make the occupying tenants the owners of the soil.

Brennan then got more practical. He stated that it would be unrealistic to expect a final settlement could be obtained at once. The immediate need was to make a stand against evictions.

Chapter Eighteen

It seemed that the new league was somewhat of an instant success. An estate near Irishtown owned by a Joseph Bourke was managed by a man named Daly who was from Irishtown. A land agent, Daily, was threatening the tenants with eviction. These farmers were in arrears and the bad harvest had made it impossible for them to meet their rents. Hearing of the meeting at Irishtown and fearing the wrath of the Mayo men, Bourke instructed Daily to lower the rent by twenty-five percent. It was the league's first victory.

"We won that battle without firing a shot," said Parnell when he heard of the incident.

Michael was pleased to hear the news, but he somehow got the facts wrong. He was under the impression that a Catholic priest, Canon Jeffery Bourke, was the owner of the estate, and it had been he who gave the order to evict the tenants. Canon Bourke was indeed a member of the family, but it was Joseph Bourke who had given Daily the eviction order to carry out. It was a regrettable mistake, and one that Michael would apologize for later.

The movement was underway and it was proceeding as if it had a life of its own. No one was exempt from it. Even Catholic priests who chose to speak out against it were not immune. This was evident in the town of Knock in Mayo when the Venerable Archdeacon Kavanagh, the parish priest, spoke out against the practice of farmers organizing meetings to vent their grievances. In a sermon, he singled out one John O'Kane of Claremorris–who had been involved in the Irishtown meeting–and claimed that O'Kane was preparing the country for revolution. A local farmer issued the following warning to Fr. Kavanagh: "Don't stand between the people and their rights; if you do, you must...accept the consequences."

The organizers were now preparing another meeting at Westport. Parnell reluctantly agreed to attend and speak there, but first he wanted to meet with Michael and John Devoy in Dublin.

"Just look at the success of our movement already, and it's just in its infancy," said Michael.

"And consider the statement made by the Irish Chief Secretary, James Lowther," said Devoy. He then read a statement which Lowther had made a few days earlier when he was asked to take action on the agrarian crisis in the west of Ireland: "The agricultural depression in Ireland is neither so prevalent nor so acute as the depression in other parts of the United Kingdom," he read.

"I know, I heard him say that," said Parnell. "In fact, I was one of the MPs that brought it up to him."

"The league needs your leadership," said Michael. "It needs a man of your standing to give it legitimacy. It won't work without you."

It was something which Parnell had to think hard about. *Was he really interested in the plight of these farmers or not?*. He was torn between his reluctance to lead what was sure to be looked upon as a "rebel" group, and his genuine concern for the Irish peasants.

"Let me reflect on it for a few days," said Parnell. "I'll let you know shortly."

But an unforeseen event would help make up his mind: Isaac Butt died suddenly. The MP who had championed the home rule movement was gone. Parnell saw no alternative, and decided to take the job of president of the Irish Land League of Mayo.

* * *

On the first day of June, Parnell met with Michael and John Devoy. It was a long discussion, but Michael and Devoy were ready. They had four conditions for Parnell to accept if he were going to lead the league.

"We don't want anything publicly to impair the Fenian movement," said Michael. "The league is not about that. You said yourself that we don't necessarily have to join forces but that we should not impede each other, either."

"I can accept that condition," said Parnell. "It's practically one I made up myself. What else?"

Devoy read the second condition. "We should not at this time publicly define the demand for self-government, but our goal should be nothing short of a national parliament with power over all vital national interests and an executive responsible to it. This is all we will accept."

"That is nothing more than home rule. Of course I will accept it," said Parnell.

Devoy went on. "In the settlement of the land question, we can accept nothing less than the eventual ownership of the land by the peasants affected by compulsory purchase."

"Compulsory purchase! That will be a tough one to get by the House of Lords," said Parnell. "But it is a goal worth having."

"We have one more condition," said Michael. "If you think that last one was tough, listen to this."

"Go ahead," said Parnell.

"The Irish members of parliament elected through the public movement should form an absolutely independent party, asking and accepting no places, salaried or honorary, under the British government, for themselves, their constituents or anyone else."

"That probably will be the toughest, but it's my favorite," said Parnell.

They went on for about another hour. There were a few more details to be ironed out, but the main points had been made.

"The first point is the most important," said Devoy. "We would not get Fenian support without it, and without that support the movement would quickly die."

"As a politician, I know that well," said Parnell.

So the stage was set. Parnell would take the leadership of the land league. Before the men parted, it was decided that Devoy would go back to New York and head the fundraising through Clan na Gael. The scheme would need money if it were going to work. Besides, Devoy was not in the United Kingdom legally and could be sent back to prison if he were caught. He was too valuable to lose.

It was also decided that Michael should eventually go to America as well. He would stay for awhile to help get the league started, but it would be better if he could help the Clan raise money by lecturing. He also thought that it would be best if he and Parnell were not in Ireland at the same time after the movement gained momentum. The movement could not risk Michael having his ticket of leave revoked and being sent back to prison. He was as valuable as anyone.

The men departed in agreement. And then it was time for the Westport meeting.

* * *

The meeting at Westport drew about eight thousand people in spite of the opposition of the local Catholic clergy. They had not been consulted, and this did not sit well with them. On the 7th of June, a letter had appeared in the *Freeman's Journal* signed by the Archbishop of Tuam, warning all the faithful against attending a meeting "convened in a mysterious and disorderly manner" and "organised by a few designing men."

Of the sympathy of the Catholic clergy for the rack-renting tenantry of Ireland, and of their willingness to cooperate earnestly in redressing their grievances, abundant evidence exists in historic Mayo as elsewhere. But night patrolling, acts and words of menace, with arms in hard, the profanation of what is most sacred in religion–all the result of lawless and occult association, eminently merit the solemn condemnation of the minister of religion, as directly tending to impiety and disorder in church and society.

"The Archbishop is eighty-nine years old," said Parnell, talking to the executive body of the league. "I don't believe this is his letter at all. It sounds more like his nephew, Rev. Thomas McHale."

The league had decided to go ahead with the meeting in spite of the clergy opposition, and it was a huge success. It seemed that the people were paying no attention to the clergy opposition. Many speeches were made reasserting Ireland's right to home rule, turning tenants into landowners, and condemning the practice of evicting tenants for the non-payment of unfair rents.

Michael, although ready to leave for America, did attend the meeting after all and made several speeches. Many more meetings were to follow; the movement was growing and getting the attention of the press. The Land League was real and it was hitting the landlords in the purse.

Chapter Nineteen

The Mayo Land League was so successful, it took only two months for the National Land League to blossom. The Westport meeting spawned much more press coverage, especially when a man with the status of Charles Stuart Parnell heading it, and now a meeting was to be held in Dublin at the Imperial Hotel on Sackville Street on the 21st of October.

The League was mainly Michael's brainchild, but he was content to stay in the background and write proposals, letting Parnell front the organization. Many prominent dignitaries were in attendance on October 21st to support it, most of them Catholics. The wisdom of letting Parnell become the spokesman for the organization was becoming a testimony to Michael's wisdom. It was one of the best public relations move ever made in Irish politics.

By the 5th day of November, the National Land League acquired offices at 62 Middle Abby Street in Dublin. Rules were laid down and the tactical methods of the League were changed as the organization matured. The biggest problem was keeping the movement from becoming violent.

The League had to deal with violence at Castlerea on the 7th day of December. This was due to the presence of police reporters there who were taking notes on speeches being made. The crowd was becoming angry at the armed police who sported rifles and had been assigned to protect the two police reporters. It was only through the strenuous efforts of Michael and Parnell that a riot was averted.

"Bring the reporters up here," said Michael. "Let them sit on the platform behind the news reporters."

"Yes," echoed Parnell, "and move those armed men back. These men will be safe here. We don't care if they take notes. We've nothing to hide from them."

It was a touchy situation, but the crowd listened to the two men.

Michael then proceeded to lecture the crowd in Irish. The two police reporters looked at each other, closed their notebooks, and left.

"That was genius," said Parnell later. "It's a good thing I understand Irish. I would hate to be there and not know what you were saying."

Michael smiled but then turned the conversation to the serious at hand.

"We cannot let this movement turn violent," said Michael. "It will destroy our public relations and undo much of our work."

"I agree," said Parnell. "We're on the verge of solving the land question in Ireland and we have the working class British on our side. Violence will only spread fear among them and set our whole movement back."

Parnell publicly condemned the violence, but was equally vocal on the floor of the House of commons speaking against the provocation that the police presence was giving to the meetings. This prompted the newly appointed Chief Secretary for Irish Affairs, William Edward Forster, to ask for a meeting with Parnell.

"If you let police reporters on to your platforms in the future, we will guarantee that no armed police will be at your League meetings," said Forster. "And speak in English, or you will just force us to use Irish speaking reporters."

Parnell looked at Forster.. He could not be speaking the truth. The police had such reporters?

Forster understood the look. "Yes, we have such men."

Parnell agreed to the deal. Later at Charleville, Co. Cork, the police reporters were barred from sitting on the platform. Parnell, hearing of this, informed the parties involved in the incident that if this happened again, he would no longer attend meetings.

* * *

1879 saw the National Land League come to prominence. Many farmers were being defended and many landlords ostracized. Since most of the landlords were absentee, it was their managers or land agents who took the brunt of the League's measures. If a farmer was evicted, the League made sure that no one else would work on that farm.

"There is a black cloud hanging over that farm," they would say. "Let no man live on or work on a farm from which a fellow Irishman has been evicted. Leave the land to the hares and rabbits, foxes and wild fowl if they are not afraid to alight upon it."

With the League going so well, Michael decided to go to America to lecture and raise money for the cause. It was expensive to feed and house people who had been evicted, but it was essential to the movement.

* * *

1 August 1879

Captain Charles Cunningham Boycott was an Englishman, a Protestant, and an ex officer who had served the Queen's army well. With his army career over, he decided to use his military skills to operate the land holdings of a Scottish Lord named Erne, a beautiful estate of lands located at Lough Mask, Co. Mayo.

"Captain," said one of the servants, "there is a note attached to the gate of the wrought-iron fence."

"Well, what does it say, man?" snapped the Captain.

"I don't know, sir, I can't read," said the servant.

"Stupid peasants," said the Captain under his breath as he walked out to the gate, his servant following.

Captain Boycott picked up the note. It read:

137

DO NOT COLLECT THE RENT
NOT UNLESS AN ABATEMENT
OF 20 TO 25% IS ALLOWED!

Under the text portion of the note was a drawing of a coffin.

"I hope they don't think this will intimidate me," said Boycott.

"What does it say, Captain?" said the servant.

"They want me to reduce the rents," he answered, "or I'll wind up in this coffin."

Back at the main house, the Captain threw the note on the table and forgot about it.

About a week passed, and when and the rents were due, three tenants refused to pay unless an abatement was given. The Captain immediately filed a legal eviction notice with the police. Then he received more threats.

"And I received this note which I found pinned to the gate," he said to the police captain. "I demand protection."

The police captain assured Boycott that the Royal Irish Constabulary would indeed send a contingent of men to protect Lough Mask. He did not know that they would be there until May of the next year.

* * *

Once he was back in Ireland after his American fund raising trip, Michael decided that a new tactic was needed to help farmers who were being evicted. The League would take advantage of the fact that the law required a process server to serve the eviction notice. This had to be done within a certain period of time or the family could not be evicted. It was decided that the League would organize and impede the process servers.

138

Michael realized that this tactic had the potential of getting out of control, but thought it was necessary since the number of evictions was on the rise.

In one town, the League organized a group of women who were instructed to surround a process server who had arrived on a horse. The women not only surrounded him, they threw mud balls at him until they succeeded in knocking him off the horse. The RIC police were called in but refused to fire on the women or otherwise disburse them. They simply took the man and ran for the shelter of their police station.

"They know better than to fool with Irish women," Michael said to the amusement of the organizers.

"I know I wouldn't," the organizer replied.

"Most of these RIC are country boys themselves. How could they live with it if they fired upon the women of their own village?"

"I wouldn't be surprised if some of the women were policemen's wives."

* * *

Michael and Parnell had to make another trip to America. Clan na Gael was forming an American branch of the National League, and it was important to have them both there to help launch the new organization, whose main function would be to raise funds for the National Land League of Ireland. But before Parnell left, he made a speech at Ennis that would prove very influential in how the League would operate in the future. Parnell directed his remarks at the land-grabbers, those who would move into a farm from which a tenant was evicted. He asked the crowd, "What would you do if you encountered such a character?"

"Shoot him," yelled a voice in the crowd.

A cheer went up. Parnell waited until it subsided, and

said, "I wish to point out a very much better way, a more Christian and charitable way which would give the sinner time to repent."

He enunciated the better, more charitable way. "When a man takes a farm from which another has been evicted, you must shun him on the roadside when you meet him, you must shun him on the streets of the town, you must shun him in the shop, you must shun him in the fair green and in the market place, and even in the place of worship. By leaving him severely alone, by putting him into a moral convent, by isolating him from the rest of his countrymen as if he were a leper of old, you must show him your detestation of the crime he has committed."

The crowd fell silent to ponder Parnell's words. He had given them a way to fight without having to plunge their souls into hell, and he had, for now, countered the inevitable violence. Backed by the civic leaders and parish priests, the League took a new direction. A form of moral excommunication for the land-grabber!

* * *

But the new direction would take an unexpected turn. It started at Lough Mask, in Mayo. Michael and Parnell had already left for America, and a group of workers who worked for Captain Charles Boycott were not satisfied with their wages.

"We cannot live on what the Captain pays us," said one worker to Father John O'Malley, the local parish priest. "I cannot feed my family on seven shillings a week. The prevailing wage in England for agricultural workers is nine shillings a week. Do we do less work?"

"No, you don't do less work," said Father O'Malley. "You are entitled to at least as much as your English counterparts."

"What do we do, Father?" asked the worker. "How do

we convince the Captain to raise the wage?"

"We will get the Land League behind us," said Father O'Malley. "They are in favor of withholding services for evictions. Why not use that tactic to help get your wages where they should be? You can strike."

Encouraged by Father O'Malley's words, the men informed the Captain that they would not work unless he paid them a fair wage.

The Captain capitulated almost immediately. Knowing that if he fired these workers, no one would risk taking their place, he agreed to the raise. It would be nine shillings per week.

But that was only a hint of things to come. It was November, and Lord Erne's rents had become due. It had been a bad harvest, and the peasants were hard-pressed to meet the rents. Lord Erne, in what he deemed to be a charitable gesture, instructed Captain Boycott to lower the rents by ten percent. The tenants, however, disagreed that this abatement was charitable. Spurred on by the League, they demanded an abatement of twenty-five percent.

Boycott was incensed, but he wrote to Lord Erne anyway. Lord Erne turned down the request, reiterating that the offer was ten percent and fair under the circumstances.

Captain Boycott immediately issued eviction notices against the tenants. "He didn't even give us time to raise the money," they told Father O'Malley.

"Even if he did," said Father O'Malley, "where would you get it anyway? The crops have been bad for three years and you're already in arrears."

* * *

David Sears was handed eviction notices to serve.

"We are sending seventeen constables to help you serve

141

these legal notices," said the police chief. "Remember, you must deliver to the head of the household, or his wife. If this is not possible, you can nail them to the door."

The first three notices were uneventful. The wives took them without incident. The fourth, however, was a different story. When Sears tried to serve the notice on a Mrs. Fitzmorris, she refused to accept it and waved the red flag, which warned the other cottages that the process server was in their midst. About twenty women descended upon Sears and his police escort and pelted them with stones, mud, and manure. The group retreated to the safety of the Lough Mask house with one woman yelling, "That'll teach ye devils to be fooling with Irish women!"

"They're like a bunch of screaming banshees, ladies from hell!" said Sears to Captain Boycott. "I'll not go out there again."

"We'll get you more constables," said the Captain. "You can try again tomorrow."

Sears looked a little perplexed. "Allright, I'll try it again," he said reluctantly. "But they need to do a better job of protecting us. I was knocked off my horse by a piece of dung!"

Chapter Twenty

The next day, Sears gathered all the remaining eviction notices and sat on his horse just outside the gate of Lough Mask waiting for the extra constables to come. He was determined to do his job. The Captain had talked to the police chief, who assured him that the notices would be served.

Sears heard a low murmuring sound coming from the road leading up to Lough Mask. When he looked up to see what was causing it, he saw a mob of men and women descending upon the estate. Fearing for his life, he rode back to the mansion to inform the Captain.

The mob stopped short of the grounds only because Father O'Malley, who had been walking with them, decided to address the crowd. "Do not use violence to deal with the Captain," he shouted. "There is a more Christian way of forcing him to change. Strike against the landlords. Do no work for them. Do not harvest their crops, cut their wood, take care of their horses, or even cut their hair. Don't speak to them when they come to town. Ostracize them!"

The crowd calmed down a bit, but began trespassing upon the estate. They talked to the workers: farm laborers, herdsmen, stable workers, servants, maids. They "advised" them not to work for the Captain. By the end of the day, the Boycott family was isolated, with no servants or laborers to do their work.

The strike against Boycott began to spread. The blacksmith left the family's horses unshod, and the laundress left their clothing unwashed. Even the young lad who delivered the post would not go to the estate.

"I'll take over for the boy delivering the post," said Arthur Boycott, the Captain's young nephew, who was living there as a ward.

But this proved impractical as well. Arthur began delivering the post, but he was stopped along the way. He was promptly advised to stop or he would find himself in danger.

The shopkeepers in Ballinrobe also joined in, forcing the Boycotts to get their food and household goods from the village of Cong, accessible only by boat, in order to avoid the Land League patrols which were guarding the roads.

* * *

In New York, a young journalist from America, James Redpath, was busy taking notes for his newspaper, the *New York Herald* and *Inter-Ocean*. He had made his reputation as an ardent supporter of the anti-slavery campaigns of John Brown. He arrived in Ireland with an open mind, in respect to the Irish land question. However, it did not take him long to take sides. Just as he had taken sides with the abolitionists in America, he quickly aligned himself with the tenants in their struggle. His stories were well received in America.

"It seems we have one well-known journalist on our side," said Michael to the American Clan na Gael members. "And he's an American, not Irish. He was neutral when he arrived in the country, but it didn't take him long to do the right thing."

Michael handed one of Redpath's articles to the Clan member, who smiled as he read it.

"It seems your Land League means business, Davitt," he remarked.

"We're putting your money to good use," said Michael. "Those Lough Mask workers could not afford to strike if the League were not able to help support them. That's how important your funds are."

"Then we will keep supporting it!"

* * *

1880

Michael had succeeded in organizing many of America's Irish-based organizations. More than any other Irishman, he was responsible for uniting these organizations behind the Land League. In fact, the Land League had united more American Irish to its cause than any other policy concerning Ireland in America.

His tour was hectic. On the 26th of June, he addressed a meeting at Jersey City, New Jersey and on the 5th of July gave a talk at a picnic in Albany, New York in the pouring rain. He then returned to New York City to plan another organizing tour, which he hoped would carry him across the country to form more chapters of the American Land League.

Michael thought about visiting his mother in Pennsylvania. He had only seen her twice since he had been in America but he had become so embroiled in the business of the League he kept putting off a vist. But one day he realized he had not seen his mother since the 13th of June, and here it was the 16th of July. He began clearing his schedule when the telegram came.

Catherine was sick. Michael immediately dropped what he was doing and set out for Manayunk. When he arrived, he found his mother sick but not seriously ill.

Catherine reached up from her bed to put her arms around him, and Michael could sense how weak she had become. He put his strong left arm under her to support her, but it seemed an effort for her just to bend at the waist so her arms could encircle him. His mind compared the memory of her strong arms with the way she was hugging him now. With her arms still around him, he bent forward and put her back down on her bed.

"Please rest, Mother," said Michael.

"I'm OK," she said. "I'm just tired. I should be up and around in a few days. I have things to do."

"Let Bina take care of you."

"Will you be staying long?"

"Not for very long. I'm in the middle of planning a nationwide tour to open new chapters of the Land League."

"That's wonderful, Michael. Perhaps you will free Ireland from the British like your father always wanted."

"I would like to. But even if we don't free her, we will at least make her an equal partner. With the support we're getting from America, I believe we will do it."

"I think I'm going to die in American and never see Ireland," said Catherine. "I'll be buried here and never touch the soil of Turlough again."

"I thought you wanted to be buried with Father."

"I am torn about that, One minute I want to be next to him, the next I want to be in Turlough. But I fear I will never leave this place."

"You have children and grandchildren here," said Michael. "They'll want you here."

"Yes, I know," said Catherine. "I don't know what to do. I'll leave it up to them. No one can afford to ship me back to Ireland to be buried, so I will probably end up here. Tell me more about Ireland, Michael. When was the last time you were there?"

Michael began to describe Mayo. He told her of the changes the Land League was making and how the people were standing up to the landlords. He described the countryside, which had not changed much in the years since she left. He even talked about some of their old friends in Haslingden. She fell asleep listening.

Michael touched his mother's hand. "God grant she may live to enjoy a few years quiet and happiness in the old land after her many years of exile from it," he prayed.

It was Friday. Michael had commitments in New York for the weekend. Catherine still seemed ill, but Michael thought

146

she would pull through. That same evening he said goodby to his family and left for New York.

$$* * *$$

On Sunday, the 18th of July, a telegram arrived from Manayunk. Michael noticed that it had been sent on Saturday, a day earlier, but had been delayed. When he opened it was tense. Catherine had taken a turn for the worse. The end of the telegram read, "...come at once if you want to see her alive."

Michael immediately boarded a train and arrived in Manayunk later that day. When he walked up to their house, he saw the family had gathered. Most were crying.

"Where is she?" Michael asked.

"You're too late Michael," said Sabina. "Mother passed away three hours ago."

He began to weep uncontrollably.

"I want to see her," he said.

"In the bedroom," said Sabina.

Michael walked to the bedroom and turned to Sabina and the others who were standing in the room. "Give me a moment alone with her," he said.

Catherine was lying on the bed, under the covers with her hands folded in front of her.

"I'm sorry, I could not get here sooner," Michael said to her as he knelt down beside her, the light of the death watch candle flickering on her face. He bowed his head, and the half-memory of Catherine refusing to let go of him in the Swineford workhouse jumped into his mind. Now he would be the one to never let her go.

"Your children and grandchildren want you buried here, and it appears you have made a great many friends in this land," Michael told her, "and I have not the means to bring you back to Ireland. But I will go to Turlough and say a prayer for you

147

there."

He got up and walked to the door. Before he opened it, he thought of what he had done in his life, all the years in prison that he could not spend with his family. He was not there when his father died, and now he had not been with his mother in her final hours. He thought of all the suffering she had to go through because of him. It was because of him that his parents had to leave Ireland and die in America. Now they had to be buried in a foreign soil, a world away from the land they loved so much. He had been too busy being a patriot. And this, he saw, was its price

* * *

"A well-born lady like myself should not have to do this," complained Mrs. Boycott as she prepared the meal for the evening.

"My hands are being ruined," said Boycott's niece, also the Captain's ward, referring to the blisters she was raising from doing the laundry.

"If I can get up at four in the morning to feed the cattle and horses, you two can cook and do laundry," said the Captain. "I have only my manager, Ashton Weekes, and Arthur to help me. Yesterday I had to muck out the stables myself, and Arthur and I milked the cows, so don't complain to me that you have to cook and wash. But this is not the worst of it. If I don't get farm help soon, my produce will rot in the field and the crop will be ruined. Do you two want to pick turnips?"

"Pick turnips!" shouted Mrs. Boycott, appalled. "You want me, a lady, to pick turnips?"

The Captain turned away, not in sympathy with his wife and niece.

"I have too much to do. I've no time to be listening to

the two of you. Get to work or we don't eat."

* * *

It was the 23th of September when James Redpath sat down with the convivial Father O'Malley for dinner and a drink.

"I'm writing the story of the Captain, Father and, I'm bothered by a word," said Redpath.

"Only one word?"

Redpath laughed and said, "Well, when the people ostracize a land-grabber, we call it social excommunication, but we ought to have an entirely different word to signify ostracism applied to a landlord or a land agent like Boycott. Ostracism won't do–the peasantry would not know the meaning of the word–and I can't think of any other."

The thought crossed Father O'Malley's mind that social excommunication sounded too much like a religious concept–something the Catholic Church would do. He did not want people to confuse the Land League with the Catholic Church.

"No," said Father O'Malley, "Ostracism won't do."
Father looked down and after some deep thought said, "How would it do to say 'boycott' him?"

A light went off in Redpath's head. Use the man's name as a verb! It had a good ring to it. He liked it! The next day he began writing the story of the Captain using "boycott" as a verb. He published an article in *Inter-Ocean* which appeared on October 12, the first such use of the word "boycott" in the English language.

* * *

The copy editor of the *London Times* was reading his copy of *Inter-Ocean* when he saw Redpath's article. He brought

149

the article to the main editor's office and showed it to him.

"This American reporter took the name of the Lord Erne's agent and used it as a verb," he said. "I believe he has coined a new word."

The editor took the paper and skimmed through the article.

"Yes, I believe he has. We need a little something to spice up that story anyway. Print it!"

The article went out in the *London Times*. The next day, the Spanish newspapers picked up the story, then the French and Russian papers. All used the term "boycott" as a verb to describe the efforts of the National Land League who were instrumental in withholding services to the land agent. "Boycott" became a word in those languages as well.

* * *

The Tory newspapers, however sympathized with the Captain. On the 3rd of November, two letters appeared in the *Belfast News-Letter*, one from the Reverend William Stuart Ross, the other signed simply "A Lover of Law and Order." The letters were an appeal for a relief fund to save Captain Boycott's crops. The Reverend's was more to the point. He maintained that relief should be sent to "our suffering fellow Protestant."

The next day, the *Belfast News-Letter* sported a column entitled "The Boycott Relief Fund." It contained a list of subscriptions already received, and a further column written about formation of a "Boycott Relief Expedition." It seemed the anti-Land Leaguers had found a way to express their frustration at the tactics of the League. A group of Orangemen was being formed to go to Mayo. However, as much as the newspapers tried to make it a religious war, the other side kept bringing up the fact that the National Land League's President was Charles Stuart Parnell, a Protestant and Member of Parliament, who was not some hot-headed, heavy-handed revolutionary. He was

Charles Stuart Parnell!

But there was no stopping the Orangemen. They would go to Mayo and save their fellow Protestant's crops.

"This might be a dangerous mission," said one of the organizers.

"We will have to arm ourselves," said another, "or it won't be safe for us in Mayo."

* * *

The prospect of an armed expedition of hundreds of armed Ulstermen going to Mayo sent the editors of the *Freeman's Journal* into a frenzy. Alarmed at a probable confrontation between an armed band of Protestants and an armed band of Catholics, the paper denounced the action.

Even the Ulstermen were having second thoughts about going to Mayo alone. They immediately petitioned the British government to send troops to guard the men who were going on a mission of mercy to help a besieged family at Lough Mask. The government agreed, and began outfitting special troop trains to accompany the charter cars that would make the trip from Ulster to Mayo but only if the men went unarmed and numbered no more than fifty.

The organizers had no choice. It was either hold the mission to fifty or not get Her Majesty's troops for protection. When it finally started out, it was a sight to behold. Fifty Orangemen boarded the special trains, followed by the several British troop cars assigned to them. Newspaper reporters descended upon the band in droves, trying to get interviews.

It was not much different in Mayo. Newspaper reporters were arriving from all over the world. The 'boycott" story had become big news.

Chapter Twenty-One

In the early morning hours of November 9th, four troops of the British 19th Hussars, a cavalry division, boarded the train in Dublin and loaded all their equipment, including their horses. Later, members of the Army Service Corps arrived with hospital equipment, ambulances, horses, and supplies. In Curragh, some four hundred men of the 84th Regiment carrying a large quantity of tents boarded their train and set off for Claremorris. They arrived to foul weather; the soldiers had to stand for hours in the rain, tired and hungry and waiting for their orders. It was not until the next day that they were ordered to march to Ballinrobe, thirteen miles away.

When they finally reached Ballinrobe, Her Majesty's soldiers looked more like Her Majesty's clowns. There was no shelter, food, discipline, or supplies. The Army Service Corps and the commissariat had not arrived, and when they did they did not have their picks, tent-pegs, or camp kettles. When they finally got organized, they pitched their tents on the green between the infantry and cavalry. The engineers dug the water troughs to carry the water away from the tents. When done, there were at least one thousand men in uniform, including the RIC who had been instructed to supplement the troops.

"What are these troops supposed to do?" said one man to a group of about ten locals sitting in a local pub.

"I guess they're here to pick turnips," answered another.

"I thought men from Ulster were coming to do that," said another.

"I don't know, I don't see anyone but the soldiers."

One man picked up a copy of the newspaper. "It says here that only fifty men are coming from Ulster to harvest crops," he read.

"It takes a thousand uniforms to protect fifty men?" the other said. "The best troops must be off fighting Zulus."

* * *

On the 10th of November the rumor began circulating that the Orangemen of Ulster were now armed and organized and ready to leave. The army troops and the local constables were put on alert.

"I don't like it," said the chief constable. "If these soldiers get trigger happy, we could be seeing the start of a full-fledged civil war. The IRB will certainly retaliate and bring armed men from all over the region. Remember the crowds that showed up at Irishtown?"

"Yes," said the assistant chief. "We should make sure the soldiers don't fire upon the people unless they are openly attacked."

The army commander agreed. He would keep his men confined to Lough Mask and the Captain's grounds. They would only go out of the compound to escort the Orangemen from the train to the fields.

The next day, the fifty Orangemen, from Monaghan and Craven, assembled on the platform of the train station at Athlone. Three men were responsible for their organization and had obtained arms and food for them: Mr. Manning, Mr. Goddard, and Captain Somerset Maxwell stood on the platform facing the and began to hand out revolvers.

"Make sure you conceal them," Maxwell said. "We are not going on this mission armed, but do not let anyone know you have these weapons. Use them only if absolutely necessary and only for your personal defense. The army is already at Lough Mask and will be protecting us."

When the train arrived at Ballinrobe in the heavy rain, soldiers of the 76th Regiment were there to greet them. The *Freeman's Journal* described the event. "...we have never seen a sorrier or more wretched crew than the volunteers." The loyalist newspapers had a different interpretation. They described the group as "...fine young men making a brave show of indifference."

It was 4:30 in the afternoon when the group finally started its march to Lough Mask in the heavy rain escorted by Her Majesty's soldiers. The downpour was turning the dirt road into mud. The road was nearly impassible, except for one part that had been paved with seashells and seemed to have adequate drainage, a leftover from the old public works days during the height of the famine forty years ago. The marchers wondered why the entire road had not been done that way.

"Probably politics," said one man. "The man who was doing it right was probably relieved by some politician who wanted to give the job to a friend."

"They should have stayed with the first man," said the other. "His replacement certainly didn't know anything about building roads."

The group reached Hollymount, where the 76th Regiment was being relieved by 84th Regiment.

"Why do we have to stand here in the rain waiting for the soldiers to change shifts?" said one Orangeman. "Why can't they go the rest of the way with us?"

"It's the way the army operates," said a second man. "I served in Her Majesty's Army and there's usually no rhyme or reason to what they do."

It took five more hours to reach Ballinrobe. The volunteers were put up in tents for the night next to the soldiers.

"Take a tent and get a good night's rest," said Maxwell.

"I'll not sleep in a tent with men from Craven," said one of the Monaghan men.

Maxwell sensed a war within a war might be immanent. "Men from Monaghan will occupies these tents," he said, pointing to the tents on the left. "Those of you from Craven, the ones on the right."

It was a cold, wet night but the men got through it. The next morning, the 13th of November, the Orangemen and their escorts made the final three mile march to Lough Mask. The weather had improved but the going was still slow. When they finally arrived, the Captain and his manager, Weekes, were there to greet them. Both were armed. The crowd of men who were expected to start the civil war, were nowhere to be seen. Only a handful of women watched as the men marched up to the house.

"Welcome, Orangemen," said the Captain. "Welcome to Lough Mask."

The Captain and Weekes shook hands with the men and invited the officers to a dinner that night. Then the volunteers went out to the fields to harvest the crop, assisted by some of the soldiers. It took them about five times longer to get the work done than if the local peasants had done it. The soldiers, not used to doing farm work, began to complain.

"We're not farm hands," said a corporal who had been placed in charge of corn threshing. "You'll do as I've ordered," said the officer in charge. But even he could see they knew nothing about threshing corn. He had to get some of the Orangemen over to direct them.

The work continued all day. The soldiers dug a cooking trench and suspended three huge pots filled with potatoes over the fire. When the day ended, the volunteers refused to stay in the tents.

"We're already soaked from those leaky tents," said the men.

Weekes intervened. "We have very large haylofts which are dry," he said. "Perhaps you can bunk there."

The men were happy to get the haylofts. They were indeed dry, and no one had to sleep on an army cot sinking into the mud.

That evening, a rumor circulated that the Irish

155

Republican Brotherhood was planning an attack on Lough Mask in order to stop the harvest. The Army immediately went on the alert and doubled the sentries. New passwords were issued, and the Orangemen were told not to leave the hayloft. They posted their own guards through the night, revolvers ready to defend themselves. The attack never came.

* * *

"This is insanity," said Father O'Malley to the Land League members. "I propose we get a delegation together and visit Lord Erne. Perhaps we can arrive at a compromise and solve this problem. I will head the delegation myself."

One of the men in the room held up a telegraph which he received from Dublin.

"Michael Davitt has returned from America," he said, joyfully.

* * *

Michael was immediately swamped by reporters as he stepped into the lobby of the hotel at Cork.

"What do you think of the activities of the Land League?" asked the reporter.

"I believe that land agitation will eventually result in the overthrow of landlordism."

"What do the Americans think of these agrarian outrages?"

"The London press agency has tried to give the Americans the impression that they are the result of Land League teachings. It is of greatest importance to disabuse the American mind of this fallacy."

Michael went on to tell of the great amount of American support for the League and its mission, and that it would be the job of the League to get the truth out to America.

* * *

With the crops picked, the Orangemen were ready to leave, and had assembled at the door of the Lough Mask house. Maxwell read them a letter from Captain Boycott, who thanked them for saving his crops. The sale of the saved corn, turnips and mangolds were enough to keep him from financial ruin. He also announced that he would now be "obliged to quit, with my wife, a happy home where we had hoped to have spent the remainder of our days."

Boycott was leaving! The reporters scrambled around trying to write down the words and at the same time to scurry off to the telegraph office. The Land League had forced him out. Boycott was leaving!

Just then the Captain appeared at the door. A great cheer went out as he walked through the crowd and shook everyone's hand. The men began singing "Auld Lang Syne" and "For They Are Jolly Good Fellows."

An army ambulance took the Captain and his wife to the train station. A few locals had come out to witness the event, Father O'Malley being one. He found an old woman who was bent upon giving her opinion of British soldiers, the Captain, and his wife.

Father O'Malley turned to the woman and said, tongue in cheek, "Did I not warn you when I said to let the British Army alone? How dare you come to intimidate those two thousand heroes after their glorious campaign? I'll make an example of you. Be off!"

The woman smiled and felt proud of herself to be singled out as a person who was intimidating the two thousand soldiers of the British Army. Also smiling was the reporter standing next to her at whom Fr. O'Malley's remarks were really aimed.

Chapter Twenty-Two

1880

After the Boycott incident, Michael continued his tour across the country. Land League chapters were springing up everywhere. The boycott incident was of immeasurable value to the League, probably the single most influential event in history and Michael constantly referred to it in his lectures. The image of a group of poor tenant Irish farmers pushing a stodgy Englishman off Irish land had caught the people's imagination, and Michael became the most popular Irish hero in America.

On the western part of his tour, Michael stopped in Oakland, California. He thought it was a beautiful city, situated as it was on San Francisco Bay. He was to be the guest of a wealthy Irish women, Mrs. Canning. When he made the five-mile journey over the bay from San Francisco to Oakland, a huge contingent of Irish organizations was there to meet him, including a band. They swiftly escorted him to an opera house, where he spoke to a huge crowd. He told them how the famine-stricken Irish were now standing up to their British landlords and would no longer suffer any landlord-created famines.

He spoke of the non-violent movement of the League, and how the people of Ireland were going to defeat the British landlords without violence unless THEY did something stupid to cause the people to become desperate.

After the speech was over, Michael retired to the home of Mrs. Canning. At her house he was introduced to her niece, Mary Yore, A beautiful, eighteen-year-old girl who was living with her aunt due to her mother having met with a fatal road accident when Mary was seven years old.

Michael liked her very much. She was full of questions and opinions. Michael saw that she had a keen mind and had studied many of the questions about the Irish land problem. She was also familiar with the book *Progress and Poverty*, by Henry George. For her part, Mary was very much impressed with Michael. She also thought he was very handsome. She had quickly gotten beyond the fact that he was an amputee, a reality that might have turned off many other women. They became good friends.

* * *

Michael was impressed with Henry George's self-published book. Essentially, George's solution to poverty lay in stopping private ownership of land. He argued that it had no moral justification anywhere, and that land should be considered like air or sunlight, which everyone had a right to own. Everyone had an equal right to land.

George's solution was very clever. Only rents should be confiscated, not land. These rents would then be applied to the equal benefit of all citizens.

Michael thought about how this would work

George wrote that this would be achieved by taxing the land up to its full value, exclusive of improvements, and by abolishing all other taxes. The landlord's unearned increment would thus be abolished without compensation, speculation in land values would be eliminated, nothing produced by human labor would be taxed, and absolute free trade would be established.

To Michael, it seemed too simple a solution to be true. But as he thought about a country under this type of economic system, the more it made sense to him. A system like this would save Ireland. All they had to do was get the land holdings away from the landlords and institute this system of taxation, and the landlord problem would be forever solved.

He returned to New York At the home of *Irish World* editor, Patrick Ford he was introduced to Henry George.

"I understand you were a printer's apprentice in England," said George.

"Yes, I did everything in the shop, including setting type," said Michael.

"I wouldn't think it was possible for a man to set type with one hand."

"When a man is determined, he can do great things."

"Have you read *Progress and Poverty*?" asked George.

"I certainly have," said Michael.

"And what did you think?"

"I believe your solution is the only solution to the Irish land problem."

"So you like the idea of making land common property?".

"That may be the only way to get the land away from the landlords," Michael said. Only the government has enough resources to compensate the landlords for their holdings. I like the idea that rent should be paid to the community and still privately owned, especially with tenure for the workers who are producing the wealth that comes from it. And I understand your distinction between common property–that which all have a right to use and enjoy–and government property–that which belongs to the state and is subject to the direction of the government. "

"And you think that the landlords should be compensated and the land made into common property?" asked George.

"We all feel that the landlords should be compensated for their property. The alternative is a violent revolution, which I think is impractical."

"Do you think that Ireland should be free and independent some day?"

"I would like to see that," said Michael. "But we must be careful. A free and independent Ireland might not have the resources it needs to support the peasant population. Right now, I feel we need to build up the country and gradually take over the land for the Irish. Getting it all at once and without the resources of the British government might cause more hardship. When we are ready, we can become independent. Someday we may achieve it, but I don't want to sacrifice any more Irish lives to get it. The Land League gives farmers a way to fight without violence."

"Well, Mr. Davitt, I hope you will succeed," said George. "It appears to me that your Land League may well be the mechanism that will effect this change and break the land monopoly of the British aristocracy. I wish you luck."

"I will be returning to Ireland soon," said Michael. "I can assure you that *Progress and Poverty* will be pushed in Great Britain. And not only in Ireland, but with the English working class as well."

Henry George smiled. His book had started out as a self-published treatise on the causes and evils of poverty in the world. It sold five hundred copies in 1879, and had later been picked up by a New York publisher. Now it was known worldwide and was about to get a boost from Ireland's premier hero of the century.

After several more appearances, Michael said goodby to the United States of America. On the 20th of November, 1880, he was back in Ireland.

Chapter Twenty-Three

Parnell addressed the Members of Parliament. "It cost a shilling for every turnip dug," he said. about the expedition to save Captain Boycott's crops.

That statement would go down in Irish history and point out the lengths to which the British aristocracy would go to protect their stranglehold on the land and the peasants of Ireland. It also showed that the Land League was a success. The only problem was with those who wanted instant gratification and insisted on turning to violence to achieve their ends.

Michael had to address this problem. In a speech in Dublin on the 23rd of November at a Land League meeting, Michael condemned the use of violence. He first spoke on the support of the American Land League and the formation of the American Lady's Land League, under the direction of Charles Stuart Parnell's sister, Fanny Parnell, and Ellen Ford, the sister of *Irish World* editor Patrick Ford. He commented on how these organizations were growing in influence. Then he hit upon the question of violence.

"The non-violent operation against Captain Boycott did more for the tenants' cause than if a hundred landlords had been shot by those who resorted to the wild justice of revenge."

* * *

The League was growing in power. Landlords all over Ireland were complaining to Her Majesty's government that they were being hurt by the League's actions. Profits could not be made without the cheap labor of the peasants, and the League was interfering with business. The House of Lords was crying for action, and Michael labeled it "The House of Landlords" in the press.

Michael suspected, without actually knowing it, that the

police had him under surveillance. Chief Secretary of Ireland, Forster had several meetings with Prime Minister Gladstone about revoking Michael's ticket of leave.

"You can do that at the discretion of the Crown," said Gladstone. "You don't have to give a reason."

Forster shook his head no. "If we did that, the press would have a field day with us. Davitt is not some common criminal who relieved someone of his purse in the street. He's become an international figure. If we revoke his ticket of leave, we want to be sure that we have a good reason to do it. I don't want to make a martyr out of him."

"Yes, of course you're right," said Gladstone. "I can just hear Parnell and O'Connor on the floor of Parliament turning him into just that. The liberal newspapers would publish a picture of him, making sure they showed his missing right arm. He would even get the sympathy of the English working class. He's a dangerous man."

Forster then produced a draft document of a plan which he called "the Coercion Act." Basically it called for a temporary suspension of habeas corpus. This would enable the police to arrest and imprison Land League leaders without having to give them a trial.

"Do we need that for Davitt?" asked Gladstone.

"No," said Forster, "he's on a ticket of leave. This Act will, however, give us the power to hold the other Land Leaguers who are causing all the trouble."

"Very good," said Gladstone. "As you know, I am very liberal when it comes to dealing with this problem, but I will not stand for violence. This measure will help the police move quickly and deal with it."

They ended the meeting with the decision not to arrest Michael. But the aristocracy would not give up. Lord Randolph Churchill made a speech to the House of Commons asking that Michael's ticket of leave be revoked, documenting statements

Michael had made in several speeches which Churchill considered inflammatory. After much consideration, and reluctantly, Gladstone finally decided that Michael had to be re-arrested. Too much pressure was being brought upon him. Michael and the League had to be considered seditious.

A warrant was issued for Michael's arrest and executed on the 3rd of February in Dublin, while Michael was crossing O'Connell Bridge in the company of Tom Brennan and Matt Harris. The arrest was made without resistance from Michael, but over the objection of Brennan and Harris. Michael quickly calmed the men down and told them it was alright. He would get in touch with them later.

Michael was put aboard a train under heavy guard. A first-class compartment was reserved for him with five police guards attending. There was also a pilot engine assigned to proceed the train. This was a security measure usually reserved only for the Queen. "It's quite an honor," thought Michael to himself when he saw the engine in front of the train. "They think I am as important as Queen Victoria herself!"

The party reached the ferry docks and then proceeded by boat to England where the formal warrant was served. Michael was sent back to Millbrook Prison where he had been ten years ago.

Egan, hearing of Michael's arrest, anticipated a move against the League by the British government, and immediately moved all the League's records to Paris. A special meeting of the League was held in Paris on the 3rd of February, whereby the IRB executive committee authorized Eagan to make Paris the financial headquarters of the League. This made sense, since this action would place the League's funds out of the jurisdiction of Her Majesty's government.

* * *

The newspaper accounts of Michael's arrest were split along Irish Nationalist and British Nationalist lines. The pro-Irish papers were filled with criticism of the British government for revoking Michael's ticket of leave. The most outspoken was *The Freeman's Journal,* which eloquently pointed out Michael's record of non-violence.

"He (Michael Davitt), has been the deadly enemy of crime; no man so often, so eloquently raised his voice against any act of violence or illegality." Almost all of the other pro-Irish papers also extolled Michael, stating that his own personal fortitude would stand up against a tyrannical government which would never beat him into the ground.

In a rebuttal, the *Nation* printed that the government could not have done any more to stem the tide of "Irish antipathy to British rule than to have arrested Michael Davitt."

In Parliament, the issue of Michael's arrest came to a boiling point when Parnell and his followers demanded to know what Michael had done to have his ticket of leave revoked. They insisted that nothing he had said was inflammatory, and that the actions of the Land League on behalf of the peasants of Ireland were consistent with the rights given to the English working class. But Gladstone and Secretary Forrest were silent. When Gladstone tried to go on with the business of the body, Parnell and his followers caused such a disturbance that thirty-six of them were suspended for the remainder of the sitting. They held a caucus outside the chamber and decided to remain. It would serve no purpose for them not to be there to vote and talk against other bills that would be brought up in the future. They must have a voice.

* * *

Millbrook Prison was a little different for Michael than it had been ten years ago. He was well known in prison circles.

It seemed that the reforms he had been instrumental in making upon his release almost a decade ago had had their effect on the system. First, he was examined by the prison doctor. He was found to have a cough, which was probably a result of exhaustion. It was recommended that he be moved to Portsmith, which would be better for his health.

When he arrived at Portsmith, he was assigned to "rest only" and was given a full meal allowance. In a few days he was much better, his cough subsided, and he was elevated to privileged status. He was housed in the center of the prison and visited by the prison governor and the Catholic chaplain. He and the governor, George Clifton, became immediate friends. Clifton was an admirer of Michael and a supporter of prison reforms. He allowed Michael the privilege of helping out in the infirmary, which became his permanent job.

On the 8th of February, Michael wrote a letter to his friend, Tom Brennan. Michael asked Tom to retain his collection of books and newspaper files for Tom's own use and send the rest of his personal belongings to a friend in Dublin. Michael also instructed Tom to use the money in his bank account to pay his rent and keep his subscriptions to the *Connaught Telegraph, Mayo Examiner* and *Nation*. He also wanted forty pounds sent to his sister Sabina in Pennsylvania, so she could erect a suitable plain tombstone over their mother's grave. Tom was also to make a contribution to a convent. Michael then wrote more letters, mostly to Sabina. This was certainly a much different situation then what he had faced the last time he was incarcerated. Ironically, he was benefitting from his own influence on prison reform.

After much consultation, the prison officials agreed to supply Michael with paper and pen so he could continue his writings. Michael thought about what he should write. After considering several titles, he decided upon *Jottings in Solitary* as the title of a book. With such a great deal of time at his disposal,

Michael poured out his thoughts on English civilization, Ireland's place in the British government and constitution, and the education of the Irish, as well as many random thoughts on the "land war" and its effects on the world.

* * *

One evening, Prison governor Clifton came to Michael's cell.

"Good morning, Governor," said Michael. "To what do I owe this visit?"

"I have something for you," said Clifton. He clutched an object under his arm, wrapped in a cloth. Then he carefully unwrapped the cloth and showed Michael an injured bird. "It's a blackbird I rescued from the prison cat. I thought you might like to nurse it back to health."

Michael took the bird gently in his hand. It appeared that the bird's wing had been injured and it did not resist Michael's touch. It was also evident that the poor creature was undernourished. Michael smiled at Clifton The gift of empathy was exactly what he needed.

"Be sure to give him a good name," Clifton said.

The bird made a small sound.

"I think he said 'Joe,'" said Michael, "so that will be his name.

"I'm sure he can use a friend," said Clifton. "I'll arrange to give you an extra portion of milk on the infirmary allowance. That should help you speed up his recovery."

"I will not forget your kindness," Michael said.

* * *

Joe became a constant companion. He perched on the foot of Michael's bed at night and slept when Michael slept. He was there in the morning, waiting for his handout of biscuit crumbs and water. Michael began to lecture him. He told Joe about the British Empire and how the class structure of Britain exploited the working people. He spoke of how the Empire used military force to protect "British interests" around the world with little or no regard for the people they were exploiting. He told Joe in detail about the landlord system, which had to be reformed, and outlined a plan to get the absentee landlords out of Ireland so the land could be given back to the Irish, the rightful owners of the Old Sod. He whispered to Joe that even though this stint in prison was better than the last one, it was still prison, at the whim of the government, and that he, Michael, was determined not to go mad, as long as he, Joe was there to listen to him.

For his part, Joe proved to be a capable audience. He would cock his head to one side when Michael was talking, and appeared to be listening carefully to everything Michael said about how the British exploited the world. He did not disagree with anything; he had his own wings to think about perhaps. He was like a homeless man in a mission who had to listen to Bible stories in order to be fed; he happily listened in order to get some of the oatmeal and his freedom back.

Joe helped save Michael's sanity. Michael tended Joe's injured wing. It was the same gesture.

Chapter Twenty-Four

March, 1888

The weather in England was getting a bit warmer. Even the prison was pleasant with the smell of early spring. But this pleasantness was interrupted by the bad news which arrived by telegram. Mary Agnes' husband, Neil Padden, had died on the 6th of March after a short illness.

Michael sat in his cell thinking about Neil and his sister, who had now been left alone to bring up their nine children. He asked the governor for permission to write to Mary Agnes via their sister Sabina, and permission was quickly granted. He decided not to strike a sorrowful tone but instead extol the virtues of Cornelius Padden, a wonderful father and husband. He had been a man who had sacrificed everything for the sake of his family. His whole life, in fact, had been a sacrifice for his daily bread and, like all workers, a constant fight against the industrialists' greed, which had put many a family man too early in his grave.

After he composed this part of the letter, Michael thought about his sister, widowed at the age of 41 and with children ranging in age from eighteen-year-old John to three-year-old Elizabeth. He decided to help them, and told Mary Agnes that she and her children would not go without assistance. He arranged to send her a draft for one hundred dollars, which he paid out of his savings.

* * *

Time continued to creep along slowly in prison. But this sentence was much different from the previous one. He was allowed reading material. He could supplement the prison library with books from the outside. The only restriction was on newspapers and other reading material which contained references to the current political situations in England and Ireland. So, he had no idea of the events that had taken place in his absence. There was also Joe, whose wing had now healed and was now taking practice flights around the small cell.

Early in the morning of the 6th of May, Michael working in the infirmary garden. He looked up to see the governor walking across the yard with a smile on his face and papers in his hand.

"You've been released, Michael. Congratulations."

Michael froze, unbelieving. Immediately the image of his old governor came to mind. In Dartmoor, he remembered the sadistic game that governor had played with him, telling him he was being released and leaving him to find out later that he was only being transferred to another prison. But this could not be the case now! This governor was completely different. He would never do such a thing.

Michael's heart began to pound. Clifton handed him the release papers.

"Is this true?" asked Michael.

"It most certainly is."

It's a mistake, Michael thought. He still could not believe it. But then he looked at the papers. It was a letter from Parnell stating that Michael was to be released. So it was really true. Parnell wouldn't lie to him. He was free!

"Parnell and others are coming to get you," said Clifton. "They were in prison as well."

"Parnell was in prison?" asked Michael, a look of disbelief on his face.

"Yes, since October," said the Clifton. "He's on his way here now to take you to London. You'll be there this afternoon."

Clifton escorted Michael back to his cell to pick up his belongings, especially his writings. Joe was still there. He took

Joe out of the cell perched on his hand.

"Shall I get another prisoner to look after him?" asked Clifton.

Michael looked down at Joe. Joe looked back up at him, cocking his head to one side. "No, I think it's time to set him free," said Michael. "He reminds me of Ireland. He came to me starving with a broken wing. I nursed him back to health and educated him. He's ready for independence. It's time to set the blackbird free!"

He gave Joe a morsel of food that the governor provided and said goodby. "I'll take him out with me and set him free outside of the prison gate."

Once outside the prison gate, Michael put Joe down on the ground. At first the bird did not seem to know what to make of it, but soon found some seeds on the prison lawn. After eating them, he spread his wings and flew up into a nearby tree. It was as if he knew that he was supposed to be free.

"Goodby Joe," said Michael. "You are on your own now. It's not going to be easy to be free but you are ready and you'll make it. I will never forget you."

* * *

When Parnell arrived, Michael was ready. Parnell was accompanied by two other men, Dillon and O'Kelly who had also been released. They began filling him in on the events that had taken place while he was in prison. Parnell told about the "no rent manifesto" the League had promulgated. Much violence had taken place, with the Tory press blaming the Land League for all of it. In October, Parnell had been arrested under The Coercion Act and sent to prison without a trial. Gladstone offered to release him and the others if Parnell would sign a treaty and call off the manifesto. The press had been calling it "The Treaty of Kilmainham." Parnell had reservations about the

171

terms of the treaty but agreed and signed it, making sure it included Michael's release.

"So you see, that's why you're out," said Parnell.

Michael could not resist looking out of the carriage so see if he could spot Joe up in the tree. He was not there.

"Michael, did you hear me?" asked Parnell.

Michael snapped back into reality. "Yes, of course I did. I was just looking for a friend of mine."

"Was someone else released with you?" asked Parnell.

"Yes, but he's gone," said Michael. Michael forced himself to deal with the conversation.

'It seems the Land League came under considerable pressure from the government while I was in prison," said Michael.

"Yes, in fact it was almost completely stymied," said Parnell. "The Ladies' Land League took over and subsequently gained a lot of power while we were away. Now they've become a major obstacle to us."

"You're talking about Anne and Fannie, your sisters," Michael reminded him.

"Sisters or not, they're out of hand," said Parnell. "They have taken the country out of our hands and must be suppressed."

"You feel that strongly about them?" asked Michael, shocked.

"If we don't stop them," said Parnell, "I will retire from public life."

Michael got the message. The Ladies had in fact taken away the political power Parnell had once enjoyed as the head of the Land League, and he was not one to give up his decision-making control so easily. Michael decided not to antagonize Parnell by extolling the virtues of the women who had kept the ball rolling while they were incarcerated. He simply let Parnell go on.

172

"Michael, we are on the verge of Home Rule," said Parnell. "We are already making plans for it. Gladstone has assured me he will help get it passed. We intend to appoint Sexton as Chancellor of the Exchequer, Dillon as home secretary, O'Kelly as head of a national police force and you as director of prisons. There is a new chief secretary, Lord Frederick Cavendish. He is one of the most modest and best man in the House of Commons and throughly committed to the new policy."

Michael was somewhat in disbelief. Was it really going to happen? Home Rule! The dream of men like Isaac Butt was about to come true. It was what he and Parnell had worked and sacrificed for all these years. Ireland would be ruled by Irishmen but still have the resources of the British Government behind them. It was too good to be true!

Michael, Parnell, Dillon, and O'Kelly arrived later that afternoon at the Westminster Palace Hotel in London and were welcomed by a host of friends. Michael was itching to get to work on the new Home Rule policy and began constructing a new Ireland. All were in a joyful mood and ready to go.

They had only been there for two hours when a bellboy came into the room with a telegram for Parnell. Parnell ripped it open and read it to himself, a look of dismay and then grimness clouding his face.

"What is it?" asked Michael, suddenly afraid.

"There has been an assassination," Parnell said in a monotone. "Lord Frederick and his under-secretary, Thomas Henry Burke, were murdered in Phoenix Park about two hours ago."

Chapter Twenty-Five

The Phoenix Park incident had become international news.

"These murders have set us back years," said Michael. "It will be difficult to keep public opinion on our side now."

"But we cannot give up," said Parnell. "We must condemn this act as strongly as possible."

"Who is responsible for this?" asked Michael.

"There's a splinter group of Fenians who call themselves 'The Invincibles.' They're out of control. We believe they are responsible."

"Do any of them belong to the League?"

"Probably. But even if they don't, the League will get the blame anyway."

"I'm sorry we ever took help from Devoy and his group. I think that ass Jeremiah O'Donovan Rossa is behind this. I intend to take that up with Devoy when I see him."

Parnell pointed to the London newspaper. He wanted to calm Michael down by changing the subject. "It seems you're a favorite of Queen Victoria," said Parnell.

"I am?".

"According to this," said Parnell, "she was asked about our release from prison. Now, mind you, we were all mentioned by the reporters, but the only one she talked about was you."

"What did she say?"

"'They didn't let that Michael Davitt out, did they?'" read Parnell.

Michael chuckled. "She was only concerned about me?" he asked. "Not about the rest of you?"

"You're the only one she mentioned."

"My father always told my mother that someday Queen Victoria would know my name."

"It seems your father was somewhat of a prophet," said Parnell.

* * *

After issuing a bold condemnation of the Phoenix Park murders, Parnell, Michael and their group formed the Irish National League, to replace the now outlawed Land League. Parnell wanted the new League to emphasize Home Rule though Michael was reluctant. Michael felt that they had the British on the defensive, and now was not the time to give up on land agitation. But the murders had changed all that.

It took only a few months until the new organization was able to negotiate an extension of the Land Act that would settle the question of rent arrears in favor of the tenants. It called for the government to pay the arrears up to the last two years. The landlords saw this as found money, since they probably would not have collected these rents anyway and would have to have gone to the expense of evictions. The government saw it as a way to avoid the violence and expense it would incur if these evictions had to be enforced. The law also provided that tenants could also apply to the land courts to fix their rents, one of the three F's, of the old Land League.

Michael and Parnell were happy that the burden of rent arrears was to be lifted from the tenants. The new Irish National League could now concentrate on the Home Rule movement. Parnell thought it would be best to disassociate the new organization completely from the Fenian movement.

"That will probably put us on someone's assassination list," said Michael.

"I know that," said Parnell. "But it's time to stand up and be counted."

"I'll be on that list with you."

In the months that followed, Parnell's new organization seemed to be achieving its goals. The Ladies' Land League was effectively snuffed out, and the new plan began to move forward. But in spite of the change of direction orchestrated by Parnell, the practice of boycotting, especially against the land-grabbers, was still taking place. It seemed that the old Land League had installed a new unity among the Irish peasants, and the demise of the League could not stop it.

Michael, having made a conscious decision to break from the Fenian movement, wrote a press release condemning the violence and named the responsible splinter groups, who were referring to themselves as "Captain Moonlight" and "The Invincibles." He also knew that he must do more than that. He decided to go back to America and confront John Devoy. But before he could make preparations for the trip, he was called in for an interview by the director of the Committee for Imperial Defense, Howard Vincent. On the 11th of May at C.I.D. headquarters, where Michael made his formal break with the Fenians.

"I am no longer a Fenian, and I am ready to cooperate fully with the C.I.D. and all other authorities in bringing to justice any who were responsible for these acts," said Michael.

"Won't this put your life in danger?" said Vincent.

"Yes, of course it will. But I have no choice. I cannot condone such acts."

Vincent took the opportunity to explore further. "Does that extend to other secret societies?" he asked.

"I am denouncing all such violence."

"Do you think there is one person who is instigating all this?" asked Vincent.

Michael paused. "At first I thought it was that arch-scoundrel, O'Donovan Rossa. But he lacks the courage to organize such a thing. I believe it was simply the work of a few desperate ruffians who are still in Dublin."

Michael fully expected that his cooperation with the authorities would get him assassinated. He began to carrying a pistol. He decided to return to America as soon as possible. He had to confront John Devoy.

* * *

In the same back room of the tavern where they had first met, Michael met once again with Devoy. The bartender didn't even ask what they wanted; he just made a pot of tea. Michael had brought W. A. Redmond with him.

"John, here is a check made out for a sum equal to the amount of money your organization gave the Land League," said Michael.

Devoy was dismayed. "Michael, why are you doing this? We have the British on the run. It won't take us too long to get independence now!"

"An independent Ireland is still my ultimate goal," said Michael. "But I don't want it the Fenian way. Our new Irish National League will do it by peaceful means. We will break the power of the landlord and be free of the dominating British aristocracy. And we will accomplish this without sneaking up on people and stabbing them. We will have none of it."

Devoy took the bank draft. "Mr. Redmond here is my witness," said Michael. "A receipt, please."

"Michael, this draft is drawn on your personal account."

"Yes. I am personally paying you back out of my own funds."

Devoy looked surprised. "This must be all the money you have."

"Close to it," said Michael. "But I feel I must do this. We ask only that your organization not interfere with the work

177

of our new Irish National League. We will not support any more violence. Parnell feels the same way."

Devoy was obviously not happy with this decision. "So be it," he said. "Your receipt will be with the bartender. You can pick it up on your way out."

He took the draft and walked out of the room. Michael and Redmond followed and picked up the receipt from the bartender. It was Devoy's way of showing Michael his displeasure. Michael knew his action would probably end his friendship with Devoy, but it was necessary. He felt that the new Irish National League must never again associate itself with the Fenian movement.

* * *

Much to his surprise, Michael was still in demand in America as a speaker and his ideas were still widely accepted. He proposed a new League which he would call "The National Land and Industrial Union of Ireland." He wrote it up in such a way that the question of land nationalization would be left open. He found many supporters in America, but was bitterly disappointed when he came back to Ireland.

Parnell rejected the new organization out of hand. It was his opinion that land agitation should rest for a while. The Coercion Act would run for three more years, and he felt the Irish National League was still on the verge of home rule; Michael's stirring up land agitation once again would ruin the chances for home rule and the British would only use the Coercion Act to stop him. Besides, he did not like the idea of nationalizing the land. Too many of his constituents were looking forward to owning their own farm, and any system of nationalization would scare them away from his new political party.

For the next few years, Michael would vacillate between

peace and aggression. He lost his temper witnessing evictions at Bodyke, County Clair, and made a statement that he regretted ever having counseled people to be non-violent. "...would to God we had the...weapons by which freemen in America and elsewhere have struck down tyranny," he shouted. His anger earned him another term in an Irish jail, which lasted seventeen weeks. This time Parnell did not come to his rescue.

Henceforth, I must control my emotions, he thought to himself in the confines of the prison. Away from the world and left to his own thoughts, he decided that he must stay on the peaceful path. *But I understand why our people turn to violence. Yet, I must show them the way. If we fight, we must fight by peaceful means.* It was easy to think that way now, he knew; it was not so easy in the frustration of witnessing families being evicted. Every time he saw it, his childhood haunted him.

However, people never seemed to lose confidence in him. He was elected to Parliament while he was still in jail, although his status as a prisoner barred him from taking the office. Once he was released, he was elected again. This would happen on two more occasions But it seemed he was not cut out for politics. He could never master the art of compromise, so essential to being an effective politician. He was too devoted to his principles, two of which would play a large part in his demise as a politician. One was his insistence on nationalization of the land. The other was his call for non-sectarian education.

"Sectarian education has divided our country," he said in a speech. It was his hope that Ireland's Catholic and Protestant populations could live and work together, and that non-sectarian public schools could accomplish this in at least the next generation. This was already being accomplished in America, and he believed that it could also benefit Ireland. But all he succeeded in doing was making two powerful political enemies: the Anglican Church and the Roman Catholic Church.

Chapter Twenty-Six

1886

Michael once again began his travels in America. He had taken his notes *"Jottings in Solitary,"* and had re-written them into a book which he called *"Leaves From a Prison Diary."* The book had been published in 1885 and was meeting with some success. The royalties from *"Leaves"* added to the payments he was receiving from other articles and the five other books he had written were not making him rich, but were keeping him comfortable.

A new landmark had been added to New York harbor when Michael's ship anchored off Staten Island. He came out on deck and gazed upon a magnificent sight: a colossus standing on a pedestal welcoming all the ships coming into New York harbor. The Statue of Liberty, a gift of the people of France, held her torch high in one hand and a book in the other.

"Beautiful, isn't she?" said a man standing next to him.

"She certainly is," said Michael. "The symbol of a great country."

The man decided to give Michael a lesson on the statue. "She was designed by the artist Bartholdi and her inner structure was built by the French engineer, Eiffel. Bartholdi used his mother as the model for her face and his mistress as the model for her body."

How French, thought Michael to himself. *And how appropriate.* Such a fitting symbol for liberty, a blend of a mother and a mistress.

* * *

In time, he arrived in Oakland, California and went to visit his old friend and benefactor, Mrs. Canning.

"How wonderful to see you, Michael," said Mrs.

180

Canning. "Did you have a nice trip?"

"I am always in awe when I see America," said Michael. "Its beauty is amazing. I never get tired of it."

"Why don't you move here permanently?" asked Mrs. Canning.

"It's tempting," he answered, "but I cannot leave the people of Ireland. I have already sacrificed most of my life for them, but that's nothing compared to what so many of them have faced. As much as I love America, I cannot abandon Ireland."

"I thought you might feel that way," said Mrs. Canning.

At that moment, Mrs. Canning's niece, Mary Jane Yore, walked into the room. Michael stood up.

"You remember my niece, Mary," said Mrs. Canning.

Michael was stunned. The last time he had seen her, she was eighteen years old. Now she was twenty-four and even more beautiful than he had remembered. There was a slight pause before Michael was able to speak.

"Yes, of course I remember her," he said. Mary walked over to him and took his hand.

"How nice to have you back, Michael," she said. "I've been following your work in the Irish newspapers."

"I'm flattered."

"I have a lot of questions to ask you."

"I am at your disposal."

For one of the few times in his life, Michael felt self-conscious about his missing arm. He wanted to make a good impression on Mary but did not know how much the loss of a limb really meant to her. Should he dare try to enter into a courtship? Could anyone want a courtship with a man who only had one arm? If he allowed himself to fall in love, would he only be setting himself up for heartbreak?

In spite of his misgivings, he and Mary did begin a courtship. Mary did not seem the least bit intimidated by his handicap. When the courtship advanced to the point where they became more intimate, Mary simply made adjustments to the missing limb. She and Michael fell deeply in love with each other.

Michael finally brought up the subject.

"Will my handicap make any difference to you?"

"Michael," said Mary, "You're a better man with one arm than most people in this world are with two. Besides, you said yourself that if it had not been for the accident, you would never had gone to school and set yourself on the path of knowledge."

"That is true," said Michael. "I probably would have remained ignorant. It's likely that I would have been shot in some Fenian operation, or maybe caught and hanged."

"As far as your missing arm is concerned, let me point out to you that a wedding ring is worn on the left hand."

How could I have found such a woman?" he thought.

* * *

They decided to get married. They would wait until after Christmas, and set the date for the 30th of December. Two friends of the Mrs. Canning, Michael Stackpool and Mary O'Brien would act as witnesses. Fr. Thomas McSweeney would perform the ceremony. The quiet family wedding would be followed by a trip to Monterey. The wedding was performed in Mrs. Canning's parlors, since holding it in the church might draw a large crowd, something Michael did not want. First they had a mass at 7:30 in the morning at the church of St. Francis de Sales, then the party moved to Mrs. Canning's house at 954 Sixteenth Street, with only relatives and a few intimate friends in attendance.

The reception followed, attended by eighty-seven guests, mostly prominent Irish and a few others, mostly politicians, all well known in the Oakland community. The rooms were expertly decorated with flowers and flower arrangements including one which spelled out the word "welcome" in white flowers. There was also a table piled high with congratulatory telegrams from all over the country.

Michael looked at some of the wedding gifts. There was one in particular which caught his eye. It was a service case made of polished oak with shamrocks inlaid in silver. On the leaves of the shamrocks were two hearts and the initials, "MD." The case was gold-lined. It was a teapot, coffee urn, creamer, two sugar bowls, and a wasting bowl. This was accompanied by another case which contained the eating utensils, a set of twelve. The two sets were a gift from a number of "...friends of the Irish cause and admirers of Mr. Davitt..." It was accompanied by a silver tablet inscribed:

Congratulations of a Few Friends
San Francisco, California

Then Michael gave Mary his gift to her: a beautiful gold watch, studded with diamonds.

At 3:30, the Davitts made the short trip to Monterey and stayed a few days. Mrs. Canning then presented her niece with a large check, as her wedding present.

Michael was no stranger to the Oakland press. When the wedding finally became public, the newspapers were filled with the story.

DAVITT-YORE
The Irish Patriot Wedded to an Oakland Bride

The announcement, which appeared in the *Oakand Enquirer* on the 30th of December, was followed by an extensive

183

writeup about "Michael Davitt, Irish Patriot ...important because of the relation he bears to the politics of Great Britain..."

The couple headed to Chicago and then Philadelphia, where they were given other receptions. They then departed for Ireland. When they arrived in Dublin, the Irish National League presented them with a "Land League Cottage" just outside Dublin. It would be the only gift that Michael would ever accept from the League.

Chapter Twenty-Seven

1888

His Holiness, Pope Leo XIII, sat in his study in Rome talking to his secretary of state, Cardinal Mariano Rampolla.

"What progress have we made with the Italian government?" asked the pope. "Are they going to stop occupying Rome and cease keeping us prisoner in the Vatican?"

"I don't think we have any hope of that," said Cardinal Rampolla. They have occupied the entire city except for the Vatican. That is all that is left of the Papal States. But we are receiving some overtures from Her Majesty Queen Victoria's government. Sir Henry Fitzalan-Howard, The 15th Duke of Norfolk, has requested a private audience."

"The Duke is a Catholic, is he not?"

"Yes, a recusant.".

"Do you have any idea what he wants?" asked the Pope.

"I believe he wants to talk about the position of Her Majesty's government as it relates to our present predicament in Italy."

"Very smart of Her Majesty to send a royal who is a Catholic to represent her."

"Shall I show him in?" asked Rampolla.

"By all means," answered the Pope. "Let's see just what Her Majesty is up to."

* * *

The reporter from *The London Times* was standing outside the Papal residence and recognized the Duke of Norfolk, who had driven up in a carriage. He tried to get close enough to ask the Duke a question, but was stopped by a member of the Swiss Guard.

"Out!"yelled the guard. The man was a menacing sight, a huge German Swiss dressed in the traditional motley Swiss Guard uniform. He held a lance, the bottom of which was anchored in the cobblestones. When the reporter tried to move closer, the guard tilted the lance forward and yelled again, this time louder.

The reporter moved back. This was not England, and there were no English laws to protect him here. It would be better to wait and try to get an interview after the Duke left the Papal Palace.

It was awhile before the Duke came out and walked over to his carriage.

"Sir Henry," said the reporter, rushing up. "I'm from *The London Times*. Can I ask you what was the purpose of your visit with Pope Leo?"

Sir Henry smiled.

"A private matter," he said.

"I know you are a Catholic, Sir Henry. Did the Pope hear your confession?"

This question would have angered most people but the Duke was royalty. He had been trained as such from the time he was old enough to talk, thus he knew just how to respond.

"I'm not saying that is what I did, young man," answered the Duke. "If that was my purpose, I would certainly not discuss it publicly."

The reporter persisted. "Then what was your meeting about?"

"All you're going to get is that it is a private matter," said the Duke. "You can print that," poking his head out of the carriage window as it drove away.

The reporter turned to his assistant, an English-speaking Italian whom the newspaper had put on its payroll.

"You're about to earn your money, Giuseppe," said the reporter. "Nose around and see what you can find out."

"I have a cousin who works inside," said Giuseppe. "He's a cook. Cooks know more about what's happening here than the Cardinals."

* * *

Michael placed his hand on Mary's abdomen and felt the baby inside her move. It was April and the trees and shrubs around the Land League Cottage were beginning to turn green. Michael opened the *Times* and the following article caught his eye.

April 21, 1888

The Pope's Domicile

REVIVAL OF A RUMOR OF A CHANGE OF LOCATION

But little doubt that Pope Leo XIII, is Contemplating a change of Base—The Strained Relations between Italy and the Vatican that Now Exist.

London April 21—At no time since the first stormy days when the Italian troops succeeded the French garrison in Rome, have the relations between the Vatican and the government of Italy been so strained. The perennial information, up on the best authority," that the seat of Papal rule is to be transferred from the Eternal City to some more congenial abiding place is again given to the public, which receives it with the usual wild incredulity, but there are many whose anxiety is wakened by the periodically recurrent rumors and several circumstances have occurred lately which cause the most unbelieving to reflect.

Michael pondered upon what he had just read. The Pope was threatening to leave Rome! Would he really do that? If so, where would he go? He read on.

Sarcastic references were made by other journals to the statement which recently appeared in the St. James Gazette that Leo XIII had determined to leave the restless old world, with its unceasing wars and muttering of wars, and seek a peaceful refuge in America. It was of course urged, as on similar occasions, that such a step would be an abandonment of the traditions of the church and that the desertion of its hallowed site would shock believers all over the world...

Going to America! Leaving the place where St. Peter was martyred and relocating to America! The situation between the Vatican and the Italian government must be pretty bad. He skimmed over the next paragraph--which talked about the last time the Papacy left Italy for Avignon--and the civil bill which was passed by the Italian chamber of deputies. It was the next part that caught his attention.

*...**Even if it could be considered necessary or refuge of the Island of Malta, the complete sovereignty of which would be gladly ceded to His Holiness by the British government.***

Michael could not believe what he was reading. Michael re-read that passage several times.

Her Majesty's government was offering the Island of Malta as a refuge to the Roman Catholic Church, with complete sovereignty! The rest of the article went on to tell how the United States and Mexico were offering the Pope sanctuary, but the British government? Why would they do that? Something was going on. He must talk to Parnell immediately. He got his carriage ready and went to find him.

* * *

"I don't like it," said Parnell. "I'm sure the Pope is mindful of the fact that one of the Fenian aims is to break the stranglehold of the Catholic Church in Ireland. Priests have been told not to support the violence. This may be one of the ways in which the Vatican is retaliating against the Fenians."

"You're right," said Michael, "and I fear the British government has convinced the Vatican that the League is behind the violence. They are probably using the Phoenix Park murders as their prime example. I supposed they were told where our money is coming from"

"And don't forget, they are all royals," said Parnell. "Leo the XIIIth is the former Cardinal Pecci, who comes from a minor royal family in Italy. His Secretary of State, Cardinal Mariano Rampolla, is a Count. Count Mariano Rampolla del Tindaro. I don't like it when these royals get together like this. I fear something else is coming. The British government knows the Pope needs their support. If they are offering him Malta, you can be sure they're getting something in return."

They did not have to wait very long to find out what the British wanted in return. Three days later an article appeared on the United Press Dispatches:

April 24, 1888

TELEGRAPH
United Press Dispatches by Special Wire

THE IRISH
*Discussions of the Controversy Between Pope Leo and the
Nationalists*

*Does the Pope Incline to Ireland's or England's Side?—What
Cardinal Newman Says—The Duke of Norfolk Not Interested.*

*London April 24—A number of Nationalist members of
Parliament were interviewed today regarding the report to the
effect that Pope Leo* **intends issuing a condemnation of the plan
of campaign, and the practice of boycotting in Ireland, and
forbidding his people to follow the direction of the National
league in these matters.** *All the members seen expressed it as
their opinion that his report was simply a revival of the like
statements made from time to time by the Tory press, for the
purpose of influencing English voters, and if possible, to
intimidate the Irish who were struggling hard against the
government's measures in the unequal fight for their liberty.*
*"Why would the Pope do this?" asked one of the members. "It
is far more consistent, to my mind, to think that the Pope is
inclined to favor Ireland, rather than to array himself on
England's side against her. In the first place consider the great
numbers of Catholics who are in Ireland, and who, in spite of
their poverty, give, not only faithfully, but very largely to the
support of the church. They constitute the truest of the Pope's
people today, and nowhere would His Holiness find a safer and*

190

better asylum from possible persecution, or more devoted defenders than in the same Ireland. Beside these considerations the Pope would hardly, for the sake of pleasing England, proceed in a direction contrary to the indicated in the various reports he has had from different authorities on Ireland. Mgr. Persico's report of Ireland was favorable in most respects and he certainly did not advise the Pope to interfere with legitimate means of warfare employed by the people. Cardinals Newman and Gibbon have both made favorable reports to the Pope in regard to Ireland: but of Cardinal Manning, who told Pope Leo, that if he were an Irishman living in Ireland today, he would consider justified in joining the plan of campaign, and of doing just what the people were doing there in defense of their rights.

The idea that the Duke of Norfolk went to Rome to influence the Pope in these matters, has no foundation in fact. He merely conveyed the congratulations of Queen Victoria to His Holiness, on his first visit, and his subsequent visit was a personal one.

Despite what the MP said, it was true: The Vatican was about to abandon the Irish peasants in order to get the support of the British. It was the ultimate political game and the British were winning. That was the purpose of earlier rumored move of the Vatican to Malta! The British were trying to "buy" the pope's abandonment of Ireland. There was little doubt that the Irish National League would be facing trouble.

Later that month, Parnell got all the Irish leaders together to meet the new crisis. The story leaked out to the press on the 4th of May:

TELEGRAPH
United Press Dispatches by Special Wire

THE LAST STRAW
The back of the Irish Camel finally breaks

But little doubt in the minds of the Irish leaders that the rumored adverse decree from the Vatican has become a reality.

London, May 4 1888—The report that a special congregation of the propaganda is deliberating upon questions relating to Ireland and the policy of her nationalist party in parliament for her better government, has been a sort of final straw on the back of the Irish church camel. **The Irish leaders doubt not now that the rumored decree form the Vatican has become a reality; that the points which the cardinals of Rome have under their august and pious consideration, will be decided in a manner which every lover of unfortunate Ireland must deem adverse to her interests.**

In view of this, and in order to anticipate the coming blow, the leaders of the National League have, it is learned, prepared a circular which has been distributed throughout Ireland to every branch of the League, calling upon the members to be firm in their advice to that body and arranging for the simultaneous meetings of the twenty League branches at a time, until all the members have met and conferred upon the line of action to be adopted in respect to the papal rescript and other emanations of Rome.

The first of this series of meetings will take place at an early date, and everything respecting the assemblings will be maintained in strict secrecy, so that the government will not be

192

able to proclaim and put a stop to them. Serious matters must now come before the national, and it means life or death, virtually to that organization whether or not its members consider that their political guidance along with their faith must come from Rome. It is expected that the best speakers the nationalists possess will address the League meetings, and thoroughly arouse Ireland of the necessity of moving forward to yet higher ground in their fight for the right to govern themselves.

Michael thought that this might end the League. He didn't think they could fight the British and the Vatican at the same time. What he did not know was that the British still had other cards to play.

Chapter Twenty-Eight

1890

The pro-Tory forces in Great Britain had decided that Charles Stuart Parnell had to be discredited. They started with a campaign to ruin his reputation. The first step in the attack was a series of articles that linked Parnell with murders which had occurred in Ireland. The so-called "proof" of this link were letters, supposedly written by him that excused the Phoenix Park murders from 1882--where Lord Frederick Cavendish and his under-secretary, Thomas Henry Burke were assassinated--and supported acts of violence against the duly constituted British government. This caused the government to set up an inquiry.

The following letter had appeared in the *Times:*

May 15, 1882.

1. "DEAR SIR - I am not surprised at your friend's anger, but he and you should know that to denounce murders was the only course open to us. To do promptly was plainly our best policy, but you can tell him and all concerned that though I regret the accident of Lord Cavendish's death, I cannot refuse to admit that Burke got no more than his desserts. You are at liberty to show him this and others whom you can trust also. But let not my address be known; he can write to the House of Commons.

Yours very truly,
CHAS. S. PARNELL.

194

Michael and Egan had also been accused in the press of supporting "outrages" committed in Ireland and England by Irish secret societies, but it was Parnell who made the headlines. Michael had contemplated the use of the word "outrages." It seemed that any crime committed by Irish were "outrages," while any committed by English were simply crimes. Yet the facts showed that more murders per capita were being committed in England by the English than the Irish in Ireland. As a journalist himself, he had to be aware of the tricks journalists used, especially if he found himself in a position where he was expected to write a rebuttal. But this attack had only been the beginning. Parnell would have to come to grips with another problem.

* * *

Katie O'Shea was the wife of Captain "Willy" O'Shea, a "Castle Catholic," meaning he was a descendant of the old Norman aristocracy. They had three children. Captain O'Shea was a Member of Parliament and had introduced his wife to Parnell in 1880. Parnell, who had never been married, fell deeply in love with Katie. She also fell in love with him.

At first they met in London and other places, but as it became apparent that they could not live without one another, Katie rented a house in Brighton. By1883, Captain O'Shea did not seem to mind that his wife had left him and was living on her own, even though they were still married. He knew what was happening, but never filed for a divorce. In Catholic Ireland, a divorce would have ruined him and probably would have cost him his seat in Parliament, so he simply went along as if nothing had changed.

After a considerable amount of moving around, Katie and

Parnell decided to live together. They rented a flat in Hove. They had three children of their own in this adulterous relationship, Katie still being married to O'Shea.

Now, in 1890, Captain O'Shea was filing for a divorce, naming Parnell as correspondent.

"Why is he doing this now, after all these years?" asked Mary Davitt. "He knew about Katie and Parnell. He introduced them ten years ago."

"It must be convenient for someone," answered Michael. "There are forces out to discredit Parnell, as you remember from the forged letters. These forces may have gotten to the government. I expect O'Shea thinks he will receive some favor from these forces, perhaps even from the government."

"Do you think Gladstone is involved in this?"

"That's hard to say. I don't think so. More likely it's members of the House of Lords or even Queen Victoria herself. In any event, I believe this scandal will ruin Parnell's political career."

It was another blow to the Irish National League, coming on top of the Pope's pronouncement against the League. Parnell was advised to leave politics temporarily, but he was stubborn and refused. It was a poor decision. His political party split, forty-four going with Justin McCarthy and only twenty-seven going with him. In Catholic Ireland, Parnell was finished politically. He was a Protestant living with a married Catholic woman, who was still married to her husband. Even though O'Shey did get his divorce, the Catholic Church did not recognize it. Even when Parnell and Katie were married in a civil ceremony, the Catholic Church still considered them living in sin.

Parnell would stay active in politics for another year, traveling the country making speeches about the Irish issue, but he was never an effective politician again. In October 1891, he got sick and died at the age of forty-five. And so ended the life of the man whose political skill had carried the Irish people to the brink of home rule, the man whom history would record as the "uncrowned king of Ireland."

* * *

Michael felt that the home rule movement had truly died. With the League condemned and Parnell gone, there was little chance that Ireland would truly attain it. No one else had the shrewdness and political savvy of Charles Stuart Parnell, and with him went Michael's dream of an independent Ireland, at least an independence that would come first from home rule and then *peaceably* move to a totally independent country. It was more likely that the Fenians would once again go to war and try to defeat the British that way. Michael did not think that would ever be successful.

However, he had other things to think about. He had a beautiful daughter, Kathleen, two years old, and another child was born on the first of December, 1890, a son, Michael Martin. A son to carry on the Davitt name.

Michael's income now came completely from his writing and his new job as a foreign correspondent for the Hearst newspapers. Mrs. Canning kept sending money to them, and between that and his earnings, he and Mary were living comfortably. The only drawback to his new job was the travel. It meant long periods of time away from his home and family. But he was doing what he loved, writing. On the long steamship journeys, he was able to work on his books and articles. During this time he produced his greatest book, *The Fall of Feudalism In Ireland,* which would also become his biggest success.

* * *

April 1, 1895

 Michael was on assignment in the Mediterranean thinking about his wife and four children. How fast his family had grown. Kathleen was seven years old, Michael Martin five, Eileen three, and his new son, Cahir, eight months. How lucky he was. A beautiful, intelligent wife and four beautiful, healthy children.

 The ship had just put into port when the telegram arrived. It was from home. Michael opened it and read every parent's nightmare. His daughter, Kathleen had gotten sick and died.

 He kept reading the words over and over, hoping that perhaps he had read them wrong, or that the telegram had found its way to the wrong person. But the reality could not be avoided. His beautiful Kathleen was dead.

 He put his head in his hand and wept. He felt weak and sat down on the bed. Burying his face in the pillow, he could do nothing but cry uncontrollably. He sat for hours clutching the telegram in his hand.

 In his grief-stricken solitude, he kept telling himself that he could not bear it. No one should have to bury a child. He sank into a semi-conscious stupor. A picture of his mother and father, standing next to Baby James' grave, with their children clinging to them entered his mind. How real it seemed to him. He could feel the March wind, blowing cold on his face. He clearly heard his father say, "How much trouble can God send us before we break under the strain?" He could see his mother looking down on the grave and his sister Anne saying. "Is James in heaven, Mum?" He heard his mother tell Anne that he was in heaven, sitting on Jesus's lap and that Jesus was smiling just as

198

he always did when he was with children. He imagined Katline sitting on Jesus' knee, with Baby James sitting on the other. He heard Anne's farewell; "Goodbye, Baby James." He saw his parents weeping uncontrollably on their way home.

He fell asleep. In his dream, his mother was in the room across from him speaking in her native Irish.

"Yes, I know how difficult it is for you to lose a child, Michael," she said, "but you are not the only one. I did, and we survived it. Think of all of our people whose children starved in the great hunger. Remember that woman we saw on the way to the workhouse who was begging for money so she could bury her dead infant. You must go on, Michael. You must have strength."

Michael woke up with a start. Sweat was pouring from his forehead and he was trembling. Once again his mother's strength was sustaining him as it had done so many times in the past. He could not get the sadness out of his heart, but he found the strength to get up and wash his face. He would have to return home immediately.

* * *

December 1899

Robert Davitt was born on a cold December day. *Three sons and one daughter*, Michael thought to himself. He looked at Mary lying in the bed holding Robert. She looked at Robert, and then at Michael. Each knew what the other was thinking. They would never be able to get Kathleen out of their minds, but they had to go on. Michael would have a few weeks to spend with his family and new son, and then it was back on assignment again. He would be hearing from the newspaper soon.

"Where do you think you'll go, Dad?" asked nine-year-old Michael Martin, an image of Michael's father, Martin.

"I'll know soon," said Michael. "It seems likely that I will be sent to Russia. There's a lot of unrest there lately, and I'm sure my newspaper will have me covering it."

"The Russians have a king, don't they, Dad?" said Michael Martin.

"Yes," answered Michael, "they call him a czar."

"Is that the same thing as a king?".

"In English we would call him 'The Emperor,' after the Roman Emperors who called themselves Caesars. "It's very much like our concept of a king."

"Is the Czar of Russia good or bad?"

Michael gave a small laugh at that question. "As a man, Czar Nicholas II is not bad, I mean he is not a bad man. But being an emperor is a bad thing as far as I'm concerned. America has no emperor, no king or queen. America is a free country. We Irish have suffered under the royal families of Britain and would like to do away with emperors in our country."

He could see he was already getting over Michael Martin's head. The boy was looking at him with a look that said "you told me more than I wanted to know."

"Enough talks about kings, queens and czars," he said. "We can talk more about the Czar when I get back."

Chapter Twenty-Nine

April, 1903

It took four years for Michael to get to Russia, on assignment in the city of Kishinev in the area known as Bessarabia, east of the Romanian border. There had been an outbreak of violence against Jews which had lasted for two days, April 19th and 20th. Michael's job was to investigate the extent of the violence, determine how bad it was, and how it started.

The official report listed 45 Jews killed, 586 injured. Witnesses said that countless other women had been raped and children tortured over that two-day period. Michael's investigation turned up many witnesses who would speak only on the condition of anonymity, fearing repercussions from the gangs who had perpetrated these crimes and from the police.

"The police!" Michael exclaimed to one of the witnesses. "Are you saying that the police took part in the riot?"

"They may as well have," said the witness. "They not only did nothing to stop it, some were telling these criminal youths to kill all the Jews."

Michael wondered what or who had started such a riot. To him, it looked like a planned effort rather than an act of random violence. He decided to investigate further. Other witnesses led him to read some recent newspaper articles published before the riots. He had to pay a local to translate for him, and concluded that the entire riot was instigated by a local newspaper editor named P.A. Krushevan, who had published and circulated a flyer claiming that the Jews of Kisninev had murdered a child for ritualistic purposes and should be thrown out of Holy Russia. The flyer had been posted in a local tavern and ended with a note saying that if the owner did not display it, the group would "smash your tavern down." All the witnesses knew the flyer was authored by Krushevan, even though it bore someone else's signature. Even though the tea house owners were against what was said in the letter, they posted it anyway, fearing for their lives and property.

Michael had the background of the story, but felt he needed to interview a minor Russian official, who would speak only if his name was not be used. Michael agreed, and wrote what the official had said in a notebook:

"What can we do with them? They are the racial antithesis of our nation. A fusion with us is impossible, owing to religious and other disturbing causes. They will always be a potential source of sectarian and economic disorder in our country. We cannot admit them to equal rights of citizenship for these reasons and, let me add, because their intellectual superiority would enable them in few years' time to gain possession of most of the posts of our civil administration. They are a growing danger of a most serious nature to our Empire in two of its most vulnerable points, - their discontent is a menace to us along the Austrian and German frontiers, while they are the active propagandists of Socialism of Western Europe within our borders. The only solution to the problem of the Russian Jew is his departure from Russia."

Michael saw that the situation was worse than he thought. Although there were laws passed against Jews in Imperial Russia, most of them had been passed after the assassination of Emperor Alexander II, which was erroneously blamed on the Jews. Jews were restricted as to where they could live and what professions they could follow.

The next step was for Michael to interview the Jews who had survived the attacks. He went to the Jewish hospital. The first man he met was Mayer Weissman, who had owned a small store in one of the poorest Jewish quarters of the Kishinev. His head was bandaged and both eyes were covered. After Michael introduced himself, Mayer said he had lost one eye in an accident as a youth. The mob arrived on Easter Sunday, dragged him out into the street, and totally demolished his grocery store. He had offered the leader, a young man, all the money he had, sixty rubles, if they would spare his life. The leader took the money and said he was going to spare his life but "...now we want your eye. You will never look upon a Christian child."

"I pleaded with them not to take my one remaining eye and leave me blind for life," said Mayer. "I asked them to be merciful and kill me instead. But they gouged out my eye with a sharpened stick and left me." He sobbed and Michael could see the tears soaking through the bandages. He took Mayer's hand and assured him that he would let the world know his story. Mayer squeezed Michael's hand.

Michael thought about his missing right arm. It was nothing compared to poor Mayer Weissman who was now blind for life, the victim of a crazy mob made up of people who did not even know him. What had he done to them? Michael remembered an old cliché he had once heard: "I cried because I had no shoes, until I saw a man who had no feet." He glanced at the stub that remained of his right arm. He felt like the man with no shoes.

Next to Mayer's bed was a man whose head had been battered with bludgeons. His skull had not been fractured but his injuries were nevertheless very severe. His head was heavily bandaged, as were his arms and hands, which showed defensive wounds. He had been left for dead but saw the same gang kill

203

his mother-in-law by driving nails through her eyes and into her brain. At first Michael could not believe the story, thinking that the man was in such shock he could have dreamed it. But, he quickly changed his mind when six others, including a Christian doctor, told him the story was true. They had seen the body. Two of the witnesses told Michael that they had dug the woman's grave.

Michael had to stop for a moment. The stories were coming at him too quickly. He was not by nature squeamish. He had seen people dead from starvation; he had been in a Victorian prison, which was no walk in Hyde Park. But this was different. This was cruelty beyond anything he had ever witnessed. He was having a difficult time, but went on through the hospital ward. In another room he saw a young girl, about seventeen years old, with her head covered in bandages. She told Michael that about a dozen young men had killed her parents and held her for about three hours. After raping her, they beat her and left her for dead.

Michael wrote their stories in his notebook and assured the victims that their stories would be told. It was all he had to give them. The look of appreciation on their faces told him how much it must have meant to them. He was all they had.

Later, he visited the rabbi's house. Several more victims who had survived the riots were there, and he interviewed most of them. They seemed anxious that the world know what had happened to them and were eager to talk, even though it must have been very painful for them.

One of the victims was a sixteen-year-old girl named Simme Zeytchik. She was very beautiful, and looked even younger than her years. She told the rabbi that fifteen young ruffians had outraged her repeatedly.

Michael looked at this poor girl, her eyes blackened and

her face bruised. He could only imagine the unspeakable terror she had gone through. Her beauty was probably the envy of every young girl her age, but her beauty had became her curse.

Michael asked the rabbi, "Were these incidents brought up to the police? Were complaints filed?"

"They most certainly were," said the rabbi. "I personally spoke to the public prosecutor. Some of the rioters were arrested. Some of them could not understand why they were being arrested. I heard one say, 'Why are you arresting me? Was it not permitted to kill the Jews?' Some even made the argument that the police were yelling to them to kill the Jews. There was even a rumor circulating that the Czar himself was encouraging the persecutions."

In October of 1903, Michael compiled his notes into a book. He called it, *Within the Pale: The True Story of Anti-Semitic Persecutions in Russia.*

* * *

Michael made several other trips throughout the world and became a popular speaker. He took an interest in Indian affairs and sided with the native population, which was under British rule. A few years before, he had befriended Mr. Dadabbai Naoroji, an Indian resident of London. He had once proposed to have him in the Parliament so as to give India a direct voice for Indian nationalism in the House of Commons, but was never able to accomplish this. He had also been invited to preside at the Indian National Congress in Madras in 1894, but had declined. His reason was that his presence would have been too big a risk for the Indian Congress to take. The British would most likely have found some way to punish India if it had allowed a former felon to preside over its congress. Naoroji

205

understood and he and Michael had remained friends.

Once, when Michael was speaking to a large group in London, his topic included the situation in India and South Africa, so many Indian nationals were there. One was an intelligent young law student named Mohandas K. Gandhi. Mohandas listened intently to what Michael Davitt had to say. He found many of Michael's ideas intriguing and recognized a man who thirsted for justice and worked for it. Mohandas took careful notes and decided he would make a further study of Michael Davitt, and intended to read his books.

Chapter Thirty

1904

June in Russia was not exactly warm, but the countryside was green. *Not as green as Ireland*, Michael thought to himself, *but what in this world is?*

He had been commissioned by his newspaper to interview the great Leo Tolstoy, considered the greatest writer of the late nineteenth century. Michael had read Tolstoy's book, *Resurrection,* and had gained a personal respect for the writer. He thought about what he would say while the troika he was riding in made its way up the winding path to Tolstoy's house. Three women were there to greet him.

"He's out back, walking the dogs," they said, without waiting to be asked.

Michael was walking down the path which led to the back of the house when he saw Tolstoy with three dogs coming toward him. A letter of introduction had preceded him, but Tolstoy had not opened his mail for the day and did not know who Michael was. When Michael introduced himself, Tolstoy, fooled by his accent, asked if he were English. He saw by Michael's reaction that he had asked the wrong question followed with a statement that it surely must be a privilege to be English. It did not take long for Michael to straighten him out. Tolstoy got the idea.

They went into the house and were served tea. Tolstoy was seventy seven years old and was showing signs of his age. He had the air of an aristocrat. Michael felt a little uncomfortable, but Tolstoy was the type of person who could easily put people at ease. He opened the conversation about the evils of war, especially the Russo-Japanese war. When Michael began to talk, however, he got himself bogged down in giving Tolstoy his opinions of the British and the state of affairs in Ireland, trying to make a case for his country with the great man. He brought up Henry George, and found that Tolstoy was also an admirer. He had read *Progress and Poverty* and supported the view of common ownership of land. He had even written to the Czar urging him to nationalize all the land of Russia, just as Henry George had outlined in his book.

"Mr. George has written me many letters. I regret I never met him," Tolstoy said.

They went on to talk about prison reform. Tolstoy listened with much interest as Michael talked about life in Victorian prison and his attempts at prison reform. Tolstoy was also interested in prison reform, and had made many efforts to reform the Russian prison system.

They talked about religion and the role of the churches, both Russian Orthodox and Roman Catholic, respectively, in the affairs of their countries. Michael sounded a bitter note when he talked about Pope Leo XIII's condemnation of the Irish Plan of Campaign, with the Pope putting politics above the needs of his subjects in Ireland.

In all, it was more like two friends talking to each other than an interview. Michael refused the invitation to stay the night and bid Tolstoy goodby. He wished he had more time, but there was work to do.

* * *

It was a cold January night, and Alexsei Volsky and his wife were sitting in a teahouse.

"Are you going to join in the strike?" asked Alexsei's

wife.

"Yes, I am," said Alexsei. "For too long we Russians have suffered under the brutal conditions these factory owners have made for us. It is time we stood together and fought them."

"But, Alexsei, if you get fired, how will we live?"

"We are not living now. We can barely exist on what I earn at the iron works. When my four brother workers were dismissed, who asked them how they could live? I must join the strike. If the workers don't stand together we will all hang separately."

"Alexsei, tell me you are not going to march to the winter palace," said his wife.

"Father Gapon will be leading us. He has asked the iron workers to stand behind him as we walk peaceably. Father has written to the Czar, telling him that we are on a peaceful march and mean him no harm. He assured the Czar that no harm would come to him. The Czar will listen to Father Gapon."

"What is this petition about? Everyone is talking about the petition."

"It is mostly about reducing the working day to eight hours, giving us the right to vote, and stopping the war with Japan, which is draining our resources and killing our young men."

His wife looked very concerned. Russia was not a place where one could be critical about the government's policies. The Siberian labor camps were filled with dissenters. But she knew she could not talk Alexsei out of it.

* * *

By the 22nd of January, 1904 the petition that Father Gapon had circulated bore the signature of over 150,000 people.

It seemed that all of them had come to march. Alexsei stood behind Father Gapon, who was holding the petition in the air. On both sides of the priest stood two men, blacksmiths, who were acting as his bodyguards. Women and children walked on the side of the crowd. More women walked in front of the priest, forming a line. Their thoughts were to protect the good Father with their bodies. But Father Gapon would not have them in front of him, and told his men to use force to remove them.

Finally The winter palace come into sight. Alexsei could see the Cossacks, sitting on their horses with their swords drawn. Suddenly, without warning, the Cossacks began galloping towards the crowd. Alexsei stepped to the side and a sword swooped down on him, making a gash in his outer coat. He was lucky. As the Cossacks cut their way through the crowds, men, women and children fell like stalks of wheat, their blood turning the snow red. When the Cossacks came to the end of the crowd, they stopped and regrouped. It was not over. This time their horses galloped at the crowd from the rear: they were coming back. Some of the wounded who were too badly hurt to get out of the way were trampled by the horses. The Cossacks cut indiscriminately through the crowd, slashing even children who were clinging to dead and wounded mothers.

When the Cossacks made it back through the crowds, they rode up to the infantry, which had formed a skirmish line in front of the palace gate. The infantry immediately opened its ranks and let the Cossacks through.

Alexsei looked ahead. The bridge over the Tarakanovskii Canal was all that separated the crowd from the infantry. The soldiers were about thirty yards away. Suddenly, the crack of rifles filled the air. The soldiers were shooting at them! A man in front of Alexsei, who was carrying the Czar's portrait, went down in front of him. Father Gapon tried to catch

210

him but was unable to hold him up. Another man picked up the portrait and stepped forward with it. He also took a rifle shot, and died instantly.

The crowd began dispersing and Alexsei ran into the courtyard of a nearby house. Alexsei saw a bullet hit the window of the building and heard someone inside moan as the bullet found him.

The infantry moved forward and began shooting into the courtyard. A man in front of him caught a bullet, which hit him with such force it turned him around. The man grabbed Alexsei in a vain attempt to keep himself from falling. When he hit the ground, the man's blood was all over the front of Alexsei's coat. Alexsei dove for the ground and the soldiers, satisfied that they had killed everyone in the courtyard, moved on.

Alexsei lay motionless for quite some time. Then he got up and began to walk home. He could feel his anger grow as he walked through the blood-soaked streets, stepping over bodies. People who were badly wounded, many of them women and children, cried out to him, but he was unable to help.

How could their Father, the Czar allow this to happen? he thought to himself. "All they had wanted was to present their petition to him. He was supposed to take care of his people, not shoot them in the street."

* * *

"The British newspapers say that the Russian people are revolting against the Czar," said Michael to his wife.

"Here It says that the Tsar's troops fired on a crowd of unarmed protesters," said Mary.

"One cannot trust the British newspapers," said Michael. "Most are in support of the Russo-Japanese War because the government of Great Britain is supporting the Japanese."

"Are you referring to the alliance Britain has with Japan?"

"Yes. The Japanese and the British protect each other's interest in China and Korea," said Michael. "It's an unholy alliance. It protects the business interests of British companies and provides Japan with resources it doesn't have otherwise. Russia is the only other nation in the Far East that is challenging them, and Britain is afraid of the Russian nation."

"But what do you make of this 'Bloody Sunday' as the press is referring to it?" said Mary. "They claim that the unrest is widespread in Russia and is the beginning of a revolution."

"Probably a lot of British propaganda," said Michael.

Just then, a telegraph arrived. It was from the Hearst newspapers in America, commissioning Michael to go Russia and investigate the circumstances of the Bloody Sunday massacre.

* * *

St. Petersburg seemed quiet when Michael arrived. He immediately contracted for the services of an interpreter and set about talking to the citizens of the city. The interpreter suggested that Michael start in a popular teahouse frequented by workers.

"That man sitting over there," said the interpreter, "was in the crowd on that day. You should start with him."

Michael nodded yes and the interpreter walked over to Alexsei Volsky who was sitting with his wife. The interpreter told Alexsei that an American newspaper reporter wanted to interview him.

When the interpreter walked away, Alexsei's wife

grabbed him "You are not going to say anything against the Tsar, are you?" she said.

"Of course not," said Alexsei. "You think I want to wind up in a Siberian labor camp?"

Michael and the interpreter approached the table where Alexsei and his wife were sitting.

"May we sit down?" asked the interpreter.

"Of course" said Alexsei.

The interpreter began. "This is Mr. Michael Davitt. He is a reporter for an American newspaper company."

Alexsei nodded.

"Mr. Davitt lost his arm in a factory accident when he was eleven," the interpreter went on, "so he knows about the conditions of the workers. You can trust him."

Alexsei could see that this was true, but it did not change his mind. He was not going to say anything that could put him in prison.

Michael began the interview by asking Alexsei if he thought the Czar had given the order to fire on the crowd.

"Not the Czar," said Alexsei. The Czar is our Father. He did not know they were going to fire. We love the Czar."

Surprised, Michael asked if the unrest in St. Petersburg was spreading throughout Russia, as the British newspapers were claiming. Alexsei assured him that this was not widespread, that the people loved the Czar and were confident that he would reform the industries, where all this had been started by a few people who did not speak for the Russian workers.

And so from interview to interview, Michael heard that the people loved the Czar. The violence had been started by a few malcontents and the Czar would protect the Russian people. Michael was confidant he had been right about the British newspapers. Just stooges of the British government. Owned by the very businesses which were exploiting the people of China and Korea. The Russian people had convinced him.

Chapter Thirty-One

May, 1906

The garden around the Davitt cottage in Ireland had turned green with the warmth of late spring. Flowers were bursting open and splashing their colors over the green background. As beautiful as it was, it was difficult to appreciate. It had been two days since he had two teeth extracted and he was feeling weak. The empty tooth sockets were causing him considerable pain.

Michael sat outside in the garden. He thought about the places he had been and the things he had seen. To him, no country was as beautiful as Ireland. He liked the United States, it was a spectacular country with its great plains and majestic mountains, but Ireland was incomparable. Perhaps it was just that it was home. So much of his soul was imbedded in this land. It had a grip on him and would never let him go.

He stood up and headed for the door of the cottage. He was feeling tired and wanted to go inside and lie down. He took a step and felt a sharp pain in his side. He stopped for a moment and put his hand on a tree to steady himself. He thought the pain would pass, but it didn't. He barely made it to the door. He called for Mary.

When she came, he was leaning up against the door jamb with his hand on his side, a look of excruciating pain on his face. She had a difficult time getting him over to the sofa. She finally managed to get him down, but the pain, he said, would still not go away.

* * *

Michael was brought to Elphis hospital in Dublin. The diagnosis was septic poisoning, a result of the extractions. The doctor told Mary that Michael would not last the day. Mary went into the hospital room, sat by Michael's side, took his hand, and held it as though she would never let it go.

"I know I don't have much time left," said Michael. Mary began to weep. He squeezed her hand. "My regret is that I will not live to see Ireland become an independent country, free from British rule."

Mary put Michael's hand to her face.

"With that strong hand, you lifted the yoke of the landlord from the back of your countrymen," said Mary. "Because of you, Ireland will become independent one day."

"It appears you have been reading, *The Fall of Feudalism in Ireland*," said Michael.

"I have read all your books," said Mary, "and many others have as well. You are a great hero to the Irish people. You showed them a way to fight the oppression that was gripping them, and no queen or pope could stop you. Because of you, we are no longer servants."

Tears began to appear in Michael's eyes. "Such a woman," he said. "How did I get such a woman?"

"She fell in love with you the first time she saw you," said Mary.

"But I didn't meet my goals. I wanted non-sectarian education, nationalization of the land, and an independent Ireland. I will die without this happening. I need more time!"

"Sometimes an idea and a man is ahead of his time, Michael. Perhaps someday in the future others will study your ideas and the right time will come."

"If I have to choose one of these goals, Mary, if God will allow only one of these, then I pray for an independent Ireland.

216

I know I'm going to die. I don't want a big public funeral. Please keep it private. Just for you and the children, please."

Mary agreed, nodding her head. Her tears were preventing her from doing anything else.

* * *

The poison in his blood did its work, Michael once again saw the roof of his house fall into the fire as the crowbar crew knocked down the walls and his father's eyes flashed in hatred. He felt his mother hold him to her breast as she refused to let him go in the workhouse. He saw the face of James Bonner lifting up the makeshift tent in Haslingden when he had the measles, and heard John Ginty's mother singing over John's dead body. He felt the pain of the cotton machine tearing off his arm. He could hear Anne say "Goodby Baby James" at the grave side of their baby brother. He heard Mr. Cockcroft compliment him on his work in the print shop, and the sound of Big Ben in Darthmoor Prison. He saw Joe the blackbird sitting on the prison bed, listening intently to his lectures and Mary taking her wedding vows. He remembered his Kathleen being born and read again the telegram that announced her death.

He looked up, and there was a great light in the room. It was as if he were looking into a tunnel, and the light was at the other end. He saw his mother beckoning to him. He reached out.

* * *

Mary tried to keep the funeral private. She arranged to have the body brought quietly to the Carmelite Friary on Clarendon Street in Dublin, but the word got out. The irrepressible news spread like a grass fire: Michael Davitt was

217

dead. He was at the Carmelite Friary.

The next day, 31 May 1906, people began appearing at dawn. At first, Mary thought only a few would come. After all, she had made no public announcement. She gave in and allowed those who were waiting outside a chance to come in and pay their last respects.

But no one could have anticipated what was to happen next. The people kept coming, and then more and more. Great lines of mourners formed outside the friary as far as the eye could see. People stopped and wept in front of the coffin. They were old and young, healthy and infirm. There were old men walking painfully with canes, mothers with small children clinging to them, blind old women who had to be helped, young men in suits, middle-aged women in black veils, farmers, workers, clergy.

And they kept coming. There seemed to be no end to them. Some had to be stopped from touching the coffin. Others were weeping uncontrollably. And still there was no end. Hour after hour they came, well into the night. When it was finally over, a local newspaper put the count at over twenty thousand mourners.

* * *

Mary decided that Michael would be buried in his hometown, Straide. She arranged for the burial on the grounds of Straide Abbey, next to the church where he had been baptized. The next day, a train brought the body to Foxford, County Mayo, where it was then brought to the Abbey. A large crowd followed the train from the station to the Abbey, and would not disperse.

* * *

"Have you chosen an epitaph for your husband's grave?" the priest asked.

"Yes," said Mary. "I want the Irish inscription to appear on the front of the stone and the English to appear on the back." She handed him the paper.

Is beannuighte iad-san a mbideann orra ocras agus tart na cora oir deanfaiodar sasugad. Mata

Mar Chuimhiughadh Gradamull

Ar

Miceál Mac Dáití

A fuar bás

Dia –ceadaoin 30[ad] Bealtaine 1906

Trí Fecid Bliadain d'aois

R.I.P.

Do Thog Maire a bhean

Is beannuighthe iad-san fulaingeas gear-leanamuint ar son na
cora oirisleobhtha
Riogact na bflaiteas

Blessed are they that hunger and thirst after justice for they
shall have their fill

IN LOVING MEMORY OF MICHAEL DAVITT

RIP

This monument is erected by his wife, Mary

Blessed are they that suffer persecution for justice sake for
theirs is the kingdom of heaven

* * *

1993

A young Indian man got off the train at Castlebar. He
checked into a hotel, ate a meal, and went to bed. Early the next
morning he walked up to the desk clerk and asked, "Could you
possibly direct me to a florist?"

After receiving directions, the young man walked to the
florist shop, which was only a block away.

"I would like to purchase a wreath suitable for a grave
site," he said.

The florist pointed out several arrangements that were
hanging on the wall. "These are our samples," she said. "But
we can make up a fresh one right away."

"This one will do nicely," said the young man, pointing
to one of the larger wreaths.

It did not take the florist long to make the wreath, and the young man paid her. "Would you happen to know where I could hire a taxi to take me out to Straide?"

The florist pointed to a man across the street standing next to a car. "O'Sullivan over there will help you," she said.

The young man hired O'Sullivan to take him to the Abbey in Straide. He bid O'Sullivan wait. He walked among the stones with the fragrant wreath in his hand until he found the grave of Michael Davitt, and placed the wreath on it. He then stood lost in thought for a time. The parish priest, who happened to be in the area, saw the young man and came out to greet him.

"You know Mayo's most favorite son?" he asked.

"Yes, very much so," said the young man. "But the wreath is really for my grandfather. He admired Michael Davitt very much. In fact, he often said that his entire campaign was patterned after Michael Davitt's Land League."

"What was your grandfather's name, son?" asked the priest.

"Mohandus K. Gandhi," said the young man.

Epilog

Although Michael Davitt did not live to see Irish independence, it would not take much longer. But his dream of accomplishing it peacefully would never come to pass. In the years that followed his death, the Fenian movement strengthened and eventually freed most of Ireland from British rule. It took violence to achieve that goal, something Michael Davitt would have opposed. But his peaceful influence, was evident. It was his Land League that had solidified the Irish into a group. Their achievements resulted in a national pride, which they eventually brought forth in everything they did. Building on Davitt's foundation, the demise of the landlord system meant that the British had fewer interests to protect in Ireland, and this fact may have prompted them to eventually make a settlement.

In May, 1914, a law supporting Home Rule for Ireland had finally passed in Parliament. However, the outbreak of World War I prevented the law from being implemented. The Irish, frustrated by the delay, began an armed uprising on Easter Sunday, 1916. Civil war followed until an Irish Free State was established in 1921. If Michael Davitt had lived, he would have been seventy-four years old. What part he would have played in the civil war is a matter of speculation.

The new republic, as Michael Davitt predicted, was very poor after the break with the British, but found some prosperity from Irish men working in the British arms industry during World War II. Being independent, Irish men were no longer subject to conscription into the British armed forces, and could work as foreign nationals in England. Many sent money home.

But the resentment against Great Britain persisted. Some wanted to grant Germany the right to submarine bases in Ireland simply because they were the enemy of the British, although this was a minority view. It would have violated the country's policy of neutrality, as well as jeopardized support the country was receiving from the American Irish. The Irish Prime Minister of the time, Eamon De Valera, wisely steered his country on the neutral path. However, the majority of the Irish people were sympatric to the allied cause. It is a well known fact that many American servicemen who were interned in Ireland "escaped" to the British territory of Northern Ireland. No Germans ever did.

Eventually, the war ended and the relationship with Great Britain stabilized, with only small groups still carrying on guerrilla warfare. This was especially true in the north of Ireland, were the Catholic-Protestant feud still smolders. In 1936, the Irish Republic outlawed the Irish Republican Army which still carried out acts of violence against the British.

Ironically, both Great Britain and Ireland have joined the European Union, whose ultimate plan is to politically and economically unite the countries of Europe. In effect, joining the EU has actually achieved a type of "home rule" for Ireland, which so many Irish wanted and so many others fought against.

As time passed, the "boycott" as it had become known throughout the world, became a weapon for the working class. Its next most effective use was implemented by a young British-trained, Indian lawyer named Mohandas K. Gandhi. Gandhi had studied Davitt's Land League methods and the Irish "Plan of Campaign," which he used in the British colonies of North Africa and India where it was so successful it caused the British to leave India and its interests there. The British eventually traded empire for commonwealth, and Gandhi gave Michael Davitt and the Irish Land League credit as the basis for his non-violent campaign for Indian independence.

In the late 1950's and early 1960's, fifty years after Davitt's death, a young minister in the United States once again

223

used the boycott. This time it was to obtain civil rights for African-Americans in the United States. The minister was Dr. Martin Luther King, Jr., and the boycott was of the segregated buses in Montgomery, Alabama.

CHAPTER NOTES

Forward

Pope Adrian IV was the only Englishman to ever become Pope. The original of the Papal Bull, *Laudabiliter* was never found in the Vatican archives. This fact added fuel to the burning issue of the Irish independence movement.

Chapter One

I made every effort to keep the story historically accurate. I relied upon Davitt's biographers, as well as Davitt's own writings. Where they disagreed, I used whatever official records were available. A case in point is the eviction of the Davitts from their cottage in Straide, County Mayo, in 1850. Davitt's own writings state that his sister, Sabina, was two months old when this incident occurred. However, the official records show that Sabina was born in Haslingden, England, and could not have been present at the time

My characterization of Michael's family is based upon his own writings. He described his father, Martin, as a man who could speak, read, and write English, as well as "Irish." Many biographers concluded that he was probably educated by a "hedge schoolmaster" and was given a basic education. Such schoolmasters were given the name because they taught clandestinely during the Cromwellian era when it was against the law to educate Catholics.

Michael described his mother as the dominant strength of the family. She was not able to handle English well, and felt more comfortable speaking Irish. He wrote that she was fond of illustrating her sentences with Irish proverbs. Like most European peasant women, she was evidently the pillar upon which her family rested, a woman whose strength, character and courage are to be admired. Often, when listening to my wife relate stories about her Irish grandmother to whom this book is dedicated, I feel her resemblance to Catherine Kielty Davitt. It made it easier to bring her to life.

As in any dramatization, some literary license had to be taken. But even here, I took great pains to follow the facts. Fortunately, Davitt's story is well documented. I have supplemented part of the story with incidents such as the reading of the letter from the fictional Brian McGinty. The letter is based upon journals of two men who described the actual events of the voyage of the "coffin ships."

Great Britain had outlawed the trans-Atlantic slave trade on their ships in 1807, and slavery itself in 1833. With the lucrative slave trade gone, the Liverpool ship captains were out of work and welcomed the additional income that transporting Irish emigrants provided them. They were also known for supplementing their profits by withholding the passengers' oatmeal allowances. For views of the famine, see appendix I.

Chapter Two

The English town of Haslingden, just outside Liverpool, was the birthplace of the Industrial Revolution.

Some biographers think the family that initially took the Davitts in were distant relatives. In his notes later published as the book *Jottings in Solitary*, Michael Davitt does not refer to this family as distant relatives, but other biographers think this was due to the fact that the family evicted them when he developed measles and he did not want to embarrass the family name.

All that was known about James Bonner is what has been included in the incident described in the chapter.

The "Irish Town" community on Rock Hill was populated by families from western Ireland. Like all immigrants in all countries, they were resented by the native population because they were seen as cheap labor and a threat to local jobs. Most started out as "hawkers," or street vendors and some worked in the factories. Before the Irish arrived in numbers, Scots had been dominating as hawkers. Haslingden was surrounded by several industrial towns and was a good place for selling merchandise. As the Scots became upwardly mobile, the Irish, especially those who could speak English, filled the gap. "Irish" speakers were at a disadvantage for hawking and factory jobs, so many had to work as day laborers.

Martin did a great deal to help the Irish children in Rock Hill learn to read and write the King's English. This seems to have been a service that was available only to boys, because Martin's oldest daughter, Mary Agnes, was illiterate.

Except for his house being torn down, Michael did not seem to have much memory of his childhood in Ireland. His attitudes were formed by being closely tied to the Irish enclave in Rock Hill.

Infant mortality was not uncommon in the nineteenth century, especially in Europe. In early twentieth century America, an influenza epidemic resulted in the deaths of thousands of people, many of them children. Both my own parents' families lost two-year-olds in 1917 from the disease.

Chapter Three

The "Mill House Rules" poster is not the actual one posted in the factory where Michael Davitt worked; they are from another facility. But they were typical of the times.

It was common for the industrialists of this era to use child labor and work them sixteen hours a day. It was also common in the United States, whose industrial base was patterned after England.

Industrial accidents, such as the one which took John Ginty's life and Michael Davitt's arm, were regular occurrences in the factories. Most accidents happened to children who did not possess the size or judgment of adults. In the seven-month period from April to October, the period in which John Ginty died, eleven fatal accidents were reported in the Haslingden area.

Chapter Four

Michael was a good student and had an excellent relationship with the teachers at the Methodist school. He later remarked that Mr. Proskett never made him feel inadequate simply because he was a Catholic.

There was a special relationship between Michael and Mr. Cockcroft. Cockcroft took a special liking to Michael and went to great lengths to protect him.

Ernest Jones had a considerable influence on Michael. There would be others who would influence him later, but the idea of land nationalization would stick with him into adulthood and would come back to haunt him later in life.

Mr. George E. Burns, a descendant of Michael Davitt, who worked as a printer points out that in Michael Davitt's time printing was a very highly skilled profession. In his day, typesetting required the operator to hand pick each individual letter from a wooden printer's box and place it on what was known as a stick. When a line of type was completed, it was spaced out to even length or justified and then set into a "chase." It then had to be leveled with a "planer-block" and mallet before it was turned over to a pressman.

The "chase" is a frame the size of the page to be printed, with no bottom. If every individual letter is not "locked," i.e. squeezed together absolutely, positively perfectly, the type will fall out when the case is picked up. This work required a highly skilled person with two hands. For Michael Davitt to be able to do it with one hand is a near miracle.

Chapter Five

The leaders of the Fenian organization generally recognized Michael's leadership abilities, and therefore he was able to rise quickly in the ranks. He proved to be very resourceful and was well respected by the men who had been placed under his direction. He was, however, reticent when it came to the indiscriminate use of violence, especially when it threatened innocent civilians.

Chapter Six

The Irish Amnesty Association

Chapter Nine

The above view shows Milbank Penitentiary as it looked in 1828. The structure is seen from Milbank Road, the River Thames being at the viewer's back.

Source: Anonymous, Shepaerd and Elme's *Metropolitan Improvements*, 1828, now in public domain.

Chapter Twelve

The incident at Nally's public house in described in T.W. Moody's, *Davitt and the Irish Revolution 1846-1842,* page 120. The passage appears as follows:

"He was accompanied by Walshe and Nally to Balla, where a deputation, supported by a host of 'patriotic young ladies', induced him to make an unscheduled stop of two hours (5-7 p.m.), in the course of which he was entertained at 'Nally's hotel.'"

I am assuming that the use of the quotation marks on 'patriotic young ladies' and 'Nally's hotel' are meant to mean other than the fact that the ladies were actually just patriots and that the specified entertainment took place at the hotel.

Chapter Thirteen

Davitt refers to the moldy bread as "poultices." The dictionary definition of poultices is:

"A soft moist mass of bread, meal, clay, or other adhesive substance, usually heated, spread on cloth, and applied to warm, moisten, or stimulate an aching or inflamed part of the body also called cataplasm. I substituted the term 'moldy bread' to avoid confusing the modern reader."

Chapter Sixteen

The story of Davitt breaking down in the meeting is based upon the journal left by John Devoy.

Chapter Twenty-One

The return of Michael Davitt had a profound effect on the League's activities. Financial aid from America was a large factor in the success of the League, and Davitt was extremely good at getting this point across to the people of Ireland, who now had an effective weapon that would eventually bring many concessions from the British government.

Although it may sound as if Davitt were a communist, there are major and essential differences between George's socialism and communism. The "Communist Manifesto" was written by Karl Marx in 1847, but was not translated into English until 1888 by Samuel Moore, with the assistance of Frederick Engels. It is not likely that Davitt would have been familiar with its contents at that time. Although he was considered a socialist, he was never considered a communist.

Chapter Twenty-Three

A writ of habeas corpus (Latin literally, "you have the body") is a judicial mandate to a prison official ordering that an inmate be brought to the court so it can be determined whether or not that person is imprisoned lawfully, and whether or not he should be released from custody. In the United States Constitution, it assures the accused of a speedy trial, or else the authorities cannot "hold the body."

In 1862, American President Abraham Lincoln suspended habeas corpus, which did not get restored until 1866.

Jottings in Solitary was subsequently published and is a significant part of the body of Michael Davitt's work. Considered a classic in Irish history, the copy I have was published in 2003 by University College Dublin Press, Newman House, 86 St. Stephen's Green, Dublin. The introduction was written by Dr. Carla King, considered to be the greatest living authority on Michael Davitt. During this time, it is believed that Davitt also wrote *Leaves From a Prison Diary*. A comparison of the two books show some overlapping of topics and some of his biographers think he took abstracts from his *Jottings* in an attempt to publish *Leaves*.

Chapter Twenty-Four

The Chancellor of the Exchequer is the title held by the British cabinet minister responsible for all financial matters.

Chapter Twenty-Five

Jeremiah O'Donovan Rossa had been released from a life sentence he received for high treason. He served eight years and was released in 1871 and exiled to America. He edited the New York edition of United Irishman and published Prison Life (1874), Irish Rebels in English Prisons (1882) and Recollection 1838-1898 (1898). He died in New York in 1915. His body was returned to Ireland and he received a hero's burial. Michael did not like Rossa and considered his writings to be inflammatory and untimely.

It must have been very difficult for Michael to make the break with John Devoy who was probably his best friend. Devoy is considered an Irish hero and one of the key figures leading to eventual Irish Independence. It was a very brave decision on Michael's part to stand on his principles and lose one of his best friends.

Davitt finally ended up resigning his position as a Member of Parliament in protest of the Boer War which he felt was being fought only to protect what he termed "British interest," in South Africa. He delivered many speeches and wrote many articles about these interests, which of course meant the commercial interest the British had there, especially those of the British royals.

Michael spent most of 1882 traveling all over the world. He visited Australia, New Zealand, South Africa and Russia. During this time he was able to finish six books.

Chapter Twenty-Six
The wedding description was taken directly from the Oakland newspaper.

Chapter Twenty-Seven
These articles are exact transcriptions of the originals. They were sent all over the United States and Europe by telegraph. Austria also offered the Pope sanctuary.

The British regarded Malta as an important naval base, and knew it would be of strategic importance if they ever had to go to war with any of the other European powers. Malta had a mostly Catholic population and the British needed to know that they could count on the help of the locals in a war; having a friendly Vatican there would have assured them of this cooperation. For the British to offer Malta to the Pope was Quid-Pro-Quo. For an in-depth look at the situation, see the *Journal of Maltese Studies,*

"The Pope Considers Seeking Asylum in Malta, 1881-1889" by Professor Dominic Fenech, University of Malta, published under the auspices of Faculty of Education, The University of Malta.

The dictionary defines "recusant" as one of the Roman Catholics in England who incurred legal and social penalties in the sixteenth century and afterward for refusing to attend services of the Church of England. In a more general sense, it is also defined as a dissenter, a nonconformist. The Catholic Emancipation Act benefitted the Catholic royalty in England, such as the Duke of Norfolk

Chapter Twenty-Eight
Many news articles of the time have referred to Katie as "Kitty" O'Shea. In her days, the name "Kitty" was a slang term for a prostitute, something like the term "hooker" is used in America today..

Chapter Twenty-Nine
The letter printed in this chapter is one of the letters actually printed in the newspaper.

Chapter Twenty-Nine
Kishinev is now the city of Chisinau, the capital of Moldova which is now an independent state following the fall of the Soviet Union. It is located between Romania on the west and the Ukraine on the east.
Michael became a Zionist, probably as a result of his experiences in Russia and elsewhere. He would later write the following in 1904:
"The Jews have never done any injury to Ireland. Like our

own race, they have endured a persecution, the records of which will for ever remain a reproach to the 'Christian' nations of Europe. Ireland has no share in this black record. Our country has this proud distinction--freely acknowledged by Jewish writers--of never having resorted to this un-Christian and barbarous treatment of an unfortunate people."

Concerning Imperial Russia, the following was contributed by Dr. Carla King, Professor of History at Saint Patrick's College, Dublin:

"There had always been laws aimed against Jews ever since, during the reign of Catherine II, they were officially permitted to live in the Empire at all. They were supposed to be limited to the Pale of settlement in Lithuania, Poland, the south-western provinces (including Ukraine, Belorussia and Bessarabia) and were only allowed to live in towns and villages. During the reign of the reforming Czar, Alexander II the situation had been relaxed somewhat, but when he was assassinated in 1881, some circles blamed this on a Jewish plot (though there was no evidence for this), and a series of pogroms took place across the Empire, with the tacit support of the authorities. In addition, the Minister of Interior, Ignatiev, passed a series of laws, called the Temporary Laws, although they remained in force until 1917, which imposed further restrictions on them. During the reign of Alexander III (son of the murdered Alexander II) and his son, Nicholas II, there were other measures passed, e.g. the expulsion of the Jews of Moscow, which took place during Passover 1891 and the limitation on the number of Jews entering university to 10% of total student intake in the areas of the Pale and 5% outside, and 3% at Moscow and St Petersburg universities. It was these pogroms and laws which led to the first large wave of emigration from Russia, mainly to the United States."

There is much speculation on weather Gandhi actually met Davitt in person. Some authors think they may have met since Davitt had such an interest in Indian affairs and was good friends with Dadabbai Naoroji. I have not been able to find any documentation about an actual meeting between them, but they were in London at the same time when Gandhi was a law student. Therefore, I did not invent a face-to-face meeting in the book. I ask the reader to keep in mind that such a meeting <u>could</u> have taken place.

Chapter Thirty-One

Regarding the Irish version of the epitaph on Davitt's grave, the following was sent to me by the staff of the Michael Davitt Museum, Straide, County Mayo, Ireland.

"The script used is the old Irish form and is almost illegible in places. The spellings and word usage are no longer used in modern Irish so may appear strange to Irish students today. We have tried to be as close as possible to what appears on the stone."

I am much indebted to the staff of the museum for this and all the help they provided me in the research of this book.

Appendix I - Views of the Famine

A special thanks must be given to Steven Taylor, who collected the "Views of the Famine" drawings reproduced here. They were sketches made by a reporter for the *London Times* who traveled with an artist. These were later made into engravings which are in the public domain. The actual scans, however, are copyrighted and are being used here with Steven Taylor's permission. You can see the complete set on Steve's web site at:

http://wassun.vassar.edu/sttaylor/FAMINE.

SCALP AT CAHUREMORE.

"Than this scalp, nothing could be more wretched. It was placed in a hole, surrounded by pools, and three sides of the scalp (shown in the Sketch) were dripping with water, which ran in small streams over the floor and out by the entrance. Yet, wretched as this hole is, the poor inhabitants said they would be thankful and content if the landlord would leave them there, and the Almighty would spare their lives. "

Illustrated London News, December 29, 1849

"Searching for potatoes is one of the occupations of those who cannot obtain outdoor relief*. It is gleaning in a potato-field-- and how few are left after the potatoes are dug, must be known to everyone who has ever seen the field cleared. What the people were digging and hunting for, like dogs after truffles, I could not imagine, till I went into the field, and then I found them patiently turning over the whole ground, in the hopes of finding the few potatoes the owner might have overlooked. Gleaning in a potato-field seems something like shearing hogs, but it is the only means by which the gleaners could hope to get a meal."

Illustrated London News, December 29, 1849
This may be a reference to soup kitchens. Many of the poor who were not able to gain admission to the overcrowded workhouses were dependent upon the soup kitchens . In some rural areas, even these were not available. It could also be a reference to the government relief efforts of public works projects, such as road building, (like the opportunity given to Martin Davitt), which were not available to everyone.

A Protestant soup school for starving Roman Catholic children. These were mostly run by the Anglican church, which was receiving subsidies from the government. There is no hard evidence that families had to convert to enter the school, but the curriculum was based upon the Anglican Church's Protestant precepts, some of which were in conflict with Roman Catholic dogma.

THE CORK SOCIETY OF FRIENDS' SOUP HOUSE.

"The Illustration shows a benevolent attempt to mitigate the suffering in the city of Cork, viz., the Society of Friends' Soup House. There are many similar establishments in operation through the county; but, we prefer the annexed because the idea originated with the Society of Friends."

Illustrated London News, January 16, 1847
The Society of Friends (commonly known as the Quakers) were instrumental in stopping the Famine. Their actions embarrassed the British Government into finally taking meaningful action.

THE WORKHOUSE, CLIFDEN.

"Clifden itself is an exotic in an unfavourable climate. It was reared by the patronage of the late Viscount; and since that ceased, it began to decline: the Poor-law has almost finished it. . . Extreme poverty exists in the neighbourhood-- the soil around is poor-- great numbers of houses have been levelled--but the poor, unlike those of Kilrush, have in great part disappeared with the houses. They have not found refuge in the workhouse-- they have not been carried away as emigrants; they have either wandered away or have died, or both may have contributed to cause their disappearance. . . I have taken a Sketch of the workhouse, which I send as a memorial of this pet place of the late Viscount Clifden."

Illustrated London News, January 19, 1850
Clifton was typical of many of the workhouses that existed in the British Isles and Ireland in the Victorian era. They were also known as poorhouses.

THE DEPARTURE

"There are usually a large number of spectators at the dock-gates to witness the final departure of the noble ship, with its large freight of human beings... As the ship is towed out, hats are raised, handkerchiefs are waved, and a loud and long-continued shout of farewell is raised from the shore, and cordially responded to from the ship. It is then, if at any time, that the eyes of the emigrants begin to moisten with regret at the thought that they are looking for the last time at the old country-- that country which, although, in all probability, associated principally with the remembrance of sorrow and suffering, of semi-starvation, and a constant battle for the merest crust necessary to support existence is, nevertheless, the country of their fathers, the country of their childhood, and consecrated to their hearts by many a token."

Illustrated London News, July 6, 1850
Ships were typically overloaded and the ship captains withheld part of the rations that the government had allotted for passengers. This added to the ship's profits.

244

WOMAN BEGGING AT CLONAKILTY.

I started from Cork for Skibbereen and saw little until we came to Clonakilty, where . . . the horrors of the poverty became visible, in the vast number of famished poor, who flocked around the coach to beg alms: amongst them was a woman carrying in her arms the corpse of a fine child, and making the most distressing appeal to the passengers for aid to enable her to purchase a coffin and bury her dear little baby. This horrible spectacle induced me to make some inquiry about her, when I learned from the people of the hotel that each day brings dozens of such applicants into the town."

Illustrated London News, February 13, 1847.
If this doesn't break your heart, nothing will.

Closing Remarks

My Grandfather, Michael Davitt was a man of many contradictions. Born in poverty in the village of Straide, County Mayo in Ireland, on a small tenant holding, from where he was evicted at the age of four, he went on to become a member of the British Parliament; a man from a mainly illiterate family who became a journalist and wrote six books; a leading member of the Fenians--the militant Irish Republican Brotherhood--; and famous for inventing 'boycotting', the ultimate means of peaceful non-cooperation; a convicted treason felonist who ended up inspecting the prisons in which he spent seven years in penal servitude; a revolutionary Irishman who was invited to stand as a parliamentary candidate for Sheffield, England, among other constituencies, at a time when Irishmen were seen as second class citizens in Britain; a man twice bankrupted who was renowned for his generosity to worthy causes; a one armed man who was appointed trustee of the Gaelic Athletic Association, founded to support the Irish Sports of Gaelic football and hurling to the exclusion of "foreign" sports and who turned the first sod at Glasgow Celtic Association Football Club in Glasgow, Scotland; Peacemaker, political and trade union arbitrator, newspaper editor, founder member of the British Labour Party, defender of the Jewish people, supporter of secular education, world traveler, this was a multi-faceted man.

But undoubtedly his greatest achievement was the part he played in the founding of the Irish Land League, the organization that, more than any other, released the Irish tenant farmer from the rack-renting landlords of the 19th century. Between 1849 and 1883, 102,366 families consisting of more than half a million people were evicted from their farms, their domiciles burnt and demolished to make room for the landlords' cattle to graze.

Davitt's demand for the 3Fs--Fixity of Tenure, Fair Rent and Free Sale--released the rural peasantry from this burden of inequity. In this year 2006, the one hundredth anniversary of his death, it is fitting that his story be retold.

-Patrick M. Davitt, Dublin, 2006

Bibliography

Davitt, Michael. *The Boer Fight for Freedom*. Funk and Wagnall, 1902. Reprinted by Scripta Africana, Capetown, South Africa 1998.

Davitt, Michael. *The Fall of Feudalism in Ireland*. Reprinted by Sequoyah Books, 2003.

Davitt, Michael, *Jottings in Solitary*. Reprinted by University College Dublin Press, 2003, with illustrations and notes by Dr. Carla King.

Davitt, Michael. *Leaves from a Prison Diary*. Chapman and Hall, Limited, London, 1885.

Davitt, Michael. *Within the Pale: The True Story of Anti-Semitic Persecutions in Russia.* Reprinted by Modern Jewish Experience Series, Arno Press, 1975.

Fenech, Dominic. "The Pope Considers Seeking Asylum in Malta, 1881–1889." *Journal of Maltese Studies,* Faculty of Education, The University of Malta, 1983.

George, Henry. *Progress and Poverty*. Originally self-published 1879, San Francisco, CA.. Reprinted by Robert Schalkenbach Foundation, New York, 1979.

Marlow, Joyce. *Captain Boycott and the Irish*. André Deutsch Limited, London, 1973.

*Moody, T.W. *Davitt and Irish Revolution, 1846–1882*. Oxford University Press, London, 1981.

**O'Hara, Bernard. *Davitt*, Mayo County Council, Castelbar, County Mayo, Ireland, 2006 (in association with the Michael Davitt Memorial Association, Straide, County Mayo, Ireland.)

Priestley, Philip. *Victorian Prison Lives English Prison Biography 1830–1914,* Methuen, London and New York, London and New York, 1985.

* Most comprehensive work on Michael Davitt

** Highly recommended

"To all my friends I leave kind thoughts, to my enemies the fullest possible forgiveness and to Ireland an undying prayer for the absolute freedom and independence which it was my life's ambition to try and obtain for her."

Last will and testament of Michael Davitt.

ISBN 141209198-5

Printed in the United States
By Bookmasters